Praise for the Downward Dog Mysteries

Karma's a Killer

"*Karma's a Killer* continues Tracy Weber's charming series."

—*The Seattle Times*

"[Weber's] characters are likeable and amusing, the background is interesting, and the story is ultimately satisfying."

—*Ellery Queen Mystery Magazine*

"Crazy, quirky critters and their odd yet utterly relatable human counterparts make *Karma's a Killer* an appealing story. But when you add the keep-you-guessing mystery with both laugh-out-loud one-liners and touching moments of pure poignancy, the result is a truly great book!"

—Laura Morrigan, national bestselling author
of the Call of the Wilde mystery series

"Tracy Weber's *Karma's a Killer* delivers on all fronts—a likably feisty protagonist, a great supporting cast, a puzzler of a mystery and, best of all, lots of heart. This book has more snap than a brand-new pair of yoga capris. Pure joy for yoga aficionados, animal lovers … heck, for anyone who loves a top-notch mystery."

—Laura DiSilverio, national bestselling author of
The Readaholics book club mysteries, two-time Lefty finalist
for best humorous mystery, and Colorado Book Award finalist

"Yogatta love this latest in the series when Kate exercises her brain cells trying to figure out who deactivated an animal rights activist."

—Mary Daheim, author of the Bed-and-Breakfast
and Emma Lord Alpine mysteries

A Killer Retreat

"Cozy readers will enjoy the twist-filled plot."

—*Publishers Weekly*

"[Kate's] path to enlightenment is a fresh element in cozy mysteries … [A]n entertaining read."

—*Library Journal*

"Weber's vegan yoga teacher is a bright, curious sleuth with a passion for dogs. A well-crafted whodunit with an intriguing mystery and a zinger of a twist at the end!"

—Krista Davis, *New York Times* bestselling author of the Domestic Diva and Paws and Claws Mysteries

"An engaging mystery full of fun and fascinating characters and unexpected twists. An intriguing read that includes yoga lessons and feisty dogs."

—Linda O. Johnston, author of the Pet Rescue Mystery series

"Weber's second yoga mystery, *A Killer Retreat*, is as delightful as her first. Readers will love the setting, the complex mystery, and the romance of Kate's second adventure. Especially noteworthy in this popular series is the appealing combination of strength and vulnerability that Kate and Bella share. Enjoy!"

—Susan Conant, author of the Dog Lover's Mystery series

"Whether yoga instructor Kate Davidson is wrestling her hundred-pound dog, her new love life, or trying to solve a murder, *A Killer Retreat* is simply a killer read! Witty, fun, and unpredictable, this is one cozy mystery worth barking about!"

—Shannon Esposito, author of the Pet Psychic Mystery series

"Fun characters, a gorgeous German Shepherd dog, and a murder with more suspects than you can shake a stick at. *A Killer Retreat* is a must-read for cozy fans!"

—Sparkle Abbey, author of the Pampered Pet Mystery series

A
FATAL
TWIST

A FATAL TWIST

A DOWNWARD DOG MYSTERY

TRACY WEBER

MIDNIGHT INK
WOODBURY, MINNESOTA

FIRST EDITION
First Printing, 2017

Book format by Bob Gaul
Cover design by Kevin R. Brown
Cover illustration by Nicole Alesi/Deborah Wolfe Ltd.

Midnight Ink, an imprint of Llewellyn Worldwide Ltd.

Library of Congress Cataloging-in-Publication Data
Names: Weber, Tracy, author.
Title: A fatal twist / Tracy Weber.
Description: First Edition. | Woodbury, Minnesota: Midnight Ink, [2017] |
  Series: A downward dog mystery; #4
Identifiers: LCCN 2016035245 (print) | LCCN 2016048176 (ebook) | ISBN
  9780738748788 | ISBN 9780738749143
Subjects: LCSH: Yoga teachers—Washington (State)—Seattle—Fiction. |
  Murder—Investigation—Fiction. | GSAFD: Mystery fiction.
Classification: LCC PS3623.E3953 F38 2017 (print) | LCC PS3623.E3953 (ebook)
  | DDC 813/.6—dc23
LC record available at https://lccn.loc.gov/2016035245

Midnight Ink   **33614057804980**
Llewellyn Worldwide Ltd.
2143 Wooddale Drive
Woodbury, MN 55125-2989
www.midnightinkbooks.com

Printed in the United States of America

*To Michelle. Of all of my lifelong friends,
you influenced me the most. I miss you.*

ACKNOWLEDGMENTS

Publishing can be a brutal industry. Most writers have days in which we wonder why we continue storytelling. For me, the answer is simple: my readers. Thank you for each email, Facebook post, letter, blog comment, tweet, and review. Without you, I'd have given up long ago.

A Fatal Twist has a special cast of supporters I'd like to acknowledge.

As always, thanks to my agent, Margaret Bail, editors Terri Bischoff and Sandy Sullivan at Midnight Ink, and freelance editor Marta Tanrikulu, who all give me invaluable help and feedback.

Special thanks go to three awesome readers: James D. Haviland, who came up with the book's title, Penny Ehrenkranz, who named the puppies in this book, and Becky Muth, who named Rene's twins.

My husband, Marc, and my real-life Bella, Tasha, will always be the lights of my life. We lost Tasha this year, but she continues to be my inspiration. Without her, this series would never have come to fruition. My new baby German shepherd, Ana, is teaching me how to write about puppies, and I'm grateful for the belly laughs she gives me each day, even when she chews up my manuscript. Marc gets extra kudos for designing and maintaining my author website, as well as for listening to all of my grumbles.

Finally, thanks go to my mother, Marcia, who was always my biggest fan, and my best friend, Michelle, who inspired Rene in the series. You are both missed.

ONE

When I entered the cold, darkened room a lifetime ago, I thought I was ready. I'd trained for this day. Looked forward to it, even. I'd prepared for the hunger, the exhaustion. Steeled myself for the blood. But I'd never anticipated the sounds. The low, tortured moans of the young blonde woman crouched before me. I tentatively reached out my hand, hoping to provide her some minimal form of comfort. She growled at me through bared teeth. A feral dog ready to snap.

"Touch me again and I'll slice off your fingers."

I could only hope that my live-in boyfriend, Michael, wouldn't want to get frisky anytime soon. Witnessing six hours—and counting—of Rhonda's unmedicated labor might put me off sex forever.

The stream of invectives she spewed next would have offended a drunken sailor, which was particularly impressive considering they came from the mouth of a twenty-four-year-old grade school teacher wearing teddy bear slipper-socks and a fuzzy pink bathrobe. I inhaled a deep breath of lavender-scented air, gave her my most serene yoga teacher smile, and backed away. Summer, my doula trainer, motioned me to the side with her eyes.

In spite of my obvious fumbling, Summer seemed unphased, which she probably was. She'd already assisted in over two hundred births. This was my first.

Like a submissive wolf pacifying her alpha, I avoided direct eye contact. I glanced around the room, pretending to take in my surroundings. The upscale birthing suite was different from any hospital room I'd been in before, which wasn't surprising. A Better Birth Association (ABBA—not to be confused with the band of the same name) was a one-of-its-kind birthing center that blended Western medical approaches with a home-birthing-like atmosphere, all housed in a converted 1920s apartment building in Seattle's Queen Anne neighborhood.

ABBA's birth center had been specifically designed to meet the need of an emerging market in Seattle's childbirth industry: parents of means who wanted low intervention, home-like births while remaining only seconds away from the latest cutting-edge equipment and liberal pain medication, should they change their minds. ABBA's tagline read, *The Comforts of Home, the Benefits of Modern Medicine.*

If these were the comforts of home, my house needed an upgrade. The interior of the birthing suite had been restored with period-appropriate touches: double-hung windows, detailed millwork, freshly painted wainscoting. Live ferns and ficus trees flourished near the windows. The soft, soothing tones of Bach's Canon No. 1 filtered through the air. A pull-out couch, a rocking chair, and an end table with a granite fountain sat across the room. The only nods to the medical nature of the facility were the hospital bed, which was covered in a purple-blue quilt, and several pieces of high-tech medical equipment that were shielded from view by bamboo shoji screens. The room was elegant enough that if giving birth weren't a requirement, I would have asked to vacation there.

Summer squatted on the ground, leaned forward, and took Rhonda's hands. Her soft, voluptuous curves and gray-streaked dark hair seemed maternal, comforting somehow. As if they were medals of honor—proof that she'd survived the birth process countless times before. The tired-looking circles under her eyes didn't detract from the power of her voice.

"It's okay, Rhonda. Look at me. Focus. Breathe. Just like we practiced. This contraction's almost over. All you need to do is hang on for a few more seconds."

Tears pooled behind Rhonda's lashes. "I can't."

"Yes, you can. We'll do it together."

For the next twenty seconds, the room was filled with deep breaths, low moans, and Summer's whispered assurances. I stood helplessly next to Rhonda's husband, who looked more distraught than I felt.

At the end of the contraction, Rhonda's eyes glazed over. She slumped against the wall.

"I think I should go back to the bed now."

I grabbed one arm; Summer, the other. I smiled at Rhonda as we guided her to the partially raised hospital bed. "Whew. That was a tough one."

Rhonda gave me a wan smile. "I'm so sorry, Kate. I never swear. It's like I've developed some sort of pain-induced Tourette's. I can't stop myself."

Her husband grinned. "I can't even say the word 'damn' in our house without putting a dollar in the cookie jar." He slid a pillow behind Rhonda's back and offered her a paper cup filled with ice chips. "Believe me, babe, I'm keeping track. At the rate you're going, we'll have enough in there for Baby Jane's college tuition." He pretended to duck, as if expecting Rhonda to slug him.

"Stop calling her that." Rhonda wrinkled her lips, but her eyes showed no irritation. "I haven't picked out a name yet, but she's *not* going to be a Jane Doe. She'll tell me her name when I see her."

I had to give the man extra-credit karma points for courage. Michael would never crack a joke while I was preparing to push a living seven-pound bowling ball out of my lady parts. I'd worked hard over the past nine months to cool down my Hulk-like temper, but all bets would be off in the middle of a contraction. One bad joke, and I'd probably smack him over the head with a bedpan.

If he was lucky.

"Don't worry, Rhonda," Summer replied. "Women say all kinds of things in the middle of a contraction. What happens in the delivery room stays in the delivery room." She leveled a stern look at the father. "And there will be no keeping track of swearing—or anything else—Dad."

The labor nurse, whose name tag read Tamara Phillips, turned to Rhonda. Her strawberry-blonde hair was tied back in a severe-looking bun, but her blue-green eyes radiated compassionate concern.

"You've been stuck at four centimeters for a while now. Are you sure you don't want an epidural? We're going to be at this for a long time. Possibly all night and well into tomorrow."

I glanced at the room's Buddha-shaped wall clock. Three minutes after midnight. Ugh.

Nurse Tamara continued. "I know you don't want Pitocin, but I wish you'd reconsider an epidural. Sometimes getting rid of the pain helps labor progress."

Rhonda's expression grew worried. "Is the baby all right?"

The nurse glanced behind the shoji screen at the monitor. "The heartbeat looks great. Steady as a drum." She furrowed her brow. "You, on the other hand, are suffering. You *can* give birth without benefit of pain medication, but you don't have to. We live in the twenty-first century. There's no reason for childbirth to be torture." She pointed to a black phone on the wall. "I can have our nurse anesthetist here with a single phone call."

Summer gave Nurse Tamara a look. The kind Dad used to give right before he dragged me out of the room for a good scolding. She spoke through clenched teeth. "Can I talk to you for a second?"

Forced smile notwithstanding, Summer's question wasn't really a request. She nodded toward the baby's father. "Dad, you stay here with Rhonda. We'll be back in a minute." She motioned for the nurse and me to follow her into the hall.

Summer spoke as soon as the door closed behind us. "I know you mean well," she began, sounding like she knew nothing of the sort, "but as I pointed out to you an hour ago, Rhonda specifically asked in her birth plan not to be offered pain medication. Giving birth naturally is important to her. If she changes her mind, she'll tell me."

Nurse Tamara's lips tightened. "There's simply no reason for her to suffer. It could be twelve hours before that baby comes."

Summer crossed her arms and stepped her feet wide. "Her birth, her choice."

The nurse's frown lines deepened.

The two women glared at each other in silence, each waiting for the other to give ground. I wondered—not for the first time today—if their conflict had anything to do with Rhonda or her supposed birth plan. From the moment I'd entered the birthing suite, I'd felt a palpable, tense energy between the two women. As if every interaction was the next move in a covert battle for dominance.

After several long moments, Nurse Tamara caved. "Fine, for now. But you're not helping her." She spun on her heel and marched back through the door.

I sagged against the wall, grateful for once that I wasn't the source of the tumult. When I'd volunteered to be the doula at my best friend Rene's upcoming birth, I'd thought a doula was a labor coach with a fancy title. Since then, I'd learned that the job included so much more: helping the couple determine a birth plan, advocating for the needs of the entire family—dad included—and occasionally running interference with the mom-to-be's healthcare professionals. I hadn't expected the last part to be quite so heated.

"Is it always this intense?" I asked Summer.

"Work as a doula can be challenging," she replied. "But honestly, we've barely been at this six hours. If I were you, I'd prepare to settle in. First babies can take a long time."

"No worries there. I'm here for the duration." I gestured to the door. "I meant with the nurse. Is a doula's relationship with the medical team supposed to be that confrontational?"

Summer's eyebrows lifted. "Oh, you mean my spat with Nurse Doom and Gloom." She frowned at the closed door, as if replaying the scene on its smooth oak surface. When she turned back toward me, her face wore a resigned expression.

"Tamara and I have a history, but you're right. I should back off. I'm being a terrible example for you. A doula's job is to facilitate, not berate." She sighed. "Take a lesson from that, Kate, especially since your friend plans to give birth in a hospital. If you want to support hospital births, you'll have to learn how to partner with Western healthcare providers."

"Is a hospital birth that much different than one here at ABBA?"

She shrugged. "Depends on the hospital. Frankly, depends on the labor and delivery nurse, too. Personally, I prefer home births. But as far as medical facilities go, ABBA is one of the best. It only grants privileges to highly regarded private practice OB/GYNs who support natural childbirth. Most hospitals advocate interventions, like that epidural Nurse Tamara keeps pushing. Drives me batty. Epidurals, Pitocin, C-sections … they simply aren't needed most of the time. Natural childbirth is far healthier for both mom and her baby."

I wasn't sure I agreed with Summer's steadfast devotion to "natural" childbirth. (Was there any other kind?) But she was right about ABBA, which was one of the most prestigious birthing centers in the Pacific Northwest. There was no better place in Seattle to have a baby. If you could afford it.

A low groan came from Rhonda's suite. "We'd better go back in," Summer said. "Tamara's right. We could be here awhile."

Summer coached Rhonda through the next set of contractions, skillfully holding her attention while the nurse did something I didn't care to think about underneath the sheets. When the contraction ended, Nurse Tamara sat back and frowned.

"Still four centimeters."

Rhonda moaned. "Seriously? Maybe I should get an epidural after all." Her eyes begged Summer for permission. "What do you think?"

Summer's face remained blank. "It doesn't matter what I think. It's your choice."

The nurse reached for the phone, preparing to dial her magic number.

The thought of watching someone insert a three-and-a-half-inch needle into Rhonda's spine made my stomach feel woozy. From the expression on her husband's face, he felt downright ill.

Rhonda seemed conflicted. "If I get an epidural, I'll be confined to the bed, right?"

Summer nodded. "Yes, for the rest of the labor. Do you want to stick with less invasive options for now?"

Rhonda didn't reply.

Summer took that to mean yes. "Good choice." She gestured toward the husband. "You look like you could use some fresh air. Why don't you take a break while I get Rhonda into the jetted tub?"

He took a step toward the door, then turned back to his wife. "You okay with this, hon?"

Rhonda nodded.

Summer patted him on the back. "Go on now. We'll call your cell if we need anything." As the door closed behind him, she pulled me aside and whispered, "You look like you're about to faint. Did you eat dinner before you left home?"

I shook my head no.

"Didn't you listen in training? Rule number one of being a doula: eat before you leave for the birth. Things can get crazy, quick." She frowned. "The last thing I need is for you to pass out on me. Go to the family room and have a snack, but don't be gone long. Bring me back a bottle of water."

The family room was another of ABBA's many perks: a lounge in which families and support staff could get sustenance without leaving the facility. I wasn't sure doulas-in-training were the intended customers, but who was I to quibble?

I stopped in the restroom for a quick bio break, then headed down the facility's light pink hallway. The spicy scent of Kung Pao Tofu taunted my stomach, courtesy of an open window and the twenty-four-hour Chinese restaurant next door.

A quick left turn later, I was foraging through the empty family room, which was furnished with overstuffed chairs, ornately detailed wooden end tables, and a large selection of puzzles, games, and current magazines. A cabinet topped with a sign labeled *Snacks* was stocked with protein bars, crackers, and single-serve packages of peanut butter. A refrigerator in the corner held sodas and bottled water. I smothered an individually wrapped graham cracker with a thick coating of peanut butter, added some honey, and placed another cracker on top—my version of a home-cooked meal. I popped the concoction into my mouth, wiped the stray honey from my lips, and groaned. Stale crackers and sweetening-laced peanuts never tasted so good. I slammed down three more, coated with an extra layer of honey for good measure.

Low blood sugar catastrophe averted, I pulled out my cell phone to call Michael.

He answered on the second ring. "Hey, babe. Are you on your way home?"

"Not even close. At the rate things are going, I might still be here next week. Sorry to call so late, but I wanted to let you know not to expect me tonight."

A cupboard door closed on the other end of the line.

"Aren't you in bed yet?" I asked.

"Nope. I can't sleep without you here, so I'm making a sandwich. If you're nice to me, I'll make a batch of those vegan brownies you love so much."

I grinned. Michael was learning. I wouldn't complain about coming home to a messy kitchen if he'd baked something worth cleaning it for.

A metallic rendition of Brahms' Lullaby floated through the birth center's sound system, signaling that a new baby had been delivered. Hopefully Rhonda's wouldn't be far behind.

"I need to get back, Michael, but I'll call again in the morning. Give Bella a kiss for me." Bella's distinctive sharp bark sounded in the background.

"Bella says she misses you."

Michael's intention was sweet, but we both knew what my hundred-pound German shepherd was actually saying: *Give me a bite of that sandwich. Now.*

I smiled. "Tell her I miss her, too. I miss both of you. Don't feed her too many treats, and try not to make a mess."

"Me? When have I ever made a mess?"

I ignored his obvious sarcasm, told him I loved him, and clicked off the phone.

Smart-ass.

A vegan protein bar and another peanut-butter-coated cracker later, I grabbed two bottles of water from the fridge and started to head back.

Whispered voices stopped me at the family room door.

"I told you, we can't do this here."

I peeked into the hall, toward the sound. Four doors down, a fifty-ish man in a white doctor's coat leaned over a woman wearing a black cocktail dress and red stilettos. The female, a mid-thirties Hispanic woman with heavily lined, deep cocoa eyes, gave him a sultry pout.

"If not here, where? I've been waiting in that hotel room for hours." She nuzzled his neck. Her right hand lay flat against his chest. Her left explored significantly farther south.

The man's voice turned low and throaty. "You're killing me." He reluctantly pushed her away, exposing his handsome face, designer glasses, and perfectly tousled George Clooney like hair. "I told you I'd call as soon as I could leave, and I will. But we can't be seen like this. Not here. Especially not now."

She ran a burgundy fingernail down the center of his sternum. "So what if someone sees us? I'm tired of sneaking around. It's time for you to get a divorce. Past time."

The man flashed a conciliatory smile. "Patience, Mariella. Patience. I told you. As soon as the lawsuit is settled, I'll leave her."

She grabbed his lapels and pulled him closer. "In case you haven't noticed, patience isn't my strong suit."

This time, he didn't resist her. Their show zoomed right past PG on the fast track to R.

And they were blocking my way back to Rhonda's birthing suite. Fabulous.

What was I supposed to do now? I considered tiptoeing past the two lovers, hoping they wouldn't notice me. I considered announcing myself loudly, in hopes that they'd scurry away. I even considered spraying them both with the nearest fire extinguisher in an attempt to cool them down before the building ignited.

Their show was that hot.

In the end, I didn't have to do anything.

Nurse Tamara appeared behind them and froze. At first she seemed angry, but then the right corner of her mouth slowly lifted, forming a grin that seemed more contemptuous than friendly. She tapped the man on the shoulder, surprising him.

"You certainly live up to your nickname, don't you, *Dr. Dick*? Can't even keep it in your pants for a few hours at work? My lawyer's going to love this."

The man's mouth dropped open, but he remained silent.

Mariella grabbed Nurse Tamara's arm. "Back off, Tamara."

Nurse Tamara shoved her away. "*You* back off, you little gold digger. If you think you two are going to live happily ever after, you're a fool." She gave Dr. Dick a scathing look. "That scumbag won't leave his wife until the day he dies."

She pushed past the shocked-looking couple and marched up to me. "Summer wants you to go back and meet the new nurse. My shift's over." She continued to the end of the hallway, then stopped at the exit and growled over her shoulder, "I'm out of here. I've had enough of this circus for one day."

"Tamara, wait!" Dr. Dick ran after her. The heavy metal door slammed behind them.

Mariella stared at the glowing green-and-white exit sign, face locked in an expression of surprised frustration. After several long, uncomfortable seconds, she frowned at me. "What're you staring at?"

"Nothing. Sorry."

I scooted past her and jogged back to the birthing suite. When I opened the door, Summer and a new nurse were whispering in the corner. Rhonda squatted on a dark green birthing ball, holding her belly and rocking back and forth.

Still at four centimeters.

TWO

Twenty-one very long hours later, Rhonda's baby arrived. A seven-pound, three-ounce girl she named Miracle. And she was. A miracle, that is. By hour fifteen of Rhonda's twenty-seven hour unmedicated labor, even *I* wanted an epidural—or at least a triple shot of morphine with a laughing gas chaser.

But when that baby finally arrived, every trace of bone-weary exhaustion evaporated, replaced by joy-filled, wide-eyed wonder. Miracle burst into the world screaming, as if she'd been desperate to belt out her message. Ten perfect fingers, ten perfect toes. A full head of perfectly curly black hair. If kidnapping wasn't a felony, I'd have gathered her up in my arms and whisked her home with me. Proof positive that sleep deprivation had drained every remaining drop of my sanity.

The second miracle of the night was that I somehow managed to drive home to Ballard without causing an accident. I stumbled into the kitchen, so exhausted that I almost didn't notice the dirty dishes Michael had stacked on every available surface. A few minutes after midnight, I took a quick shower, slipped into a well-worn T-shirt, and brushed my teeth. Michael stirred but didn't awaken, so I gave him a kiss on the cheek, crawled into the Kate-sized hole between him and Bella, and closed my eyes, determined to not stir until the next evening's yoga class. Or Armageddon, whichever came last.

Seven blissfully unconscious hours later, I awoke to a low, desperate moan.

"Not today, sweetie. Michael's in charge." I reached across the bed to nudge my sleepy-headed boyfriend awake and found nothing but the heart-shaped note he'd left on his pillow.

Sorry, hon. Tiffany needs the morning off, so I have to open Pete's Pets. Love you. See you tonight.

Ugh. Why did Michael insist on opening his pet supply store before eight? I flopped back on my pillow and groaned. Bella, like Dr. Dick's red-stilettoed companion, wasn't known for her patience.

Bella whined again, punctuating her point by scraping her polar-bear-sized paw across my lips. I rolled over and covered my face with my elbow. "No. Give me fifteen more minutes."

She replied with a single sharp bark.

An inch away from my ear.

Then another.

Then another.

I rolled to face her and stared into her gorgeous, deep brown eyes. "Fine, you win. But Michael better have made coffee."

She didn't give me a chance to change my mind. She flew down the stairs like a coal-black jetliner, skidded to a stop in our newly remodeled kitchen, and plopped into a perfect sit in front of the blender. I staggered like a zombie behind her.

She barked again.

"I know. I get it already."

The bittersweet smell of hazelnut coffee lured me to the counter, where I claimed the last semi-clean mug and filled it with the delicious brew. Between sips of life-restoring stimulant, I gorged on Michael's brownies and surveyed the kitchen. All in all, the damage could have been worse. Every dish in our combined-household kitchen was stacked on the counter, and Michael had strewn what appeared to be three weeks' worth of junk mail across the table. But at least he hadn't sullied Bella's sacred food-preparation area. Thirty minutes of dishwashing and a good counter scrubbing from now, the place would be worthy of the cover of *Kitchen Digest* again.

I still couldn't believe that I—a yoga teacher with zero cooking skills—lived in a house with stainless steel appliances, stone flooring, and custom maple cabinets, but who was I to complain? Michael loved cooking. The kitchen made him happy, which made me happy. Besides, now that the construction was finally over, I loved our new home upgrade. I especially loved Michael's new bathroom, which he could trash to his heart's content.

I swallowed the last bite of brownie, then carefully measured Bella's special low-fat, grain-free, organic kibble and ground it into a fine powder. Then I added eight ounces of warm water and mixed in Bella's prescription enzymes. My dog suffered from Exocrine Pancreatic Insufficiency (EPI), an autoimmune disease that had destroyed her pancreas and left her permanently unable to digest food without added medicine. Fortunately, she'd been stable for almost a year now, knock on wood. I finished stirring the disgusting-looking concoction and set the timer for twenty minutes.

Bella barked again.

"I'm sorry. You know the drill. No food until the timer goes off."

I won. Sort of. Bella moved to the kitchen door and whined, clearly asking to be let outside.

"Sweetie, Michael put in a doggie door for you." I pointed at the huge white plastic monstrosity bisecting my otherwise perfect kitchen door. "All you have to do is push on it."

Bella sat, stared at the door, and barked.

"Seriously, Bella. You're smarter than I am. You can figure this out." I opened the flap, exposing the paved walkway that led to her destination: the immaculate, newly planted yard Michael had created for her enjoyment. "See? The yard's right there."

Bella lifted her paw and scratched near the door handle, as if demonstrating what I was supposed to do. I considered crawling through the dog door myself in hopes that she'd follow, but that strategy had already failed. Three times.

"Fine, you win."

I closed the door behind my self-satisfied-looking dog and loaded dishes into the dishwasher. I was scrubbing what appeared to be desiccated hash browns and gelatinized ketchup off of a plate when Bella barked at the door, ready to come back inside.

Seriously?

I trudged to the door and opened it again.

"I wish Michael were here so I could say 'I told you so.'"

Michael had insisted on making several dog-friendly modifications to our yard, claiming that they would decrease Bella's separation anxiety. He'd fortified our six-foot-tall fence, secured it with a mailman-proof lock, and installed a sign that read *Caution: K-9 on Duty*. He'd added a designated digging area and a plastic wading pool to one end and planted dog-friendly plants at the other. Over my many objections, he'd finished by installing the ugly white dog door that Bella had thus far refused to use. Evidently going outside wasn't fun unless your human slaves accompanied you.

Intelligence tally so far? Bella: 537. Humans: 0. Not that I was counting.

All things considered, Bella's reticence might not have been a bad thing. Six-foot-tall locked fence notwithstanding, leaving Bella on unsupervised guard dog duty seemed like a horrible idea. I'd been working hard to overcome my aversion to beards, but my dog had no such inclination. As for other dogs? Suffice it to say, if either furry man or furry beast entered Bella's property, it might not end well.

As soon as the timer went off, Bella slurped down her breakfast while I finished downing my second cup of coffee. Fully caffeinated and daily futile cleaning complete, I was too wound up to go back to bed. Plan B it would be.

I opened the cabinet and pulled out a package of unsalted peanuts—the favorite snack of Blackie, a crow Bella and I had befriended a few months ago. I grabbed Bella's leash.

"What do you think, girlfriend? Want to go to Green Lake?

Bella responded with an enthusiastic bark.

So it was decided.

By the time five o'clock rolled around, the prior night's exhaustion had ripened into a happiness hangover. I felt positively giddy. I understood now why Summer was so passionate about being a doula. The pay was below poverty level; the schedule, unpredictable. From my experience over the past two days, the hours slid well beyond brutal to practically criminal. But the high at helping a new soul enter the world? It was like nothing I'd ever experienced. Beyond even Michael's and my toe-curling ... well, you know what I mean.

I serenaded Bella with Taylor Swift songs on the drive to Serenity Yoga and parked in my reserved spot in the building's underground parking garage, or what I referred to as "Bella's Happy Space." Even though there was a surface lot nearby, I rented this coveted spot in the resident parking area specifically for Bella's comfort. It was well worth the extra cost.

Figuring out what to do with Bella while Michael and I were at work had always been a problem; she suffered from significant anxiety when alone for more than a couple of hours, so she couldn't be left at home for a full workday. She hated other dogs and was unpredictable around bearded men, so ditto on taking her into the yoga studio or leaving her at a doggie daycare. Fortunately, she loved hanging out in the back seat of my ancient Honda. Leaving my dog to guard my car wasn't the most politically correct solution, but her vet and her trainer approved as long as I always parked in a cool, covered space and took her for a walk every few hours.

I filled Bella's water bowl, cracked the windows two inches, and promised to come back and walk her soon. Usually I took the shortcut through the lobby to see if my friend and landlord, Alicia, was in the office, but she was enjoying a two-week vacation in Maui, so I skipped the long way around the apartment building, window-shopping at the street-level businesses and picking up a bouquet of vibrant yellow sunflowers at the PhinneyWood Market. I glanced through the window of Pete's Pets but didn't see Michael, so I headed to Serenity Yoga. I was still humming chipper breakup tunes when I floated through the studio's front entrance.

Tiffany Kobrick—Michael's (and currently my) employee—sat behind the desk, grumpily updating the studio's database. Every cell in her body vibrated annoyance, from the tips of her greenish-blue toenails to the roots of her bleached blonde hair. She stood as I entered, exposing her newest yoga outfit: black and aqua capri yoga pants with a matching, form-fitting tank top. The words *Love All*,

Serve All stretched across her barely contained breasts. If her annoyed scowl was any indication, she wasn't in the mood for either at the moment.

She slammed a file folder onto the desk with an irritated thunk. "Kate, these intake forms are impossible. Can't you ask your students to write legibly? If I have to work two jobs, they should both at least be possible. Pete's Pets may have sucky hours, but at least I don't have to decipher bad handwriting."

Not even Tiffany could ruin my postpartum-by-proxy elation. I floated up to the desk, wearing a warm smile. "Come here, you. Give me a hug." I opened my arms wide. Tiffany's eyes opened wider. Her pupils contracted to the size of ultrafine pencil leads. I wrapped my arms around her and squeezed. She stiffened, as if expecting me to thrust a knife into her spine. When I let go, she backed slowly toward the wall, like a camper backing away from a grizzly.

"N-never mind. I shouldn't have complained."

I softened my eyes and tried to appear nonthreatening. "No, you're right. Deciphering the handwriting on those forms is impossible. I gave you all of the crap jobs, and it isn't fair." I placed the file folder in the desk drawer and closed the laptop's lid. "Take the rest of the day off. I'll clean the studio so you don't have to."

"But the data—"

I held up my hand. "No arguments. The database can wait. You've been working hard, and you deserve a break."

Tiffany peered at me, head cocked to the side, clearly wondering if I'd contracted some reverse form of rabies. "Thanks, Kate, but I still owe you another hour of work today, and I can't violate Michael's work-release program. He's worse than the guards at the King County Jail. He told me that if he catches me slacking off, he'll make me scrub out the dog waste containers with my toothbrush."

She was referring to Michael's keep-Tiffany-out-of-jail community service program. In short, Tiffany had agreed to give me 200 hours of work to make up for trashing my car a few months ago. In exchange, I'd agreed not to report her to the police. When Michael first proposed the arrangement, I'd balked. But I had to admit, his plan—which was to straighten out Tiffany while simultaneously forcing me to spend time with her—was working. Although Tiffany was nowhere close to being my friend, I despised her a little less every day.

I reached into my purse and tossed her my car keys. "How about a different job, then? Bella's in my car. Take her to Greenwood Park for a walk and then clean up after Mister Feathers. After that, put Bella back in my car and go home. You deserve the rest of the evening off."

Tiffany skillfully avoided acknowledging that I'd asked her to clean up the pigeon droppings decorating Serenity Yoga's back entrance. Either that or my suggestion had shocked her deaf.

"You trust me with your car keys?"

My answer surprised both of us. "Yes, I do. When you're done, put them in the top drawer of the filing cabinet. Remember to keep Bella at least fifteen feet away from other dogs. If Pete's Pets is empty, you can take her inside to visit Michael. That way he'll see that you're working."

Trusting Tiffany with Bella was a much bigger leap of faith than handing her my car keys. Damaging my dented old Honda Civic had been the reason she'd gotten into trouble in the first place, and she would never risk lengthening her stint of hard labor. Asking her to walk Bella, on the other hand, was huge. I never left Bella with anyone other than Michael or Rene, and even then I obsessively worried. I was obviously still high on baby juice.

Tiffany skipped out the back door, wearing a surprised-looking smile. I said a quick prayer to the universe that Bella would behave herself, then shifted gears and prepared the practice space for my six o'clock class: Yoga to Overcome Grief.

Tonight's class was special, as it was the last class in a series designed to help students find new meaning after loss. Everything needed to be perfect. I placed the bouquet of golden sunflowers on the altar, lined the walls with flickering tea lights, and set two large bamboo bowls on the floor next to my mat. One contained unlit candles; the other, purple envelopes that I'd filled with Pacific Northwest wildflower seeds. Seeds of joy, if you will, that I would ask each student to scatter someplace special. I finished by burning sage to clear the room's energy and chanting "Om Shanti," the ancient Sanskrit mantra for peace.

The chime on the front door rang, announcing that the first students had entered the reception area. I scanned the yoga space a final time to make sure everything was perfect, turned on my favorite Deva Premal CD, and headed to join them.

Justine Maxwell and Rachel Jones, two of the workshop's fifteen students, loitered uncomfortably by the front desk.

"Sorry, Kate. Are we too early?" Rachel asked.

"Not at all, I'm glad to see you."

I never got used to seeing Rachel in yoga clothes. I'd met her only two months earlier, at the Lake Washington Medical Center when Rene was hospitalized there for preterm labor. At the hospital, Rachel wore a dishwater-blonde ponytail and a brightly colored nurse's uniform. Tonight she wore a black yogatard, a purple headband, and a worried expression. Her normally lively blue eyes seemed clouded.

"Everything okay?" I asked.

"It's Nicole."

Nicole Amato, Rachel's sixteen-year-old daughter, normally attended class with her. I glanced out the window, expecting to see her sulking outside. The sidewalk was empty.

Rachel chewed on her thumbnail. "She was supposed to be home from a school event over an hour ago. My husband is going to be furious. He hates it when she's late."

"I told you," Justine replied. "If Richard can't handle Nicole acting out like a normal teenager every now and then, don't tell him about it." She grabbed a paper cup and poured hot water over a bag of chamomile tea. The sweet floral scent clashed with the room's tense energy. "What Richard doesn't know won't come back to bite you."

"I suppose, but ... " Rachel's words trailed off.

"But what?" Justine asked.

"What am I supposed to tell him if she doesn't show up at all? I have to get home somehow."

Justine replied with a tired smile. "I'll drive you home. It'll be no trouble at all."

We all knew she was lying. Justine had very little spare time and no extra energy. She worked as a labor and delivery nurse at the same hospital as Rachel. When she wasn't helping deliver babies, she was the sole caretaker of a mother with advanced Alzheimer's. Her deep brown eyes were almost always underscored by purple-gray half moons, and her graying brown hair usually seemed wilted. Although she'd recently celebrated her forty-second birthday, Justine looked at least a decade older.

I circled the conversation back to Rachel's daughter. "So, it seems Nicole isn't coming tonight?" The absence disappointed me. The often-sullen teenager seemed to be benefiting from the class, though I doubted she would ever admit it to her mother. Or to anyone else, for that matter.

Rachel's lips wrinkled. "Honestly, I have no idea *what* Nicole is doing tonight. She's up to something again, and it can't be good. I swear that girl is going to be the death of me."

I paused for a moment, trying to formulate an appropriate response. I wanted to tell Rachel not to worry—that all sixteen-year-old girls drove their mothers nuts. I wanted to encourage her to have patience. Nicole's father had died of cancer two years ago, and his death had been devastating for the young teen. I especially wanted to ask her to give Nicole a break; she was finally adjusting to life without her father. A minor indiscretion could surely be forgiven.

In the end, I said nothing. Before I could get out my first word, the studio's front door crashed open. A furious-looking man stormed through it, followed by a small, hesitant group of my students. Frankly, I was a little taken aback myself.

What on earth is he doing here?

The man I knew only as Dr. Dick glanced through me as if I were invisible. He glared at Rachel, then whipped his head left and right, clearly searching for someone. If he remembered me from last night at ABBA, he didn't show it.

"Where in the hell is she?" he snapped.

I suppressed my surprised recognition, pasted on my take-charge, business owner expression, and marched directly up to the rude stranger.

"I don't know who you are, but unless you're planning to take a yoga class, I'm afraid you'll have to leave." I hesitated a millisecond before adding, "Or I'm calling the police."

Rachel's face reddened. She stepped between us, whether to block me from Dr. Dick or him from me, I wasn't quite sure. "It's okay, Kate," she said. "Please don't call anyone. This is my husband, Dr. Richard Jones."

THREE

I stepped a few feet away to give Rachel the illusion of privacy, but stayed close enough to intervene if the confrontation turned violent. Justine huddled near the schefflera tree and stared into her tea as if reading her future in a bag of Cozy Chamomile. The rest of the students loitered in front of the yoga room's entrance, shifting back and forth and murmuring at the commotion.

Rachel placed a calming hand on her husband's arm. "What are you doing here, Richard?"

"Looking for that daughter of yours."

"Nicole's not here. She had an event after school today, remember?"

Dr. Dick's—I mean Dr. Jones's—face burned so hot, I was surprised the sweat dotting his forehead didn't steam up his glasses. "Don't make excuses for her. She promised to be home in time for yoga, and you know it. Besides, I went by the school. That good-for-nothing delinquent lied to us. They had early release today. If she's not here with you, then she's up to no good."

"Calm down, Richard. She's probably just running late."

He crossed his arms and scowled. "She's not late, she's a thief. She stole fifty dollars out of my wallet." His hands formed tight fists. "That little tramp is off doing drugs with her friends again, and I will not stand for it."

Rachel flinched. "Are you sure? She's seemed better lately. She passed her last three urine tests." She lowered her voice as if suddenly aware that she had eavesdroppers. "Can we talk about this at home?"

Dr. Dick grabbed Rachel's arms and yanked her to within an inch of his face. "I warned you both. One more strike and she's out. If you won't control that girl, I'll send her someplace that will."

Rachel froze, but she didn't give ground. She narrowed her eyes and hissed through clenched teeth. "Let go of me. Now."

I backed slowly toward the desk and laid my hand on the phone, ready to dial 911.

After several long seconds, Dr. Dick roughly released her and made one final proclamation. "When Nicole comes back—if she comes back—tell her to pack her bags. She's no longer welcome in my home."

The door's chimes clanged forcibly behind him, as if punctuating the seriousness of his threat.

Rachel stared after him, absently rubbing the finger-shaped welts he'd left behind. "He doesn't mean it. He'd never send Nicole away." Her voice didn't sound confident.

I stepped away from the desk and gestured to the gawkers. "Hey, everyone. Go inside the studio and set up your mats. We'll join you in a minute."

Justine hovered near the entrance to the yoga room, seeming conflicted—as if she wanted to escape Rachel's drama but felt compelled to stay behind. I motioned toward the door. She mouthed the words "thank you" and disappeared behind it.

I gently placed my arm around Rachel's shoulders and guided her to the bench. "Are you okay?"

"Yes. Or at least I will be."

I hesitated before speaking. The question I was about to ask was important, but I wasn't sure how Rachel would receive it. "I don't know how to say this, so I'll just blurt it out. Are you safe at home? I can help if you need—"

She cut me off. "Don't worry about that, Kate. Nicole brings out the worst in Richard, but he's never been violent." She examined the marks on her arms, which had already begun to fade. "These aren't as bad as they look. The only thing Richard bruised was my ego." She buried her face in her hands. "I'm so mortified."

"Don't worry about it. You should see some of my fights with Michael." I poured a glass of cool water. Rachel's hands trembled as she took it.

"Richard and I never fought until Nicole moved in. Now arguing seems to be all that we have in common." She took a small sip, then a larger one. "I feel like a terrible mother for saying this, but some days I wish he *would* send her away. Maybe then our life could go back to normal."

"Normal?"

"The way it was before Nicole joined us. Parenting was a heck of a lot easier when it was two weekends a month." She covered her face again and moaned. "Oh good lord, I *am* a terrible mother." When she looked back up, her eyes begged for understanding. "Please don't hate me. It's been a hard adjustment—for all of us. Nicole adored her father. She'd lived with him since she was three. She and I, on the other hand . . ." Her voice trailed off.

I considered, not for the first time, asking Rachel why her ex-husband had raised Nicole, but I didn't. The answer was likely painful, private, and complex. Definitely too complex for a five-minute conversation in a yoga studio lobby. If I'd learned anything during my reconciliation with my own mother, it was that good parents sometimes made terrible choices. Choices they later regretted.

Rachel sighed. "Sometimes I think Donny got off easy by dying. He's beyond earthly problems now. The rest of us are still trying to piece our lives back together."

She stood, drained her cup, and tossed it into the garbage can. "Thanks for listening. I'm okay now. Time to slink into the studio and pretend that the whole scene with Richard didn't happen." She paused at the door. "Will you do me a favor?"

"Sure."

"If Nicole comes, don't say anything to her. I'll talk to her after class."

While Rachel joined the others, I moved behind the desk and absently checked in the last straggling students, none of whom were Nicole. My body sat firmly in the present, but my mind was trapped in the past. Nurse Tamara had been right last night: Dr. Dick truly lived up to his name. Not only was he a first-class jerk, he was also a cheater. A cheater who might be planning to divorce Rachel.

All of which left me with a true dilemma. What was I supposed to do with that information now?

———

Ten minutes later, I walked into the yoga room wearing a serene—and entirely fake—smile. This wasn't the first time I'd learned that a friend's husband was cheating, but that didn't make having the unwanted information any easier.

No matter how hard I tried to come up with a solution, my heart and my mind refused to agree. My heart begged me to tell Rachel what I'd seen last night, and quickly. Living with a cheater couldn't possibly get easier with time. My mind warned me to keep my mouth shut. Rachel was a student, not a friend. For all I knew, she was already aware of Richard's infidelity.

I shelved my conflicting impulses and invited everyone to sit in a circle for a final pre-class check-in. "Since this is our last class, I don't have any lecture material prepared. This is your time to talk, if you want to. Do you have any questions or thoughts you'd like to share?"

A few students asked questions. Most simply listened. Rachel glanced at the door every ten seconds, looking for her daughter. I was about to send everyone back to their mats when Justine spoke.

"I don't have any questions, but I want to say something." She paused as if searching for the right words. "I told you all in our first class that I lost my husband and daughter—" Her throat caught. "I lost Bob and my baby Anya in a car accident three years ago. She was only two." She looked down at her hands. "What I didn't tell you is that I was injured, too. A piece of metal penetrated my abdomen. They had to do a hysterectomy to stop the bleeding. I'll never have any more children." She took a deep breath and continued. "For the longest time, I wished that I had died that day, too."

The yoga room door cracked open. Nicole eased through it and quietly unrolled a mat in the back. Her mother gave her a dark look.

Justine continued speaking. "Some days I still don't think I can bear the pain, but maybe … I'm beginning to think that maybe I'll survive. The breathing, the movement … It helps more than I ever could have imagined." She made eye contact with me and smiled. For the first time since I'd known her, she didn't look tired. "Thank you."

Justine wasn't the first student to tell me that yoga had changed her life, and I prayed that she wouldn't be the last. Stories like hers made the stresses of small business ownership worthwhile.

She gave me a hug, and then everyone returned to their mats.

I led a gentle, emotionally balancing class for the next forty-five minutes, trying to connect with each of my students. The grandmother in the second row had lost her husband to lung cancer six months ago. The young couple in front, their child to whooping cough. The heavyset man in the back recently lost the love of his life, a tiny black poodle named Lucy. I mentally sent each of them positive energy, each of them strength.

But no matter how hard I tried to focus on all of my students, my gaze kept landing on two: Rachel and Nicole.

Was Nicole high? Yoga was a relatively safe form of exercise, but all things considered, I preferred that my students be sober. Nicole had seemed flustered when she'd entered the room, but that wasn't surprising. She'd arrived over twenty minutes late. Her dark, shoulder-length hair could have used a good washing and her black sweats had dirt encrusted on the knees. But her movements seemed easeful. Her breath, fluid. If she was high, she was good at concealing it.

Her mother's movements, on the other hand, were erratic. Not at all linked with her breath. Her shoulders were still tense from the fight with her husband, but that didn't surprise me, either. Not even the best yoga practice could make up for being married to a jerk.

Admittedly, the thought wasn't yogic. *The Yoga Sutras*—yoga's key philosophical text—ask us to be neutral toward evil, and my attitude toward Dr. Dick was anything but neutral. Still, I had to believe that whether he was handsome—and likely rich—or not, Nicole and Rachel could do much, much better.

I finished the movement portion of the practice and asked the students to close their eyes for a brief meditation.

I sat crossed-legged on my meditation rug and spoke. "Take a moment to reflect on your life. Not as it was in the past, but how it can be in the future. As you've all discovered, we can't always control the events in our lives. We *can*, however, choose how we react to them. Tonight, if your future feels dark, lighten it."

"How?"

Nicole's question surprised me. Talking during yoga class is a well-known taboo. Even outside of our formal practice time, Nicole had asked at most two questions in the past six weeks. Evidently her third was going to be a doozy.

The girl's lower lip trembled. Her eyes glistened. Her expression held yearning, as if begging me to draw her a road map home. If the confused expressions on the room's other fourteen faces were any indication, she wasn't the only one lost.

I gazed at the hardwood floor for a moment and thought back to the first horrible years after my father's death. Before Bella and Michael, I had also been lost, though I didn't realize it at the time. Bella and Michael had been my road map home. But telling the overweight, likely depressed teenager that her problems would be solved by getting a boyfriend and a dog didn't seem helpful—or truthful, for that matter. I thanked the universe for Michael and Bella every day, but I'd become stronger in the past year. Strong enough that if by some unfathomable chain of events I lost them both, I knew I'd survive.

Which brought me back to Nicole's question.

How?

The answer came to me as a single word. I lifted my eyes and said it out loud.

"Hope."

Fifteen confused pairs of eyes stared back at me. The man who'd lost his dog frowned at his mat. The couple leaned subtly away from each other. Nicole rolled her eyes.

"Seriously," I said. "No matter how tough life gets, we can always find hope. Hope sustains us, lifts us up, and motivates us to move forward."

They still didn't get it. Frankly, I wasn't sure I did, either.

"Let's try a different meditation. Close your eyes again, and notice your breath." Everyone except Nicole complied. She crossed her arms and scowled. I kept speaking. "Whether you can see it or not, hope exists all around you. You just have to allow it inside."

Nicole pretended to gag herself with her index finger. "Whatever."

Rachel stood, I assumed to chastise her daughter. I motioned for her to sit again. Nicole finally closed her eyes.

"Imagine that hope is a bright yellow light filling the space around you. Every time you inhale, breathe that light into your lungs and feel it soak into your heart. Each time you exhale, imagine it moving through your entire body, illuminating every cell."

It wasn't the meditation I'd practiced, but it was the one I was meant to teach. As the minutes passed, the creases in the grandmother's brow smoothed. The couple who had lost their child reached out and held hands. The tension in Rachel's shoulders finally released. Nicole's energy shifted; her protective armor softened.

By the time my students lit the candles and gathered their seeds, the room seemed lighter somehow. I, more than anyone, understood that yoga wasn't magic. A single ninety-minute practice hadn't fundamentally changed anyone's situation. But I had no doubt: my teaching had made a positive impact.

On nights like tonight, I loved my job.

Nicole smiled and gave me a hug before leaving.

"Thanks, Kate. This class didn't suck too much."

Nicole's smile didn't last long. Rachel started scolding her the minute the door closed behind them. Filled with a deep sense of foreboding, I watched the two women cross the parking lot. If the earlier scene with Dr. Dick had been any indication, Nicole's night was about to get significantly worse.

FOUR

I USHERED THE FINAL student out the door, locked up the studio, and hustled home to Michael. I needed his help to decide what I should— or more likely, what I shouldn't—tell Rachel about her husband's affair. Hopefully he'd come up with a solution that would keep me from practicing my least favorite yoga posture: foot-in mouth pose.

I arrived home to a dark house and a spotless kitchen. Irrefutable evidence that Michael hadn't been home since I'd left.

I performed my futile teach-Bella-how-to-use-the-doggie-door ritual, made her dinner, and curled up on the couch with the day's junk mail and a glass of oaky Chardonnay. The clock read almost ten o'clock when Michael opened the front door. The sweet, spicy scent of General Tso's tofu wafted in with him. Michael's curly brown hair was messy—the way it got when he was stressed and ran his hands through it.

"Wow. You had a long day," I said.

He hadn't made eye contact, so I couldn't be sure, but I would have sworn that his blue-green eyes were missing their normal mischievous sparkle.

"You don't know the half of it." He stood hesitantly near the door, keys in one hand, white plastic takeout bag from PhinneyWood Mandarin in the other. "I wasn't sure if you'd already eaten, so I picked up Chinese food. I brought steamed snow peas for Bella." He handed me the bag, then took off his jacket and hung it in the coat closet.

I sat up straight and set my glass on the end table. Something was wrong. Michael never hung up his jacket. He never hung up anything. I declared victory if he tossed his clean and dirty laundry in separate piles on the floor.

"Michael, what's wrong?"

He ignored my question and flashed a smile so fake it could have been molded from plastic. "Do you want another glass of wine to go with dinner?"

No doubt about it, the man was up to something. And it couldn't be good.

"I'm good, thanks."

Bella sniffed the air and then padded into the kitchen, uncharacteristically ignoring the bag of food in my lap. For several long seconds, Michael's and my silence was broken only by the sound of German shepherd toenails on stone.

Michael sat next to me on the couch and cleared his throat. "I was thinking on the drive home. You know what they say about making the best of a bad situation?"

Finger-like tendrils of tension knotted my shoulders. "What bad situation?"

"Hear me out. Sometimes what you think is bad actually turns out for the best. Like when Tiffany broke into your car. You wanted to report her to the police, but I talked you out of it. That's worked out pretty well, don't you think? You're getting free help at the studio, and she's taking the work seriously. I swear she's getting more mature every day."

Oh good lord. Tiffany.

Michael had a serious soft spot for that girl. What had she done this time? It couldn't be that bad. I'd just seen her a few hours ago. All she had to do was walk Bel—

My breath caught. *Oh no. Bella.*

Visions of dog fights, veterinary hospitals, and future visits from Animal Control officers flashed through my head. I grabbed Michael's arm. "Bella didn't get into trouble when Tiffany walked her, did she?"

"No, this has nothing to do with—" Michael stopped, mid-sentence, and gaped at me, his mouth open in a wide O. "Wait a minute. You let *Tiffany* walk *Bella*? What were you, stoned?"

I didn't reply.

He shuddered, as if shaking the image out of a mental Etch-a-Sketch. "This has nothing to do with Bella. I'm just saying, what happened with Tiffany is a good example. Doing the right thing is important, even when it's difficult."

Now I was frustrated. "Michael, stop stalling. What's going on?" With my luck, he wanted Tiffany to move in with us. "Did Tiffany get kicked out of her apartment?" I vigorously shook my head. "Uh uh. No way. Having Tiffany as a minion is bad enough. She is *not* living with us."

"Who said anything about—"

A rubbery-sounding *thwack* came from the kitchen. Michael froze, as if every muscle in his body had spasmed at once. "What was that sound?"

35

I shrugged. "Bella must have finally figured out how to use the doggie door."

"The dog door? Oh no, the puppies!" Michael leaped from the couch and tore through the kitchen. The door slammed behind him.

Puppies?

Surely I'd misheard him. Michael would never be stupid enough to bring puppies here. Bella would tear them to shreds.

In an instant of terrifying clarity, I got it.

Bella. The dog door!

Bella had never harmed another dog, but she'd never encountered one on her property, either. I loved my overly territorial German shepherd to a fault, but I held no illusions. If Bella found a strange dog in her yard, she would hurt it.

Or worse.

I jumped up and scrambled after Michael.

What felt like five years later, I skidded to a stop at the edge of the patio and gaped.

How much wine did I drink?

I had to be hallucinating. I turned on the porch light and rubbed my eyes. My alcohol-addled brain still saw them.

Puppies. Two of them.

Tiny, curly-haired fluff balls, one golden, one black, at most six weeks old. The gold one was sucking on Bella's ear. The black one nuzzled the fur on her belly. My hundred-pound puppy eater was bathing them both with her long, black-spotted tongue.

Michael glanced my direction and gave me a tentative smile. "Kate, meet Mutt and Jeff."

"Seriously, Michael? What were you thinking?"

He shrugged. "I had to call them something."

Michael knew I wasn't referring to his poor choice of names, but I let it go. I was too dumbfounded to argue. I sat next to Bella and rubbed the soft spot behind her ears. "Good job, Bella. What a gooooood girl." Bella ignored me. She was too busy grooming her new charges to bother with anyone else.

I pointed at the black pup, who had evidently found one of Bella's nipples and was contentedly, although unsuccessfully, nursing. "Why hasn't Bella eaten these guys yet?"

Michael's expression was as confused as mine. "I've heard of puppy license before, but never like this. Not with a dog as reactive as Bella. I thought we'd have to keep them completely separated."

"Puppy license?"

"That's what it's called. Adult dogs often allow behavior from puppies that they would never tolerate from an adolescent or another adult." He shook his head in disbelief. "Still, this is amazing. Do you think Bella has had puppies before?"

"I doubt it. She'd already been spayed when George died and I adopted her. George had his faults, but he was a responsible dog owner. He never mentioned puppies."

Michael shrugged. "Before George, maybe?"

"He stole her from that horrible Trucker Man when she was only six months old. She would have been too young then." I pointed at the gold-colored pup, which had joined the black one at Bella's stomach. "Why are they nursing? Bella doesn't have milk."

"They don't know that yet. Besides, it probably comforts them, poor little guys."

Bella sighed, rested her head in my lap, and narrowed her eyes in pure German shepherd bliss. "Such a gooooood girl," I crooned. I shook my finger at Michael in not-quite-mock indignation. "You, on the other hand, have some serious explaining to do."

A half hour later, Michael and I sat on the couch eating cold Chinese food while Bella stared adoringly at her new best friends. Thus far, the pups seemed completely safe with Bella, but we couldn't be sure, so Michael put them in an indoor exercise pen ("ex-pen") that he'd brought home from Pete's Pets. Michael drank a Guinness while I sipped a second glass of Chardonnay—my new self-imposed limit.

I finished the last bite of tangy, deep-fried tofu and set my plate to the side. "Okay Michael, spill. Where did these little guys come from?"

"Not guys. A girl and a guy." He pointed at the gold puppy. "Mutt is the girl. The black one, Jeff, is a boy." I gave him a droll look.

He shrugged. "I don't know where they came from. I heard whining outside Pete's Pets earlier this evening, and when I opened the door, that *Dollars for Change* vendor with the weird hat scurried away. I think she dumped them there."

"Momma Bird?"

I'd met Momma Bird while I was investigating the murder of Bella's prior owner, George. She worked for a homeless advocacy newspaper, *Dollars for Change*. Like most *Dollars for Change* vendors, Momma Bird was homeless. Although she usually worked in the University District, she occasionally took George's old spot in front of the PhinneyWood Grocer.

"Where would Momma Bird have gotten puppies?" I asked. "She doesn't own a dog, at least not one that I've seen."

The lines around Michael's mouth hardened. "I don't know, but if they're hers, she better give us some explanation. What kind of person leaves a box of helpless puppies alone on a doorstep? What if I hadn't seen them?"

"If it was Momma Bird, she did it because she knew they'd be safe with you." I smiled at the puppies, who were now wrestling with each other and growling. "Abandoning an animal doesn't seem like her, though. She's eccentric, but she's kind. The homeless people I've met take better care of their animals than they do of themselves."

"These pups were *not* well cared for. I wanted to make sure they didn't have any puppy diseases before I brought them home, so I took them to the emergency clinic. The vet says they're underweight and malnourished. They were so infested with fleas that they're anemic."

I cringed. "Fleas?"

"Relax, Kate. The vet bathed and flea-treated them before we left. She gave them a thorough checkup, and except for poor nutrition and anemia, they seem basically healthy. We'll have to give them special supplements and keep a close eye on them, just in case." Before I could argue with the word "we," Michael gathered our dishes and carried them to the kitchen.

The gold puppy toddled to the edge of the ex-pen and whined at me adorably. I could barely resist the urge to pick her up and cuddle her.

Well played, little monster. Well played.

I yelled over my shoulder, toward the kitchen. "What kind of dogs are they?"

Michael emerged, carrying the last two vegan brownies. "The vet isn't sure, but she thinks they might be labradoodles—young ones, around six weeks old. I wanted to vaccinate them, but the vet wouldn't do it. She says we need to wait a week or two until they're healthier. If Momma Bird let them get in this condition, she should be ashamed of herself."

He handed me the biggest brownie and I took a bite. "Don't be so quick to judge her, Michael. She might have found the pups somewhere. Just be glad she didn't leave the mother. Bella would have never..."

I set my brownie on the coffee table, appetite suddenly gone. "Michael, where is the mother? You don't think she's..." I didn't want to say the word.

Michael's expression was grim. "I don't know what to think, Kate. Wherever she is, I doubt she's in great shape." He laced his fingers through mine. "I promise, if I find out who dumped the puppies, I'll grill them about the mother. Maybe we can help her, too. The immediate question is, what are we going to do with these two?"

I glanced at the two sleeping fur balls, curled together in an almost perfect yin-yang symbol. Bella stared at them through the expen's wires, as if guarding them from evil puppy-nappers.

"They seem safe enough here for tonight," I said. "But I don't fully trust Bella. We should keep them separated unless we're able to watch them."

Michael agreed. "You sleep in the bedroom with Bella. I'll stay down here on the couch tonight with the pups."

"Good idea. I'll call Betty at Fido's Last Chance first thing tomorrow."

Michael looked horrified. "You want to send Mutt and Jeff to a rescue? Kennels aren't safe for unvaccinated puppies. What if they get Parvo?"

"Maybe Betty can find a foster home for them."

"I suppose..." Michael's words trailed off. He stared at the floor as if searching for strength in the carpet's worn fibers.

I knew what Michael was thinking, and I didn't like it. Not one bit. Taking care of Bella was already a full-time job. Adding two more—likely unhousetrained—dogs to the mix? One of us would have to quit working.

Michael's eyes implored me. "I feel responsible for them, Kate. Somebody left Mutt and Jeff where they knew I would find them. They must have had a reason. If it wasn't that Momma Bird character, then who was it? What if they come back to get them?"

"What if they do? You said yourself that the puppies haven't been well cared for. Would you seriously give them back to a negligent owner?"

"No, of course not. But before we do anything rash, can't we take a few days to figure out what's best for them?" I didn't reply. He continued. "You always say that the universe does things for a reason. Maybe we're meant to have these dogs."

I placed my hand on his arm. "Michael, sweetheart, we can't keep them. We have a hard enough time taking care of Bella. She has to come first."

Michael pointed at Bella, who was resting her chin on her paws, staring at the sleeping puppies. "I know that, Kate, but look at her. She wants to protect them, too. Besides, there might be a positive side. Having Mutt and Jeff around might reduce Bella's separation anxiety. Heck, it might teach her how to get along with other dogs."

I'd already been beaten and I knew it. I shook my head no, anyway. "Puppies are a lot of work, Michael. We don't have the time. Bella seems happy enough now, but how do we know it will last? What if she hurts one of them?"

"I agree. We'll have to keep them separated from Bella when we're not with them, and we probably won't adopt them."

Probably?

Michael kneeled in front of me and placed his palms on my knees. "Can't we at least foster them until they're healthy enough to rehome? I've been with them for almost five hours now, and they're super mellow. They've hardly done anything but sleep. They'll be no trouble at all. Give me time to find out where they came from. I promise, I'll do most of the work."

When Michael flashed those sexy blue-green eyes my direction, I could never refuse him.

So I avoided eye contact.

I stared silently at my lap for several long seconds, trying to dredge up the willpower to say no.

I failed.

"Okay, Michael."

A grin spread across his entire face. "Thanks. You won't—"

I held up my index finger. "Don't get too excited. I'm still only agreeing for tonight. First thing tomorrow I'm calling Betty, and Bella's trainer, too. If they think it's safe, the pups can stay here for a couple of weeks. But if either one of them says no, then we have to come up with an alternate solution. Agreed?"

He nodded his head yes.

"In the meantime, you need to start looking for their owner."

"Deal."

FIVE

I HAD TO GIVE Michael credit. He was a man of his word. As soon as Betty and Bella's trainer gave our plan two thumbs up, he conned Tiffany into working overtime while he took the next few days off to work on "Project Puppy." He bathed; he fed; he made a valiant attempt at potty training. He listed the fur balls' information on Petfinder and placed a found-dog advertisement on the PhinneyWood blog. He even posted flyers around the Greenwood neighborhood, asking anyone who had lost two dogs to dial his cell number and describe them. Except for a call from a woman searching for two escaped Rottweilers, his phone remained silent.

The puppies—whose names still hadn't changed from Mutt and Jeff—got significantly more rambunctious; Bella, more exhausted. After losing two pairs of shoes, his favorite Shania Twain CD, and a brand-new pair of reading glasses to two mouthfuls of puppy teeth, Michael was seriously reconsidering my positive-reinforcement-only training philosophy. Betty at Fido's Last Chance was on standby in case we needed help, but so far, there hadn't been any signs of aggression toward the pups—from either man or beast.

Two days after the puppies mysteriously appeared, I escaped to the relative calm of Rene's house to join her and her husband Sam for the grand opening party of Lake Washington Medical Center's new birthing facility. Rene would have preferred to give birth at ABBA, but her two-baby pregnancy didn't qualify for a low-risk birthing center not associated with a full-service hospital. We hoped that the fancy new facility at Lake Washington, which was scheduled to open next week, would be the next-best thing.

Rene opened the door before my first knock. She glanced surreptitiously left and right, tucked a strand of shoulder-length, dark brown hair behind her ear, and gesticulated vigorously for me to come inside. "Quick! Get in here before he sees you." She peeked over her shoulder to make sure we were alone, then leaned toward me and whispered, "Did you bring it?"

Sam, her gorgeous blond husband, wandered out of the kitchen, drying his hands on a dish towel. He stopped at the door and reached for my purse.

"Give it to me, Kate."

I cocked my head to the side in feigned ignorance. "Give you what?"

He reached out his hand and repeatedly curled his fingers toward himself in the universal *fork it over* sign. "Whatever junk food you've smuggled in for Rene this time."

Sam and Rene had always been fitness obsessed, but since Rene's pregnancy, Sam had also become a junk food Nazi. I understood his point. Sort of. Rene's typical diet was more of the Willy Wonka than the Jenny Craig variety. But his obsession with prenatal nutrition had gotten ridiculous. At this point, Rene was more likely to die of carbo-hydrate withdrawal than her twins were to suffer from malnutrition.

I reached into my purse and pulled out a package of dark chocolate M&Ms. Sam stared at me, not breaking eye contact.

"Give me the rest of it, too."

I sighed, dug to the bottom, and handed him the second package.

Sam scanned the ingredients. "Seriously, Kate? There are ten added food colors in this garbage. And corn syrup? That's nothing but empty calories. You're a yoga teacher. I expected better from you."

"Why should I waste my money on organic chocolate when I know you'll just throw it away?" I pointed to the label. "Besides, it's not all junk. Look right here. Two grams of protein."

Sam shook his head in disgust, tore open both packets, and poured their contents into a garbage can next to the door. I winked at Rene before following Sam into the living room. I'd slip her the dark chocolate peanut butter cups I'd held in reserve later.

I froze at the entryway. "Wow, Rene. You've been busy."

Rene's *Architectural Digest* worthy living room had been torn apart by a baby-focused tornado. The floor-to-ceiling windows that nor-mally showcased the room's Olympic Mountain views were now blocked by boxes. Stacks and stacks of boxes. Every available surface—including two large folding tables that hadn't been there three weeks ago—was covered with patterns, fabrics, and brightly colored baby bibs. The couches had been pushed to the side to make room on the wool rug for a disorganized collage of 8 x 10 infant portraits. A Jenga-like stack of full-color brochures teetered next to Rene's laptop, which was positioned haphazardly on the edge of the end table.

"Aren't you supposed to be resting?" I asked.

Sam grumbled something unintelligible under his breath.

"Knock it off, Mr. Grumpy Pants," Rene replied. "The doctor said I needed to stay home for the final two months of my pregnancy, and I have. I stopped doing Hot Yoga. I gave up jogging, for goodness sake. Sorting through pictures and glancing at a few fabric samples never hurt anyone."

Sam opened his mouth to argue, but she turned her back to him and spoke to me. "Besides, Sam has been doing all of the heavy lifting. I have to occupy my time with something, otherwise I'll go insane. Not being able to exercise all these weeks has been driving me batty. No offense, Kate, but those breathing exercises you gave me don't cut it." She tapped an index finger against her temple. "These mental muscles need to burn off some serious calories. The girls certainly won't benefit from having a looney tunes mother."

Rene had come up with the idea for her infant accessory line during her two-week hospitalization for preterm labor. At the time, I thought her obsession would end as soon as the morphine wore off, but if anything, she'd grown *more* committed to the business since she'd been home on modified bed rest.

She kept talking. "Besides, the designs are all mine, but I've hired out most of the leg work. I hired a seamstress to make the samples, and an advertising firm is creating the catalogues." She pointed at two mirror-image photos taped next to the window. "What do you think of those two toddlers as my first cover girls? My twins will be prettier, of course, but they won't be able to smile until they're a couple of months old, and the catalogues need to go out in five weeks."

"They're adorable," I said honestly. I picked up the world's tiniest pink and yellow handbag. "What's this?"

Rene grinned. "Why, a pacifier purse, of course. All of the cool babies will be carrying them this season." She picked up the purse's twin and tied the ribbon attached to it into a tiny bow. "They can be tied to the baby's wrist or onto a stroller. I wanted to make shoulder bags, but I was afraid the straps would strangle the babies. Besides, this is cuter, don't you think?"

I ignored her question and asked one of my own. "Isn't all of this expensive?"

"Yes, but as they say, you have to spend money to make money. Besides, Sam doesn't mind." She smiled teasingly at him. "A divorce settlement would cost a lot more, right, honey?"

Sam's caterpillar-like blond mustache twitched.

He might not have approved of Rene's newest venture, but she was right. They could certainly afford it. Sam's uber-successful software company had made enough money to start a dozen baby boutiques. Add his financial success to the couple's Ken and Barbie looks, and I would have hated them if I didn't love them so much.

Rene grabbed a handful of brochures off of the end table and thumbed through them. "Would it be tacky to hand these out at the reception?"

Sam swiped them out of her hands and thunked them solidly back on the end table. "Yes. The hospital is advertising *their* services today, not yours." He leaned across Rene's three-person belly and gave her a kiss. "I love you. And believe me, I know that once you get your gorgeous, stubborn mind set on something, no one can stop you. But today is about preparing for the birth of our family. We'll have plenty of time to promote Infant Gratification after the twins are born."

"'Infant Gratification'?" I asked.

Rene grinned. "Sam came up with it. Isn't it a great business name? And since Sam named the business, I get to name the twins. Laverne and Shirley."

"Absolutely not," Sam replied. "We're naming them after our mothers. Wanda and Darlene."

Sam and Rene had been good-naturedly bickering about baby names—and almost everything else—ever since she'd told him about her pregnancy. After months of playing "Name that Baby," I halfway expected them to stick with their placeholder names, Twin A and Twin B. I changed the subject.

"Infant Gratification is a great business name, but Sam's right. Everyone at the party is going to be interested in seeing the new birthing suites, not checking out pacifier purses."

Rene rubbed her palms together. "I can't wait to finally get out of this house. I hear the party's going to be huge."

"I'm surprised your doctor is letting you go," I said. "I thought you were on house arrest except for medical appointments."

She shrugged. "Well, we *are* going to a hospital. Besides, my doctor's getting mellower now that the twins are past thirty-four weeks. We'd like them to percolate another couple of weeks, but they'll be safe if they're born now."

Sam put his hand on her forearm. "Remember, you're still not supposed to wear yourself out."

"Wear myself out? Don't be silly. If I get tired, Kate will push me around in a wheelchair."

I nudged her ribs with my elbow. "Maybe I should drive you around in a dump truck."

"Not funny, Kate." Rene's lips wrinkled in pretend insult, but her eyes sparkled with excitement. "Come on, you guys! Let's go!"

While Sam went into the kitchen to grab his car keys, I slid the stowaway candy out of my purse. Rene did a little bounce and slipped it inside her jacket pocket. I had a feeling that her first stop at the hospital would be the ladies' room, where she could devour her new treasure in private.

I was wrong.

The moment we arrived at Lake Washington's new birthing center, Rene beelined it straight to the buffet table, claiming it was time for her second lunch. Sam followed hot on her heels. I left them to argue about the nutritional value of catered hospital food and wandered around to check out the facility. I knew the hospital's old building almost as well as I knew my own home; I'd visited Rene in the perinatal unit daily while she was hospitalized, and since then I'd been hired to teach in-room yoga to the unit's patients. So I'd been curious about this new addition—specifically, what it offered that was worth the expense of constructing an entirely new building.

A lot, as it turned out.

The smaller, adjacent building was only a sky bridge away from Lake Washington's main campus, but it felt miles away from the older, more austere hospital. Photographs of stern-looking administrators had been replaced by pastel stencils of baby animals—lambs, puppies, kittens, and ponies included. Pink and blue ribbon arrows pointed the way to admitting, the nursery, a family area, and the neonatal ICU. The door to each patient suite was decorated by a stork whose beak held a removable sign: a baby swaddled in blue, pink, or green—depending, I assumed, on the gender of the child about to be born inside.

A voice spoke from behind me. "Aren't those signs cute?"

I turned to see Justine, dressed in blue hospital scrubs.

"Volunteers will hang them on the door when the mom checks in," she explained. "Once the baby is born, they'll paint its name on the sign and give it to the parents. It's my favorite perk of the new facility."

"They're adorable," I replied. "My friend Rene will go gaga. I hope everything's open by the time she delivers."

"Unless she goes into labor this weekend, it will be. The Labor and Delivery Unit starts moving over first, on Monday. The Perinatal Unit will transition in stages a few days later. Our new Neonatal ICU will open last, hopefully by early the following week."

"Rene will be happy to hear that. Are you working today, or are you here for the open house?"

Justine tugged on the fabric of her scrubs. "Do you think I'd wear these if I wasn't working? I'm on break." She pointed to the huge slice of chocolate cake she was carrying. "There's a staff cake in the old break room, but it's white. I prefer chocolate. I'd steal a piece to take home for my mom, but she doesn't eat much these days." Her eyes grew wet. "Alzheimer's destroys more than memories."

I reached out to hug her, but she took a step back.

"Sorry. Didn't mean to be a Debbie Downer." She smiled, but it didn't look sincere. "I need to get back. My patient will be pushing soon." Turning, she headed toward the old building. When she reached the sky bridge, she called over her shoulder, "Enjoy the festivities."

I watched her disappear, wishing I could wave a magic wand and make her life easier. No amount of yoga—or chocolate cake, for that matter—could erase all of life's heartaches, and Justine had endured way more than her share. Hopefully the yoga practices I'd taught her would make at least a small difference. I vowed to check in with her in a week or two and headed back to join Rene.

If I could find her.

The new facility's lobby was teeming with people. Hundreds of them, many of them expecting. Sam waved to me from the buffet table. I steeled my shoulders, took a deep breath, and edged my way through the crowd. The hospital had spared no expense. Lavish trays of crackers, cheeses, fruits, and vegetables vied for dominance with fancy *hors d'oeuvres* and Martha Stewart worthy desserts. Wait staff circulated with champagne for the non-expecting guests and sparkling ciders for the moms-to-be. From the mountain of food on Rene's plate, she'd taken three of everything.

I pointed to her plate and gaped at Sam. "I can't give her a candy bar, but you don't stop that?"

"I've force-fed her two green smoothies today already. How am I supposed to argue with food served at a hospital?"

He had a point.

I left Rene to her unimpeded gluttony and wandered around the crowded area, waiting for the program to begin. Based on the number of baby bumps present, I estimated that at least half of the assembled crowd was made up of expecting parents and their families. The rest were probably off-duty staff and OB/GYNs that the hospital hoped to woo away from competing birthing centers, like ABBA.

Summer, my doula trainer, waved at me from across the room. I gave her a big hug.

"I'm surprised to see you here," I said. "I thought you didn't support hospital births."

"I don't, as a general rule. I wasn't planning to come today, but I figured I owed it to my future clients to at least have a look. I just finished the tour."

"Ours is in forty-five minutes. What did you think?"

Summer frowned. "Honestly? I'm not sure. They're certainly trying. The rooms are fabulous, but the place still reeks of hospital." She wrinkled her nose. "I don't like it. Birthing at home is far safer. Hospitals have an astronomical number of C-sections. It's barbaric."

Rachel appeared behind me. "You're not making a fair comparison. Of course hospitals have more complications. We take on all of the high-risk births." Her outfit—a wispy, bright-colored sundress, red sandals, and a large red shoulder bag—contrasted dramatically with the harsh tone of her voice.

I smiled, hoping to ease the tension. "Summer, this is my friend Rachel. She's a nurse in the perinatal unit here."

Summer wrinkled her lips. "I'm afraid we'll have to agree to disagree. High-risk births explain *some* of the increased complications, but not all of them. Not by a long shot."

Rachel's facial expression remained tense, but she changed the subject. "Have you seen Nicole? She was here a few minutes ago, but now I can't find her."

I glanced around the room. "Sorry, I—"

A microphone's high-pitched squeal interrupted us.

A balding man wearing a beige suit and wire-framed glasses stared uncomfortably across the crowd. "Sorry about that, folks. Never can figure out how to work these things."

"I'm not interested in the sales pitch," Summer grumbled. "I'm going to take off. I'll talk to you later." She nodded toward Rachel and disappeared into the crowd.

The man at the microphone continued. "If you'll gather around, I'd like to say a few words."

The room grew quiet.

"Please give a warm welcome—"

A loud crash interrupted him. The entire room turned toward the sound. A thirtyish man with dark eyes, a deep black goatee, and a purple-red face stood amid a jumble of spilled food and broken glass. Droplets of liquid dotted his T-shirt and jeans.

The man at the microphone smiled. "You know what they say. It's not a party until something gets broken. We'll get maintenance to clean the mess up. Please help yourself to more food. Now, if I can have everyone's attention again ... " He resumed his speech.

If the man with the goatee heard him, he gave no indication. He stood motionless, hands clenched in white-knuckled fists, staring hostilely at the back of the room.

Rachel followed his glare. She sucked in a quick breath, then spat in a low, whispered growl, "That cheating son of a bitch."

I glanced the same direction, but all I saw were pregnant women and their bored-looking partners. Unease prickled my shoulders. "Rachel? What's going on?"

She didn't answer.

I leaned toward her and craned my neck to see through the crowd from her vantage point.

Oh, crap.

Dr. Dick.

And Mariella.

They stood with an attractive silver-haired man I didn't recognize.

Mariella glanced our direction. The corners of her mouth lifted into a calculated grin. She ran her hand down Dr. Dick's arm, not stopping until her fingers lingered on a body part normally reserved for a married man's spouse. Dr. Dick seemed surprised by her touch but not affronted. He eased away from Mariella and smiled. I'm no lip reader, but I could have sworn that his lips formed the words, "Not here."

Rachel's lips, on the other hand, barely moved. Her voice hissed with venom. "I swear, someday I'll take a knife to that horse's—"

She stopped mid-sentence. She and her husband made eye contact. Dr. Dick's overly friendly smile disappeared, replaced by an expression of horror. The star quarterback, caught being fondled by the coach's daughter. I reached over and touched Rachel's trembling hand.

"Are you okay?"

She replied in short, choked sobs. "I'm sorry. I ... I have to get out of here."

Two things happened at once. Rachel bolted toward the exit, and the man at the microphone spoke. "Please give everyone responsible for organizing today's event a huge round of applause." The room burst into whistles, claps, and happy pandemonium.

I wanted to run after Rachel. I wanted to offer support. More than that, I wanted to march up to Dr. Dick and knee him in ... well, in his namesake. But I couldn't make it through the crowd in time. Rachel and Dr. Dick collided near the entrance, and he grabbed her to stop her from leaving. I couldn't hear their words over the room's thunderous applause, but the exchange didn't look friendly.

Rachel yanked her arm away and ran from the lobby. Dr. Dick hesitated for several seconds, looking stunned. Then he chased after her.

Mariella didn't move. She waited for a chance to make eye contact with me, then tipped her champagne glass in the air, lifted her lips in a slow and satisfied smile, and winked.

By the time I turned back around, the man with the goatee was gone.

SIX

THE NEXT FIFTEEN MINUTES passed without incident. The man at the microphone finished his speech while Sam commandeered two folding chairs—one for Rene's rear and one for her feet. Rene entertained herself by groaning in mock ecstasy over each bite of "real food," meaning nothing resembling a fruit or a vegetable. I made small talk with my friends, but my mind refused to focus on the conversation. It wandered the hallway, wanting to hunt down Dr. Dick so I could knock some sense into him. How could he let Mariella publicly humiliate Rachel that way?

Rene's voice startled me back into the conversation. "Earth to Kate. Are you with us?"

"Sorry. I spaced out for a second."

"I asked you what time it is."

I glanced at my watch. "Twelve-forty."

Rene jabbed Sam in the ribs with her index finger. "See? Told you so. Our tour doesn't start for another twenty minutes. You have plenty of time. "

"Time for what?" I asked.

"To call work. I forgot to tell Sam that his secretary called this morning." She waved her hand through the air. "Pregnancy brain. I can't remember squat."

Sam looked dubious. "Whatever it is, I'm sure it can wait until Monday."

Rene shrugged. "Your funeral. You know how cranky Peggy gets when you ignore her phone calls..." She turned her back to him and winked at me. "So, Kate, while we're waiting, I have a question about those pelvic floor exercises you gave me. How firmly am I supposed to contract my vagi—"

"Cripes, Rene!" Sam covered his ears with his hands. "All right already. You win. I'm going." He tromped halfway to the door, then stopped and gave her a stern look. "You'd better not be up to something."

"Don't be silly. I'll be right here when you get back." Rene's plastic smile remained firmly in place until Sam disappeared around the corner. The moment his rear was no longer in view, her head whipped back toward me.

"I can't believe he fell for it. We don't have much time. Go grab me a piece of cake." She held her hands three feet apart. "A big one."

"No way, Rene." I narrowed my eyes and frowned. "Did Sam's secretary even call?"

"Of course she did." Rene's voice softened. "Though it might have been last week..."

"Forget it. I am *not* your sugar mule. You already had one piece of cake. If you want to gorge yourself into gestational diabetes, you'll have to get off your butt and grab another one yourself."

"Puh-lease. The pieces they cut were *tiny*. The twins barely got a taste. I've already been on my feet too much today." She pointed at her ankles, which bulged over her Skechers like skin-colored water balloons. "Look at the size of these things. If I don't keep them elevated, I'll fill up with so much water, the twins will drown."

"If you're that desperate for sugar, eat the peanut butter cups I gave you."

"I'm saving those for an emergency. Come on, Kate. You know my cells are glued together by white flour and sugar. If I don't get enough junk food, I'll die of good nutrition." Her face assumed Bella's wide-eyed, I'm-about-to-die-of-starvation expression. The only things missing were a long line of drool and a demand bark.

Ugh.

It worked every time.

Part of me agreed with her, anyway. I wasn't sure if it was because of Sam's militant diet or in spite of it, but Rene had gained extraordinarily little weight during her pregnancy. She claimed that her belly was the size of a small towing barge, but the rest of her body was still a highly toned size four. An extra slice of cake might live forever on my hips, but it wouldn't last a millisecond on hers.

"I'll be back in a minute."

I left my drooling friend behind and wove through the crowd toward the remaining two-and-a-half layers of white-frosted chocolate dessert. A ceramic stork stood on the cake's top. Pink and blue edible ribbons decorated its sides. I carefully balanced three pieces of cake—two for Rene and one for me—in my right hand, grabbed two glasses of sparkling cider with my left, and worked my way back to my friend.

Rene pulled her feet off the chair and furtively glanced toward the hall. "It's about time you got back. I was ready to pass out from low blood sug—" She froze. "Oh no. Watch out, Kate! Incoming!"

Sam yelled from across the room. "I knew it!" He lowered his head and charged, like a bull charging a cake-wielding matador.

Several things happened in horrifyingly inevitable slow motion. Rene defied all laws of gravity and leaped to her feet. She dove for the cake, on my right. Sam swatted it away from her, on my left. I tried to dodge both of them, catching my foot on a chair leg in the process. Three pieces of cake, twelve ounces of glorified apple juice, and the metal back of a folding chair collided as one with my chest. At the end of the train wreck, pink, white, and baby-blue frosting coated my breasts like a faded flag from last year's Fourth of July.

Rene took a step back and cringed. "Uh oh."

Sam stepped forward and reached for a napkin. "I'm so sorry, Kate."

I stood my ground and glared at them both.

I silently begged myself not to react. As a yoga teacher, I was supposed to be above petty outbursts of anger. Besides, I'd been working on controlling my Mount St. Helens like temper for months with surprising success.

Until now.

Frustrated irritation zapped down my spine and exploded my eardrums. My face burned so hot I was surprised my eyelashes didn't ignite. I scraped smashed chocolate cake from between my breasts and slammed the now-empty dishes onto Rene's chair.

"That's it. I've had enough for one day. I didn't sign up to be the human punching bag in your stupid food fights. Call me after you two work out your marital problems. I'm out of here."

I marched three steps away, then turned back, snatched Rene's purse off the floor, and rummaged through it until I found the peanut butter cups. I waved them through the air like a dark chocolate victory flag. "And I'm taking these with me!"

Rene's voice quavered behind me. "Kate?"

I whipped around and growled in response. "What now?"

"The tour starts in ten minutes."

I glowered at my two friends, wishing Bella were with me so she could bite them both. I wanted to be a better person, but this was ridiculous. I was a yoga teacher, not a saint. The impassioned pleas of Patanjali, Gandhi, and Buddha combined wouldn't have stopped me from marching out of that room. Michael might even have taken my side.

But the thought of missing out on an important part of Rene's birth experience glued my feet to the ground. Either that or my shoes were trapped by three layers of frosting.

I closed my eyes, took a deep breath, and replied through clenched teeth. "I'll be back."

I didn't inhale again until I reached the hallway, afraid that if my mouth opened wide enough to oxygenate my lungs, my tongue would spew out words I'd forever regret. Once Rene and Sam were out of verbal striking range, I consciously relaxed my jaw and tried to unclench my teeth. I would have plenty of time to tongue lash my friends later. Right now, I needed to wash away my frustration. Literally.

I glanced around, trying to get my bearings in the still-unfamiliar space. The hallway's pink and blue arrows—annoyingly similar to the frosting ribbons decorating my chest—seemed to mock me, pointing to every location except the one I needed: the public restroom.

I considered sneaking into one of the delivery suite bathrooms, but somehow that seemed sacrilegious. The women who christened those facilities should be trying to push out a baby. I wasted one of my precious ten minutes scanning the hallway, then I opted to head for the familiar: the perinatal unit. I crossed the sky bridge to the older building and beelined it to the employee break room. I wasn't scheduled to teach today, so, strictly speaking, I wasn't supposed to be in the employees-only area. Hopefully drowning in frosting would earn me emergency dispensation.

Now that I'd seen the new birthing center, the older building seemed institutionally stark. Bright white paint, echoing hallways. Astringent, hospital smell. Thankfully, Rene's girls would meet the world in much more welcoming surroundings.

I reached for the break room door the same time it opened. Rachel and I collided; her purse crashed to the ground. Smudges of blue frosting transferred from my chest to hers.

"Oh no! I'm so sorry, Rachel." I reached down to pick up her shoulder bag, but she snatched it away. Her face matched the hallway's ultra-white, ultra-glossy walls.

She glanced over her shoulder as if afraid someone was chasing her. "Don't worry about it."

I reached out to squeeze her arm. "I saw what happened with your husband. If you need to talk, I—"

"Not now, Kate," she snapped. "I can't do this now." She raced down the hall toward the exit sign.

I stared after her, torn between incompatible priorities.

Should I follow her?

Rachel was my student, and she was upset. I wanted to help her.

I needed to get back to Sam and Rene.

Rene's pleading voice ticked down the time in my head.

Only five minutes left.

I'd call Rachel later this afternoon. Rene and Sam were my priorities now.

I scooted into the break room, wetted a handful of paper towels, and scrubbed futilely at my chest. After two minutes of intense effort, I'd successfully turned the front of my shirt into a wet, sticky, pastel-smear painting. The staff cake on the counter mocked me like a buttercream terrorist. Same pink and blue ribbons as the cake at the party. Same smart-assed stork, this time molded from frosting. I didn't see a knife on the counter to stab it to death, so I satisfied my bloodlust by breaking off the stork's head and eating it.

I tossed the paper towels in the garbage. "This is useless."

I'd need a new outfit, a huge glass of wine, and at least three hours of browbeating Rene to overcome my foul mood.

I had three minutes.

I settled for emptying my aching bladder instead. I trudged toward the women's bathroom, barely noticing the dark smudge on the floor. I certainly didn't stop to consider what the inch-long burgundy smear might imply.

I flung open the door and froze, unable to process the scene in front of me. An inane thought flew through my mind:

What's a man doing in the women's restroom?

He lay on the floor, glasses askew, body crumpled in a twisted jumble of arms, legs, and bodily fluids. It didn't even occur to me—at least not at first—that I might be able to help him. All I could think about was my friend.

Oh Rachel, no...

Had she been running from this?

My father's admonishing voice jolted me into action:

Don't just stand there, Kate. He might still be alive!

I ran to Dr. Dick's body, rolled him onto his back, and screamed. The bloody handle of the missing cake knife protruded from beneath his rib cage.

———

There's a plus side to finding a body in a hospital. When you yell for help, it arrives quickly. Within seconds, a crowd of white-coated and blue-scrubbed professionals had lifted Dr. Dick onto a gurney and whisked him away, presumably to try to save him. I was no doctor; I was certainly no psychic. But after staring into those lifeless blue eyes, I had a hard time believing there was still hope.

Hospital security arrived a few moments later and asked me to wait for the police in a nearby conference room. I called Rene's cell phone to tell her what had happened, but the call went directly to voicemail. She and Sam must have gone on the tour without me. Guilt-induced tears threatened my eyes. What if Rene thought I'd actually deserted her? Hair-trigger temper notwithstanding, I would always have Rene's back. She knew that, right?

The tears stopped threatening and spilled down my cheeks. This couldn't be happening to me again, not if the universe was the slightest bit fair. The third—obviously murdered—body I'd found in less than two years? Fourth, if you counted the one I'd seen the police drag out of Green Lake. I had no idea what sins I'd committed in my past lives, but they must have been despicable. This was some seriously, ugly, god-awful bad karma.

Dad's voice echoed inside my head. *Stop being so melodramatic, Katie Girl. You think you had a bad day? Dr. Dick's day was worse.*

I mentally rolled my eyes, but the tears stopped flowing. Three years after his death, Dad's no-nonsense, no-self-pity-allowed chastising still kicked me out of a stupor. He was right. This wasn't like the other times I'd stumbled across death. All things considered, I was lucky. The victim wasn't a friend this time. He was barely an acquaintance. The police would have no reason to suspect me. They wouldn't arrest one of my family members, either. For once, I could give the police my statement and walk away, guilt-free.

My stomach constricted. *Unless they suspect Rachel.*

My statement would point the police straight to her. Not only had I seen her run from the crime scene, I'd heard her threaten the victim. Deep in my core, I knew Rachel hadn't killed her husband. As a nurse, she'd devoted her entire professional life to healing. Nurses might not take the Hippocratic Oath, but they worked forty-plus hours a week easing the suffering of others. How could they *not* buy into the precept of "doing no harm"?

More than that, the Rachel I knew wasn't violent. Frustrated with her teenage daughter? Yes. Angry about being cheated on? Definitely. Filled with enough rage to plunge a knife handle-deep into her husband's torso?

Not a chance.

Unfortunately, the police would never buy that logic.

I was too agitated to sit, so I began pacing. Could I withhold what I knew from the police? Rachel's mumbled threat meant nothing. If every idle threat led to murder, the human race would have died out with the dodo bird. Besides, if I saw some woman's hands idling near Michael's privates, I'd mutter a few choice words myself.

Rachel's flight from the scene didn't convince me of her guilt, either. I knew from experience that being discovered near a body didn't make you the killer.

It did, however, make you a pretty darned good murder suspect.

My heart thudded heavily against my rib cage. I felt like a goldfish trapped in a blender. I hadn't started giving my statement yet, and I already felt like a traitor. I might be able to justify not volunteering information, but I could never lie to the cops. It would go against everything Dad had ever taught me.

I glanced around the empty room, searching for an escape route—hopefully one that would lead to the truth. Nothing but a sealed fourth-story window and a solid wood door with a hospital security guard standing on the other side.

Panicking wasn't working, so my stressed-out mind switched to denial. Maybe I was freaking out over nothing. Dr. Dick hadn't been breathing, but I didn't see all *that* much blood, either. A half-dozen medical professionals had scurried him out of the room for reason. Maybe he wasn't beyond hope after all. Maybe he'd wake up, apologize to Rachel for being a cad, and identify his true attacker. Maybe we could put this whole nightmare to rest.

And maybe Rene would sign up for a thirty-day smoothie fast.

I stopped pacing and thumped down in a chair, still desperately clinging to denial. Maybe my testimony wouldn't matter. The blood-coated knife might be covered in the true murderer's fingerprints. And what about that burgundy stain? The small amount of blood inside the bathroom had been soaked into Dr. Dick's shirt and pooled under his body. Maybe the smear on the break room floor came from the murderer. Maybe it contained her—or better yet, his—DNA.

I continued my self-delusional pep talk for a good forty minutes before I heard a knock on the door. A female uniformed officer greeted me.

"Ms. Davidson? The detectives are ready to speak with you now."

I followed her down the hallway to a small office, took one look at the man seated behind the desk, and groaned.

"Well, well, well. So we meet again." Detective Henderson gave his partner, Detective Martinez, a knowing look and then stood and marched toward me. When he stopped, his substantial belly was three inches from mine. "You certainly have a habit of getting yourself mixed up in trouble, don't you?" He crossed his arms and smirked. "At least this time you didn't throw up all over my crime scene."

I might not have vomited yet, but if he came much closer, all bets were off. Henderson's gristly beard brought back PTSD-like feelings of fear, revulsion, and dread. Especially dread. If I was being questioned by Henderson and Martinez—the homicide detectives who'd investigated my friend George's murder—Dr. Dick was dead. So were my hopes of a happy ending for Rachel.

I took several steps back.

Henderson pointed at the frosting still decorating my chest. "Looks like your shirt wasn't so lucky."

"That's not vomit, it's ... Oh, never mind."

Detective Martinez intervened. "Cut her some slack, Henderson. You know this isn't her fault." Pretty, petite, with dark brown eyes and medium-length hair, Martinez was the natural good cop to Detective Henderson's bad one. She'd been an ally of sorts when I investigated my friend George's death. At least until I'd screwed up and accused her of not doing her job.

Hopefully she'd forgotten that part.

She nodded my direction. "Sorry to see you under these circumstances again, Kate."

I suspected I wouldn't like the answer, but I asked the question anyway, hoping—praying—that the day's story would have a surprise ending.

"The man I found ... Dr. Jones ... is ... is he dead?"

"I'm sorry, Kate," she replied. "Yes."

Henderson returned to the desk and pulled out a notebook. "You called the victim by name. Dr. Jones. That mean you knew him?"

Here we go, Kate. Watch what you say ...

"No ... Yes ... I mean ... " I shook my head, trying to clear the fog enveloping my brain. "I mean no, not really. I knew who he was and I'd seen him around a couple of times, but I didn't know him."

"So you'd never met him?" Martinez asked.

"I didn't say that. We … we might have been introduced once, but … " My voice trailed off. Why was I stammering so much? They hadn't even asked me about Rachel yet and I already sounded like I was lying.

Henderson tapped his pen on the notebook and peered at me through suspicious eyes. I didn't blame him. I wouldn't have trusted me either.

Martinez gave him a let-me-handle-this look.

"Take your time, Kate. You're among friends. Tell us what happened."

And so I did.

I told them everything. The fact that the murder victim was Rachel's husband, that he was cheating on her, and that I suspected she knew about the affair. No matter how hard I tried to avoid volunteering information, Martinez and Henderson wiggled it out of me. They asked all the right questions, in exactly the right order. I shouldn't have been surprised. They were, after all, trained police detectives. In spite of my frustrations with them after George's death, they weren't exactly incompetent. They even managed to get me to admit that I'd seen Rachel run away from the break room shortly before I stumbled upon Dr. Dick's body.

"That doesn't mean anything," I assured them. "I didn't actually see her with the body, and I have no idea how long it was in the bathroom. He could have been there for up to a half hour."

Henderson peered at me over his notes. "That's pretty specific. What makes you think a half hour?"

"It couldn't have been much longer than that. I saw him around twelve-thirty at the reception. My point is, I never saw Rachel with the body. When I went into the break room, the door to the women's restroom was closed. For all I know, Rachel ducked into the break room to grab a piece of cake."

"And ran out of the room crying?" Martinez's voice was kind, but her implication was clear.

"I know it looks bad, but I also know Rachel. She would never hurt anyone. Someone else is the killer." I doubted it would help, but I reminded them anyway. "You didn't believe me about George's murder, and I was right then."

Henderson closed his notebook and thunked the pen solidly on top of it. "I'll say this for you, Ms. Davidson. You're loyal." He leaned back and crossed his arms. "Somehow I doubt your friend Rachel's story is going to be nearly as convincing. If we ever hear it, that is."

I sat up straight, surprised. "Wait a minute. You haven't spoken with Rachel yet?"

"Nope." Henderson scowled. "We haven't been able to find her. She disappeared right about the time you found the body."

My stomach dropped to my toes. "Does she know that her husband is dead?"

The two detectives shared a knowing look, but otherwise ignored my question.

Martinez handed me a business card. "Thanks for your cooperation, Kate. We'll likely have more questions for you later. In the meantime, if you think of anything else, please give me a call."

She stood and walked me to the door, signaling the end of our discussion.

I hesitated in the doorway and said the words again, as if a mantra-like repetition would make them more convincing. "I mean it. Rachel is not your killer."

Martinez's eyes remained serious. "We'll look at all the evidence, Kate. I promise."

"Of course we will." Henderson's gruff reply sounded insulted. "That's our job. We follow the evidence trail." He mumbled under his breath as the door closed between us. "And ninety percent of the time, that trail leads right to the spouse."

SEVEN

THE UNIFORMED OFFICER ESCORTED me from the interview room to one of the hospital's waiting areas, where Sam and Rene were—appropriately enough—waiting for me. One glimpse of Rene's concerned expression and I burst into tears.

"I'm sorry, you guys. I didn't mean to stand you up."

Rene wrapped me in the deepest hug her three-person body could accommodate. "Of course you didn't, sweetie. We knew that."

"I found another body."

"They told us," she replied. "It sucks, big time." Accurate, if a bit of an understatement.

"Are you okay?" Sam asked.

"Not now, but I will be. Can we get out of here? I want to go home."

Rene and Sam peppered me with questions all the way to the parking garage. After receiving a half-dozen monosyllabic replies, they took the hint and remained uncharacteristically quiet for the rest of the drive home. I felt bad for shutting them out, but I couldn't focus well enough to make conversation. My brain had been shocked into traumatized, numb mush.

The three neurons still firing tortured me with a relentless litany of questions. If Rachel hadn't killed her husband, obviously someone else had. The "how" was obvious. But who did it, and why? Would Rachel ever forgive me for talking to the police? What would happen to Nicole if Rachel was arrested? And the question that yelled at me the loudest: how could I put the brakes on this freight train before Rachel and Nicole both got dragged underneath it?

I'd start by making two phone calls. One to Dale Evans, my friend and defense attorney from Orcas Island, and another to John O'Connell, my father's old partner at the Seattle Police Department.

Then I had to figure out what to tell Michael.

Selfishly, I hoped Michael wouldn't be home when I arrived. I'd tell him about finding Dr. Dick's body eventually; I'd rather teach Hot Yoga in Hades than deceive him. But I wanted to get advice from Dale and John first.

Sam's Camaro had barely come to a stop in his driveway when I flung open the door. "I'll talk to you guys later, I promise. I have to go now."

Fifteen minutes later, I parked in my own driveway—right next to Michael's Explorer. I considered driving to Green Lake to call Dale and John on my cell, but I was too tired to keep running.

Bella greeted me at the gate, which should have been my first clue that something was wrong.

I reached down and scratched her neck. "Why are you out in the yard all by yourself?"

She followed me into the kitchen, where we were greeted by a cacophony of loud crashes, high-pitched screams, and vicious, flesh-ripping growls. I couldn't be positive, but I was pretty sure the screams came from Mutt. The growls were one hundred percent Michael.

"What's got Michael so worked up?"

Bella didn't speak English, but I wouldn't have heard her reply anyway. Michael's swearing obliterated all sound within a five-hundred-foot radius. She tucked her tail between her legs, cowered behind my knees, and whined.

I didn't blame her.

I could count on one hand the number of times my normally sweet-natured boyfriend had yelled, and each of those times he'd been angry with me. Usually because I'd gotten involved in a murder investigation.

Fabulous.

I kneeled next to Bella and rubbed her ears. "It's all right, sweetie. If Michael doesn't calm down soon, I'll get him a muzzle." I opened the kitchen door again and Bella scampered outside to safety. I considered grabbing a frying pan to use as a weapon but decided it might be overkill. Instead, I steeled my shoulders, yelled "Honey, I'm home!" in my happiest voice, and walked into the living room.

To Defcon Puppy.

Michael stood bent over, using a terry towel to wipe something brown, soft, and decidedly smelly from the bottom of his bare foot. A considerable collection of his belongings—which normally lived in disorganized harmony on top of the end table—were scattered all over the floor. My three couch pillows lay in ruins among them. One had a large wet spot that looked suspiciously like something that had come out of the wrong end of a puppy. The second and third may have been soiled, too, but we'd never know unless we found and assembled their assorted pieces. White fluffy stuffing floated around the room in air-conditioned bliss. Several wispy pieces found respite in Michael's curly, dark hair.

Mutt and Jeff, for their parts, pawed at the edge of their ex-pen, screaming as if Michael had trapped them inside to gas them. From the look on his face, they might well have been right.

"What happened?" I asked.

Michael threw the soiled towel on the floor and picked up another, which he used to scrub at the carpet. "You were late, that's what happened. You promised to be home no later than two so I could give Tiffany the rest of the afternoon off."

I glanced at my watch. Almost six-thirty.

I would have told him that stumbling over a dead body makes you lose track of time, but I didn't think now was the time to talk about murder. He was too close to committing it himself.

"I'm so sorry, Michael. The afternoon took a different turn than I'd hoped."

He ignored my apology and continued grumbling. "I waited until three, then I went to Pete's Pets without you here." He gestured around the room. "I came back ten minutes ago to this."

"Why didn't you take the dogs with you?"

He shook his head so violently I was surprised his neck didn't snap. "Absolutely not. Not until they've had their shots. Do you *want* them to get sick?"

"Of course not. But honey, we agreed that the puppies are too young to have full run of the house. You're supposed to crate them if you have to leave. What if something had happened with Bella?"

Michael's expression could have curdled cheese. "I'm not stupid, Kate. I *did* crate them. They got out somehow. I could have sworn that I latched it, but I was in a hurry. I must have forgotten. When I came home, Bella was hiding upstairs in the bedroom, and these two little monsters were destroying what was left of that pillow."

Mutt scratched at the bars, screaming for attention. Michael, who was a better boyfriend than dog trainer, reached over the expen, picked her up, and cuddled her. Mutt rewarded him with blissfully silent kisses.

Michael must have gotten a deep whiff of puppy-breath aromatherapy, because his shoulders relaxed. The wrinkles in his brow softened. His lips even lifted into a close approximation of a smile.

I knew my words were futile, but I said them anyway. "You know you're teaching her to scream by picking her up like that, right?"

He ignored me and cooed into her soft golden fur. "You don't mean to be evil. You're just a baby." When he spoke to me again, his voice sounded apologetic. "Most of the stuff they destroyed was yours."

"Don't worry about it, hon. It's only a couple of pillows. Nothing that can't be replaced."

Michael tilted his head as if first noticing my appearance. "You look like you had a bad day, too. Everything okay?"

I didn't lie, but nodding yes wasn't entirely truthful, either.

He pointed at my sternum. "What happened to your shirt?"

"I got trapped between Rene and her sugar fix."

He grinned. "I guess your pillows weren't the only casualties today."

I internally winced at Michael's more-appropriate-than-he-knew word choice. I knew I should tell him what had happened at the hospital, and I would. But not now. I chose diversion instead.

"Why don't you get cleaned up?" I said. "I'll order a Tree Huggers pizza from PhinneyWood Pizza and entertain the little monsters while you pick it up. When you get back, we can drown our troubles in alcohol and carbohydrates."

Michael set Mutt on the ground and picked up Jeff, who was still trapped in the ex-pen. "Be sure to order enough liquid to drown these two little slugs, too." His words were stern, but his eyes held nothing but affection. "Momma Bird had better steer clear of me for a while. I might punish her for abandoning these guys by giving them back."

I smiled. "There's always Betty . . . "

"Don't tempt me."

Michael showered off the puppy dung and headed for Phinney-Wood Pizza, which gave me approximately forty-five minutes to make phone calls.

I started with John, but the call went directly to voicemail. I told him that I had witnessed another murder and asked him to call Martinez. I finished by saying that I'd visit him in person the next morning.

My next call was to Dale, defense attorney extraordinaire, who also happened to be the founder of Dale's Goat Rescue on Orcas Island. Dharma—Dale's new girlfriend and my no-longer-estranged mother—answered.

"Kate. How nice to hear your voice. When are you coming for a visit?"

The honest answer was *not soon enough*. I was surprised at how much I missed Dharma, considering that I'd only known her for two months. Dad would always be the parent who'd raised me, but Dharma and I were rapidly becoming family.

"Michael and I will come up for a long weekend soon, I promise. Is Dale around? I actually called to get some legal advice from him."

Dharma's voice grew serious. "That doesn't sound good. Are you in trouble?"

"I'm fine. The advice is for a friend."

"I'm sorry, Kate. Your friend should probably ask someone else. Dale's in Mexico for a week, picking up donkeys. You can try his cell, but I don't think you'll reach him. His phone gets terrible reception there."

"Donkeys? From Mexico?" That was a new one, even for Dale.

"It's my fault, I'm afraid. I got a call from one of my old El Paso buddies last week. She rescued 150 donkeys from a Mexican slaughterhouse. Half of the females are pregnant. Those butchering monsters were going to slaughter them anyway. Can you believe that?"

Unfortunately, I could.

"Dale and I talked, and we decided to expand the rescue. We're going to call it Dale's Goats and Dharma's Asses." I heard the grin in her voice. "What do you think?"

I smiled. "It's perfect."

"Dale and a crew of volunteers left the day before yesterday. They're bringing back the fifty or so donkeys that are healthy enough to travel, including twenty of the pregnant females." Her voice grew wistful. I imagined her winding her gray-streaked braid around her index finger. "Kate, I think I'm falling in love with that man."

"I'm happy for you." And I was. Dharma and my father hadn't been able to make their marriage work, but she and Dale seemed perfect for each other. "Why didn't you go to Mexico with him?"

"The last time I went to Mexico I spent six weeks in jail, remember? Dale didn't want to risk a repeat performance. He'll be back in five or six days."

I chewed on my thumbnail. "Darn. I really wanted to talk to him today."

"Can I help?"

I filled her in on my day, including what I'd told the police about Rachel. "I feel guilty. Like I betrayed her."

"You didn't have a choice, Kate."

I flopped heavily on what was left of my couch. "Do you think I should call her?"

Dharma paused for a moment. "You'll likely be a witness for the prosecution. We both know what Dale would say."

I imagined Dale's white-bearded lips. They formed a stern, no-arguing-allowed, absolute *no*.

I sighed. "I'm on her side, Dharma."

"I know that, Kate. But that still doesn't mean you should call her. Anything your friend tells you could end up in court."

We both sat silently for several long moments. When I spoke, my voice was soft. "Dharma, I have to help her."

Her reply was matter-of-fact, as if I'd just told her that I needed to buy toilet paper. "Of course you do, Kate. It's your dharma—your duty. You help people find justice."

As soon as Dharma's words bounced off my eardrums, I knew they were true. Maybe that's why they made me so angry. Frustrated self-pity spilled from my throat. "Getting involved in four murders in the last eighteen months is my *duty*? It feels a hell of a lot more like punishment."

"Punishment? For what?"

I stood and began pacing. "I don't know. What do you think? Maybe for all those times I lashed out in anger." Like I was doing right now.

"Kate, I thought you let go of that guilt nonsense months ago."

I stopped pacing and planted my feet wide. "I'm not guilt-ridden, Dharma. I'm pissed. People keep dying around me, and I'm sick of it. If the universe wanted to teach me a lesson, fine. I got it already." My voice cracked. "The flogging can stop any time now."

"None of this is about punishment, Kate. That's not how dharma works."

"Finding dead bodies certainly isn't my *duty*. Neither is figuring out who made them that way. I'm not a cop. I didn't choose this."

My mother's reply held no sympathy. "Who told you that you get to choose? I didn't *choose* to be an animal activist, either. Who in their right mind *chooses* to spend most of her adult life living in villages where outhouses are an unaffordable luxury? Animal activism chose me. Seeking justice chose you."

She paused for several long, uncomfortable seconds, letting her words sink in. After what felt like a century, she continued speaking. "Did I ever tell you how I got my name?"

"Dharma? No. Dad always called you Daisy. I figured you wanted to go by something that sounded less trivial."

"That was part of it, but only a small part. My name is a symbol. True dharma—life work—isn't something that you pick out of a college catalogue. It's a calling. A compulsion. I changed my name to Dharma to remind myself that my life's most difficult choices—including leaving you as an infant—weren't choices at all."

Two months ago, her words would have struck me as the lame justifications of a deadbeat mother. Now that I knew her side of the story, I understood.

She continued. "Kate, you and I are still getting to know each other, but from what I've seen so far, you are the perfect amalgamation of your father and me. I've spent my life trying to end the suffering of innocents. Your father worked to make sure that the guilty were punished. You do both. Frankly, if I were you, I'd stop fighting it."

I didn't speak. For the first time since I'd seen the knife protruding from Dr. Dick's sternum, I felt a weird sense of peace. Maybe Dharma was right. Even if she wasn't, her explanation was significantly more palatable than my "the universe is out to get me" theory.

Dharma filled the silence. "I don't think you should quit teaching yoga to become a cop. I certainly don't want you to put yourself in unnecessary danger. But rather than feel sorry for yourself, why not embrace all of life's experiences as gifts? That way the next time you get involved in a murder—and I have a feeling you will—you won't waste time asking why. You'll spend your energy searching for the truth."

Her voice faltered. "I haven't earned the right to give you advice, Kate, but I hope someday you'll listen. I think it might help."

I smiled. "It already has. Thanks, Dharma. I mean it. You've given me a lot to think about."

I hesitated before I said the next words. Not because I didn't mean them. Because it was the first time I'd said them to my mother. "I love you."

As I hung up the phone, I felt an odd combination of frustration and relief. If Dharma was right, I would continue stumbling into murder investigations. That was the frustration.

And it didn't mean that I'd done anything wrong. That was the relief.

I wouldn't sign up for Private Investigation for Dummies any time soon, but I could at least stop driving myself crazy trying to atone for imaginary sins.

Michael's car pulled into the driveway. I would come up with a strategy for helping Rachel tomorrow. Tonight, I needed to fess up to my boyfriend. Whether he liked it or not, I was officially involved in another murder.

EIGHT

My discussion with Michael went surprisingly well. At first I thought he'd been sedated by puppy-breath Valium and the three Guinnesses he drank with his pizza. Then I assumed he was trying to make up for my couch's destruction. Finally I realized he simply wanted to be a nice guy, and that he hoped John would bring me to my senses.

He should have known better.

Whatever the reason, when I drove south on Aurora Avenue North toward the West Precinct the next afternoon, I had Michael's blessing. John replied to my message with an email saying he was working all weekend, so if I needed to talk, I could either call him or meet him at the station. I chose to speak face-to-face, hoping my sweet baby browns would convince him to share more information.

Fortunately for me, Sunday parking in Seattle's Denny Triangle was both free and abundant. I found an open spot in front of my father's old workplace and turned off the ignition. My body felt unaccountably heavy.

Maybe this isn't such a great idea.

The rational part of me understood that the police station was simply a physical structure made of steel, cement, and other miscellaneous construction materials—no more powerful than my destroyed couch cushions. But it didn't feel that way. The sprawling, drab-gray space seemed too much like the dark cavern Dad's death left in my heart. It reminded me that I'd never again see him inside these cement walls—or anywhere else, for that matter. I'd never have an opportunity to pick an argument with him. I'd never be able to tell him that I loved him. I'd never be comforted by his gruff embrace.

I shook off the sadness and forced myself to climb, step by memory-filled step, the three cement stairs to the entrance. The door, when I opened it, seemed lighter than I remembered. Perhaps I was moving on after all.

John met me in the lobby a few minutes later.

"Katydid!" He wrapped me in one of his famous bear hugs. "Why is it that you can't stay out of trouble for longer than two minutes at a stretch?"

"I'm not in trouble this time, John. I just need some advice." We continued our normal banter. "Why do you insist on calling me Katydid? I hate that nickname. It makes me feel like I'm five."

John grinned. "You'll always be a cute little Katydid to me. Would you rather I called you Bug?" His expression turned serious. "You know I'm always glad to see you, Kate. But if you came here hoping I'd encourage you to solve another murder, you're wasting your time. My advice is going to be the same as it was the last three times you poked your nose into an investigation." I mouthed the words as he said them: "Stay out of it."

He gestured for me to follow him. "We may as well sit at my desk. I can tell you to mind your own business from there."

We made small talk as we meandered down the long hallway. "You look good, John."

He patted his receding stomach. "My new girlfriend's put me on one of those low-carb diets. If I'm not careful, she'll make me start exercising."

"I'm glad. I already lost Dad to a heart attack. I couldn't bear to lose you, too."

He squeezed my shoulder. "I know, Katydid. I miss him, too." We walked the rest of the way in silence.

John pulled out a guest chair and motioned for me to sit. "So tell me. How'd you get mixed up in a murder this time?"

I told him the full story, starting with how I knew Rachel, why I was at the hospital, and how I happened upon Dr. Dick's body. I finished by telling him the details of my statement to Martinez and Henderson. John listened to me intently, stopping only to ask an occasional clarifying question. When I finished, he lifted his shoulders and stared at me questioningly.

"Katydid, I'm not sure what you expect me to do here."

"You can start by filling me in on what's happened since last night."

John frowned. "I was afraid you'd say that. I'm not working the case, but I quizzed Martinez this morning, since you asked. If you think she and Henderson are going to phone it in on this one, you're wrong. A well-regarded doctor murdered in a public hospital? The press is all over it. She told me they even got approval for overtime. That's saying something."

John was right. Dr. Jones's murder had been the leading news story since his death. Which might not be a good thing, at least not for Rachel. Martinez and Henderson would be under pressure to make a quick arrest.

John kept talking. "They pushed the autopsy through last night, but the lab is still processing evidence. They haven't made any arrests so far."

"Rachel isn't under arrest?"

John shrugged. "Not that I know of."

My heart lightened. Maybe I was worried about nothing. "That's great news!"

John was ominously silent. My chest grew heavy again.

"You know something you're not telling me, don't you?"

John rubbed his eyes, whether in exhaustion or resignation, I couldn't tell. "I hate talking about cases with you, Kate. You know that. It feels disloyal to your father."

"Dad's dead, John."

"You think that makes me feel better?"

I stared at him, refusing to break eye contact.

"Fine," he grumbled. "If I don't tell you, you'll just harass someone else. The autopsy was definitive on cause of death. The victim died of a stab wound to the heart."

Gruesome, but I wasn't sure how that implicated Rachel. "I already knew he was stabbed to death, John. I found the body, remember?"

"Killing someone with a single stab wound is harder than you think. It could have been a lucky shot, of course, but it's more likely that the assailant had a reasonable understanding of anatomy." He paused. "A nurse, for example."

"Come on, John. The murder took place in a hospital. The *janitor* probably has a reasonable knowledge of anatomy. That doesn't make Rachel the killer."

"Maybe not, but you'd better prepare yourself, just in case." John's smile was kind, but the muscles around his eyes held tension.

"There's something else, isn't there?" I asked.

He didn't reply at first. We stared at each other in an uncomfortable silence broken only by the muted voices of distant conversations. After what felt like a century, he sighed. "I shouldn't tell you this, and I can't go into the details, so you'll have to trust me. Martinez and Henderson have physical evidence that will help them identify the murderer. They think it will implicate your friend."

"What physical evidence?"

John scowled. "I told you, I can't give you any details. But it's the kind of evidence that holds up in court. They're getting a search warrant for your friend's house. If they find what they think they will, she'll be behind bars within a day or two." He leaned forward and peered at me earnestly. "I'm trusting you not to warn her, Kate. It will be my badge if you do."

"I won't say anything, I promise." And I wouldn't. But that didn't make me feel any less guilty.

John must have noticed my discomfort. "What are you thinking, Katydid?"

I stared down at my fingers. "I won't betray your trust, John, I promise. The thing is, I know Rachel. I don't think she did it, and—" My voice cracked.

"And what?"

I met his gaze again. "I feel responsible. What if my testimony helps put her in prison?"

"You saw what you saw, Kate. You have to tell the truth." He reached across the desk and took my hand. "I don't know how to say this, so I'm just going to spit it out. I'm glad that you reunited with Dharma, but you don't have to emulate her. It's not your job to cure every social ill."

"Maybe not, John, but I can't sit back and let the police arrest my friend."

"You don't have a choice." His tone left no room for argument. "If your friend is innocent—and I'm not so sure she is—the best thing you can do to help her is get out of Martinez and Henderson's way and let them do their jobs. Will you do that for me, Katydid?"

I considered arguing, but what was the point? John was set in his ways. Nothing I said would change his mind. I'm pretty sure he was thinking the same thing about me.

I didn't lie to him, but I didn't tell him the truth, either.

"I won't interfere with their investigation, I promise."

I'll be too busy conducting my own.

NINE

I SPENT THE REST of Sunday scanning the Internet for news of Rachel's arrest, teaching yoga classes, and laughing at puppy antics. I wanted to convince Martinez and Henderson that Rachel wasn't their killer, but I wasn't sure how. So I waited, hoping that Dale would get my message and call with some ideas.

My phone was never more silent. Even telemarketers took the day off. I finally decided that if I didn't hear from anyone by Tuesday morning, I'd come up with a plan on my own.

Michael had to work Monday at Pete's Pets, so I stayed home with the pups in the morning and left for the studio around one. I placed Mutt and Jeff inside their crate, told Bella to be a good babysitter, crossed my fingers, and promised to come back no later than three to give them all a mid-afternoon bio break.

I pulled into my reserved parking spot and headed to the studio's back entrance. Contented cooing filtered from the rafters. "Hey there, Mister Feathers." The "Mister" part was an obvious misnomer. The gunmetal gray pigeon (who I now knew was female) was currently nesting. But I'd given her that name when I'd saved her life a few months earlier, and I couldn't bring myself to change it.

"It's nice to see you, too," I continued. "You keep those babies warm now." I checked my watch to make sure that the noon Flow Yoga class had finished, then used my key to enter through the back entrance.

Tiffany's voice greeted me from the front. "Is that you, Kate?"

She wandered into the yoga room, this time dressed in psychedelic yoga pants and a T-shirt decorated with a cartoon frog balanced in Tree Pose. The teal polish on her nails matched the swirls on her legs.

I pointed to Tiffany's top. "At least *someone* you hang out with does yoga." In spite of her new obsession with yoga clothes, I'd yet to convince Tiffany to try a single Downward Facing Dog.

She ignored my well-placed jab, refolded a yoga mat, and placed it neatly on the shelf.

"I wasn't expecting to see you today," I added. "I thought you were working for Michael."

"I've worked so much overtime for him lately that I'm behind on the work I owe you. He gave me a few hours off and sent me here."

It didn't sound like time off to me, but I didn't argue. I'd speak with Michael about giving her some extra vacation days later.

"I told the Flow Yoga teacher that she could go home, since I was planning to clean anyway." Tiffany gave me an uncertain look. "That was okay, wasn't it?"

I felt a strange tickling inside my rib cage. If I'd been speaking with anyone else, I'd have sworn it was affection.

"It's great, Tiffany." I smiled. "You know, you really *are* doing a good job."

She pretended to examine her fingernails, but her cheeks flushed bright pink. "You probably say that to all of your slaves."

I would have assured her that my compliment was sincere, but the chime on the front door interrupted. When I entered the reception area, Rachel and Nicole hovered near the desk. I rushed toward them. "I'm so glad to see you two!"

They didn't seem glad to see me. Or anyone else, for that matter. Nicole looked guarded, sullen, and like she wished she were standing anywhere but my studio's lobby. Bright red blemishes dotted her forehead and nose. Rachel's eyes seemed hollow, as if hope were a distant memory. Cherished but relegated to another, happier lifetime.

I ignored John's no-contact order and wrapped Rachel in a firm hug. "I'm sorry about your husband. Are you okay?"

Her body stiffened under my embrace. I released her and stepped back. "Are *we* okay?"

She smiled, but her voice sounded flat. "We're fine, Kate. That's why I'm here. I need to talk with you about what happened." Her eyes darted to Nicole, then back to me again. "Is there someplace private we can talk?"

Nicole scowled. "She means someplace where I won't be able to overhear. We wouldn't want me to know what's going on with my own life, after all."

Rachel's tone flipped from flat to annoyed in a heartbeat. She whipped toward her daughter. "I told you before, young lady. Drop the sarcasm."

I would have intervened, but I didn't get the chance. Tiffany stepped between them, facing Nicole. "Let's get out of here." She gestured toward me with her thumb. "Who wants to hang out with these old farts, anyway?"

Nicole hesitated. "Go where?"

Tiffany frowned, as if thinking. "Do you do yoga?"

"A little."

"Let's go into the yoga room, then. You can teach me how to do Hand Stand."

Nicole didn't make eye contact. "Um … no thanks."

Tiffany shrugged. "You're right. Yoga's lame. I have a better idea. I live in the apartments upstairs. Let's go to my place. I'll give you a makeover." She pointed to Nicole's forehead. "I have a concealer that will totally cover those zits."

I cringed, fully expecting Nicole to break Tiffany's kneecaps. Instead, she smiled and nodded yes.

"We'll be back in a half hour," Tiffany said. She grumbled to Nicole as the door closed behind them. "Parents suck, don't they?"

"Sorry about that," I said to Rachel.

"Don't be. That's the first time Nicole's listened to an adult in months."

Calling Tiffany an adult seemed like a stretch, but I let it go. I locked the front door, gestured for Rachel to sit on the bench, and poured her a cup of rose petal tea. She cradled the cup between her palms and inhaled, as if drawing sustenance from its sweet floral scent.

"Nicole didn't have school today?" I asked.

"I kept her home because of Richard's death, but I'm beginning to regret it. I swear that girl gets more hardheaded every day."

"The last few days can't have been easy for either of you."

"I suppose. Still, after all I've done for her, she should be grateful."

I didn't reply. Who was I to offer teenage parenting advice? I couldn't control two six-pound puppies.

Finally, not wanting to delay the inevitable, I asked my main question. "I'm surprised you came here today. I wasn't sure you'd still be speaking to me after I..." I hesitated, not sure how to continue.

"After you ratted me out to the police?" Rachel took a slow sip of her tea before continuing. "We're fine, really, Kate. I know you had to talk to them." She shuddered. "I hope they were nicer to you than they were to me. That Henderson cop tore into me Saturday night like a pit bull ripping apart a used tire. I'd just learned my husband was dead. Couldn't he have given me a day to grieve? Then, as if that wasn't bad enough, he and Martinez and a half-dozen of their cronies showed up at my house with a search warrant this morning." She shuddered. "It's unnerving."

I pretended to be surprised. "The police searched your house? What were they looking for?"

"How should I know? As far as I know, they're still searching. I called my lawyer, grabbed Nicole, and got the heck out of there. I came here because..." Her voice trailed off. "I guess because I always felt safe here. And I wanted to tell you that I'm not angry."

I hesitated before speaking. "Rachel, I'll probably get called to testify, so don't answer this if it might incriminate you. But I have to ask. What were you running from when I crashed into you?"

She stared down at her hands. "I'm sorry, Kate. I can't talk to you about Saturday. At all. Lawyer's orders. He'd have a fit if he knew I was here."

Dale would approve. At least she had a competent lawyer.

"I understand," I replied. "How can I help?"

"I'm not sure that you can. I'm not sure anyone can. I just wish this whole nightmare would go away." Her eyes grew wet. "I still can't believe Richard's gone."

Rachel's pocket buzzed. She pulled out her cell phone and glanced at the screen. "Excuse me, I have to take this." She set her cup next to the water dispenser, walked a few feet away, and spoke in a low voice. "I see. Can it wait until—" She stopped, mid-sentence, and listened. Her complexion turned ashen. "Yes. As soon as I can. Thank you. Goodbye."

She stared at the phone for at least twenty seconds, as if the screen held an important but completely indecipherable message.

"That was my lawyer. The police need me to come down to the station. Now."

Cotton lined the roof of my mouth. Henderson and Martinez must have found whatever they were looking for.

Rachel held her breath for a moment. When she released it, she seemed to grow three inches taller. "Kate, there *is* something you can do for me."

"What's that?" I was tempted to say I'd do anything for her, but I'd already proven that wasn't true. I wouldn't lie.

"Nicole's not..." Her voice trailed off. "She's sixteen, but she's young for her age. She shouldn't be by herself right now. Can you watch her while I'm gone? If I can't come back to get her—"

"Don't say that."

"I don't have the luxury of denial, Kate. My lawyer thinks the police are going to arrest me. I don't want Nicole to see it. Can she stay with you while I go to the station?"

"Of course."

She swallowed. "If I'm not back by five, call Justine. I spoke to her last night. She agreed to let Nicole stay with her until school lets out for summer. If I'm in jail longer than that, Nicole will have to go to Atlanta and live with my parents."

Tiffany rattled the front door, then opened it with her key. I almost didn't recognize the young woman who walked in behind her. The blemishes on Nicole's skin were barely visible, and expertly applied eyeliner made her eyes pop dramatically against her pale skin. Her lips were a little too cherry red for my taste, but I had to admit: Tiffany was a makeup magician.

If Rachel noticed her daughter's transformation, she didn't mention it. "Nicole, I need you to stay here with Kate while I go to the police station and answer a few more questions."

"Stay with Kate?" Nicole glared at her mother, then at me, then back at her mother again, as if she wasn't sure which of us to loathe most. "I don't need a babysitter."

"I know you don't," Rachel snapped. "But please, for once in your life, would you not argue with me?"

I offered the teen a conciliatory smile. "Believe me, Nicole. I'm not a babysitter. Ask Tiffany. Anyone who hangs out with me has to work."

"She's not kidding," Tiffany replied. "She's a freaking slave driver."

I ignored Tiffany's quip and focused on Nicole. "If you stay with me, you'll have to help with the puppies."

The girl's energy softened. "Puppies?"

"Yes. I'm fostering two labradoodle puppies. They've been home alone for the last couple of hours. I need someone to watch them while I take my older dog for a walk. If we have time, maybe you can show me some of those makeup tricks Tiffany taught you. You look great."

Nicole's eyes didn't meet mine, but I swore that she almost smiled. "Okay."

Rachel gave Nicole a one-sided hug, mouthed the words "thank you," and walked out the door. Nicole stared out the window until long after Rachel's car disappeared down Greenwood Avenue.

TEN

Forty-five minutes later, I left Tiffany in charge of the studio and drove with Nicole to Ballard. The grumbling started as soon as she latched her seat belt.

"I can't believe my mom is making you watch me like some sort of toddler. It's like that stupid party at the hospital all over again."

"You didn't want to go to the open house on Saturday?"

"Why would I? Did you see anyone else my age there?"

Now that I thought about it, I hadn't. I'd seen adults of all ages and plenty of younger kids, but not a single teen. Not even Nicole. I shook my head no.

"Mom only made me go so she could keep an eye on me."

"If that's true, she didn't do a very good job of it. When I saw her, she was trying to find you."

"The party was lame. I figured I couldn't get any more grounded than I already was, so I took off."

"To where?"

She shrugged. "Around. I hung out at a coffee shop for a while, then I grabbed a bus home." She frowned. "That woman is seriously obsessed with keeping me under observation, like I'm some sort of lab rat. If she actually *does* get arrested, she'll probably make the cops put me in the cell next to her. That way she can glare at me through the bars."

I smiled. "Hopefully it won't come to that."

Nicole crossed her arms and slumped against the seat. "Prison might not be so bad. Her real plan is worse. She told me today that if she gets arrested, I'll have to stay with Justine."

"Justine seems pretty cool. You don't like her?"

"She's okay, but the old woman who lives with her is gross. She drools all the time and chews with her mouth open. She even wears a diaper." Nicole wrinkled her nose. "The last time I was there the living room smelled like urine."

This wasn't my battle—at least not one I cared to join—so I didn't comment. Nicole sulked for a few minutes, but then her demeanor changed. She dropped her bitter facade long enough for me to glimpse her vulnerability.

"Hey, you don't think my mom will actually get arrested, do you?"

I paused for a few seconds, unsure how I should answer. I settled for honesty.

"I don't know, Nicole. She might. I wish I had a better answer, but I won't lie to you. You deserve the truth."

Nicole leaned toward me earnestly. "You know my mom didn't kill Richard, right?"

I nodded my head yes.

"Then tell the police you were wrong. Tell them you didn't see her or that you got the time mixed up."

"I can't lie to the police, Nicole. Even if I did, they'd figure it out. That would make your mom's case worse."

"There has to be something we can do. What if she goes to prison?"

"What your mom needs most is for you to be strong," I said.

Nicole rolled her eyes.

"And by that I mean cut her some slack. She's under a lot of stress. I know you two have issues, but can you try to not fight her for now?"

Nicole didn't say yes, but she didn't argue, either. I took that as a good sign.

"Good," I said. "I'll send you both positive energy."

I planned to do significantly more than telegraph good intentions, but I didn't share that with Nicole. The last thing she needed was false hope.

We drove the rest of the way to my bungalow in silence. Nicole grabbed my arm as we pulled into the driveway. "Kate, you shouldn't leave puppies outside alone. It's not safe!"

She was right. The puppies *were* in danger. From Michael. He'd strangle them the moment he saw today's carnage. Mutt was currently digging a hole in Michael's freshly planted vegetable bed. Jeff gnawed on what was left of a tattered tennis shoe—men's size ten.

"The little Houdinis escaped again."

Nicole leaped out of the car and ran toward them. I sprinted a millisecond behind her. The gold and black monster-pups glanced up from their pillaging and chose a new game. Keep away. As in, keep the heck away from the buzz-killing humans determined to catch you.

I crushed Michael's prized Sungold tomato plants and knocked over the pea trellis, but I finally cornered Mutt on the front doorstep. Jeff dropped the tennis shoe and scampered toward the street.

"Nicole, grab the black one before it gets hit!"

She scooped him up inches from the sidewalk.

Mutt wiggled happily at the end of my arms, covered in something brown, crumbly, and decidedly smelly. "What's that all over your neck?" I leaned forward and took a deep whiff.

Chicken manure.

From the wrinkled expression on Nicole's face, Jeff smelled no better.

Old Kate would have chosen this moment to throw an ill-advised temper tantrum, but New Kate was in charge now. And New Kate looked on the bright side. The puppies may have destroyed Michael's dream of home-grown salsa this summer, but at least they had stayed on the property. If they'd gone wandering...

Oh no.

If the puppies had escaped both the house and my fenced back yard, where was Bella?

I thrust Mutt into Nicole's arms. "Wait here. I need to see if my German shepherd got out, too. She's not always good with strangers."

My mind whirled with nightmarish scenarios as I ran to the back yard gate. Dog fights, car accidents, mauled Santas, stern Animal Control officers. Bella was huge, powerful, and easily frightened. She often acted like Cujo on steroids. She'd never harmed anyone, human or animal, but that gave me little comfort. Frightened dogs, when cornered, were the most likely to bite. With Seattle's tough dangerous dog laws, Bella's first bite could well be her last.

I pulled on the padlock. Still locked. That was good, right? My hands shook so hard, I couldn't insert the key.

Take a deep breath, Kate. Slow down.

The lock snapped open on the third try. I charged through the gate, tore across the yard, and peered through the kitchen blinds, desperately hoping to see Bella. She sat at perfect attention, staring at the doggie door.

My hands—in fact my entire body—still shook. I slumped against the window and took several long, steadying breaths, then looked at the sky and whispered a quick prayer to God, the universe, or anyone else who might be listening.

"Thank you."

Bella greeted me in the kitchen with wet, sloppy kisses and a full-body wiggle. I greeted her with a huge, full-Bella hug and a few sloppy kisses of my own.

"Gooooood girl."

After a moment of relieved bonding, I clipped on her leash, grabbed a handful of dog cookies, and led her outside.

"It's safe now, Nicole. Come on into the yard."

Nicole closed the gate and set the two writhing puppies on the grass. They scampered away, no doubt searching for something new to destroy.

I laid my hand on Bella's shoulders and pointed to Nicole. "Bella, this is Nicole. Nicole is our friend." At the sound of her favorite F-word, Bella lowered her head, woo-wooed, and gently swished her tail back and forth—the trademarked I-am-a-sweet-and-friendly-dog greeting she used with new friends. "Bella, say hello."

As trained, Bella walked up to Nicole, went into a sit, and offered Nicole her paw.

"How cute!" Nicole grabbed Bella's paw and gave it an enthusiastic shake.

"Good girl, Bella," I said. I gave Bella one of the cookies and handed the rest to Nicole. "Give her these and she'll be your friend forever."

Bella stared at Nicole—or more likely at the dog treats—with an expression of unbridled adoration. A long line of drool dangled from her lower lip all the way to her elbow.

"Are you comfortable with big dogs?" I asked.

Nicole's smile enveloped her entire face. "Absolutely."

I left them to bond while I explored the devastation.

Mutt and Jeff could only have been out an hour or two, but they'd made excellent use of their time. A half-dozen new holes dotted the walkway. The corpses of Michael's newly planted geraniums lay beside them. The petunias hadn't fared much better. The ones still attached to their roots had been flattened into petunia pancakes, the obvious victims of some serious puppy rolling.

Three feet from the gate, I discovered their escape route. An impossibly small break in the fence with a labradoodle-puppy-sized hole dug underneath it. Ingenuity score? Puppies: 237. Human prison guards: 0.

And I hadn't looked inside the house yet.

I took a deep breath and steeled my shoulders. No time like the present.

Nicole hugged the pups to her chest and followed me inside. "Eww." She pointed at the living room carpet. "You don't expect me to clean that up, do you?"

"No." I sighed. "Unfortunately, that's my job."

A large pile of puppy droppings and a softball-sized wet spot decorated the floor. Half of a second puppy pile had been smashed into the carpet. The rest had been tracked around the room. I wasn't sure which of the three dogs had received the day's poopie pedicure, but I could easily track the creature's movements—across the carpet, onto the couch, and out to the kitchen.

Mutt began to sniff and circle, a clear sign that she was about to desecrate the carpet again. I scooped her up and accidentally dug my fingers into her bladder, with the expected outcome. Urine splashed down my shirt and onto my jeans.

Nicole burst into laughter, a sound so rare that hearing it was almost worth being drenched in dog urine.

"Gross!"

"You think that's funny? Wait till it happens to you." I handed her the still-dripping dog. "Take her outside while I change clothes." She held the puppy at arm's length and marched it to the door. I ran upstairs and quickly changed into sweats and a torn T-shirt, the perfect clothes for dog washing.

I grabbed a week's supply of terry towels from the closet, wetted half of them, and cleaned up the mess as best I could. Next up: a kitchen sink bath for the two evildoers. I found Nicole and the puppies in my office.

Mutt, Jeff, and Nicole were cavorting like long-lost friends. The puppies nibbled; they licked; they yipped their affection. Nicole giggled and rolled on the floor, covered in crawling fur monsters. This was not the angsting teenager I'd loaded into my car at Serenity Yoga. Not even close.

The Yoga Sutras posit that within each one of us resides a perfect being. An all-knowing soul, if you will. But we rarely show it. Instead, we cover it with filters—layers of conditioning that color how we interact with the world.

Nicole was no exception. By the age of sixteen, she had experienced traumas that would have broken many adults. The gray fog of addiction, the purple bruise of heartache, the black nothingness of death. That dark-shrouded Nicole was the person I knew. That dark-shrouded Nicole was the person she shared with the world.

As she interacted with those puppies, her resentful shield lowered. For the first time since I'd met her, sullenness was replaced by something that looked an awful lot like joy.

Even when Nicole's eyes met mine, her shield stayed down. "Oh my gosh, Kate. They are so adorable. What are their names?"

I smiled, puppy-induced irritation forgotten. "Michael calls them Mutt and Jeff, but we'll eventually come up with something better." I gestured with my thumb toward the kitchen. "Come on, let's give these monsters a bath."

I filled the sink with warm, sudsy water and scrubbed the chicken doo out of Mutt's fur. Bella sat ten feet away, ears flattened in helmet-head position, undoubtedly worried that she was up next. For a while, Nicole and I worked in silence. As I rinsed the suds from Mutt's fur, I asked Nicole about the one thing we had in common: yoga.

"So, what did you think of the Yoga to Overcome Grief class?"

She didn't answer at first. She stalled by taking the pup from my hands and rubbing it dry with Michael's favorite bath towel. "To be honest, Mom forced me to take it."

I teasingly nudged her shoulder. "So your mom sentenced you to spend time with me, kind of like today?"

She blushed. "It's not you. I just ... I never thought I could do yoga." She looked down at Mutt's fur. "I'm not ... you know ... "

I'd heard the start of that sentence many times before. It usually ended with one of three misconceptions: that only fit, flexible people did yoga; that yoga was Hinduism, and therefore violated the principles of Christianity; or that all yogis looked like the models on the cover of *Yoga Journal*.

I gestured at my mismatched sweats and torn T-shirt. "You didn't think you could rock the yoga fashion world the way Tiffany and I do?"

Nicole's lopsided grin hinted at the mischievous teenager she kept hidden inside. "I hate the tight yoga pants people like Tiffany wear, but that's not it. I don't like working out." She shuddered. "I hated gym. So no offense, but watching a bunch of rubber-band Barbies shove their butts in the air didn't sound all that fun to me."

I didn't consider yoga a workout—it was a practice that integrated the full human system, body, mind, and spirit—but I didn't correct her.

She continued. "But then I came to your studio, and you turned out to be okay. You don't focus on what the poses look like at all. When I practice, I feel like I'm alone. Yoga class is the one time I don't feel self-conscious."

I knew what she meant. When I practiced yoga, the world evaporated. In a good way.

She lifted her eyes to meet mine. "They should offer yoga classes in high school. It would totally beat weightlifting and track."

"I'm glad it helps."

I handed her the black puppy. Nicole nuzzled his belly with her nose. "You're so lucky to have three dogs. I wanted a pet, but Richard hated animals. A friend gave me a kitten after my dad died, and Richard threatened to drown it. Mom made me give it back."

I bit back the vile words threatening to spew from my lips. Dad taught me to never speak ill of the dead. But when they threatened a kitten? That had to be some sort of exception. Still, badmouthing Nicole's dead stepfather wouldn't help anyone. I stuck with a safer topic.

"I *am* lucky. Bella is the love of my life." I pointed at Mutt, who had toddled to the water dish and appeared to be slurping her weight in water. "The little ones aren't mine, though. My boyfriend and I are just fostering them until we find the jerk who abandoned them. Whoever they are, I could kill them."

Nicole jolted as if she'd been slapped. Her angry-teenager expression snapped firmly back into place.

I felt like an idiot, which made total sense since I'd just acted like one. I placed my hand on Nicole's arm. "I'm a moron, Nicole. I should never make light of murder, but especially not now. I'm sorry about your stepfather."

She frowned. "I'm not. Sorry about his death, that is. Dickhead was a jerk." She flinched. "Don't tell Mom I called him that."

"Don't worry, I won't." I knew the answer, but I asked anyway, hoping she'd volunteer more information. "You didn't get along with your stepfather?"

"Richard liked me about as much as he liked that kitten. He was nice enough until my dad died and I had to move in with Mom and him. After that, he just wanted to get rid of me."

"Get rid of you?"

Nicole's expression was tough but her voice quavered. "He was going to send me to boarding school, like some untrainable dog that you send to the pound. I guess he wanted to make me someone else's problem."

I watched Nicole closely, trying to unlock the secrets that lay behind her dark, unreadable eyes. She didn't regret her stepfather's death—that much was obvious. But did she cause it? I didn't sense violence in her energy, but I didn't sense drug addiction, either.

I softened my voice. "Nicole, I overheard your mom and your stepfather fighting. Are you using drugs?"

She squeezed Jeff so tightly, I was afraid she might hurt him. "No! Why does everybody always take Richard's side?"

The puppy squirmed, clearly uncomfortable. I was about to ask Nicole to loosen her grip when she kissed the top of his head and set him on the ground. He scampered off to join his littermate, unscathed.

When the girl faced me again, her eyes were wet. "Look. I got into some trouble after Dad died, but it wasn't nearly as bad as Richard made it out to be. I stole some tranquilizers from my grandmother's house, and I got caught smoking pot at school. Getting high made me feel better. It was dumb, but Richard made it seem like I was smoking crystal and shooting up heroin on the side. I hated the rehab place he and Mom sent me to, but it worked. I'll never smoke weed again if I have to go back to that hellhole."

"Your stepfather said he was missing some money. Did you steal it?"

Nicole looked down at her shoelaces. She gave a single small nod.

"Why?"

She opened her mouth, then closed it again. "I don't want to talk about this anymore." She tossed the towel on the counter. "I'll wait for you outside." The kitchen door slammed behind her.

I stared after her, conflicted. Nicole was hiding something. What, why, and how it related to Dr. Dick's death remained a mystery. My heart would break if Nicole was the killer, but that didn't make the possibility any less likely. Did I really want to uncover the truth?

I shoved the unwelcome thought firmly to the back of my mind, moved the puppies' crate upstairs to the bedroom, and locked them inside it. I double-checked to make sure the bedroom door was latched shut. Twice.

"Let's see you get out of there, you little tricksters."

Hopefully they wouldn't take that as a challenge.

"What do you think, Bella Girl? Want to leave the little monsters alone and go to the studio with me?" Bella didn't answer verbally, but her eyes clearly said yes. I clipped on her leash and joined Nicole outside. She stood next to my Honda, smoking.

My mouth opened before I could stop it. "Don't you know how bad smoking is for your health?"

"This isn't a cigarette. It's an e-vape."

I had a feeling the distinction wasn't nearly as important as she thought.

She cringed and stared down at her feet. "You won't tell my mom though, right?"

I shook my head no. Nicole and her mother had much bigger issues to deal with than steamy inhaled nicotine. "Come on," I said. "Let's head back. I'll bet your mom's already done with the police. She's probably waiting for us at the studio."

Nicole didn't reply. Then again, she didn't need to. Her grim expression made it clear that she didn't believe me.

ELEVEN

THE INSTANT NICOLE AND I walked through the studio's back door, I could tell something was wrong. Tiffany greeted us in the yoga room, clearly fighting off tears. "Nicole, someone's here waiting for you."

Justine stood up from the bench in the lobby. A weak smile touched her lips, but her eyes remained hollow. "Hey guys."

Nicole's face—in fact, her entire body—sagged. The sulking teenager who'd attended my yoga classes disappeared. The smiling young woman who'd frolicked with the puppies left, too. For the first time in the six weeks I'd known her, Nicole looked defeated.

"You're here for me, aren't you." Nicole's words were a statement, not a question.

Justine hesitantly lifted her arms as if to hug her, then lowered them. "I'm sorry, sweetie. Yes. You're going to stay with me for a while. Your mother has been arrested for your stepfather's murder."

For several seemingly interminable moments, I kept my eyes locked on Nicole. Her face cycled through multiple emotions. Horror, disbelief, anger, fear. It landed on resignation. When she spoke, her voice was devoid of emotion.

"I'll need to go home and pack."

"Of course," Justine replied. "But we have to go now."

I hesitated, wondering how I could help. Part of me wanted to reassure Nicole—to find the magic words that would convince her that everything was going to be okay. But we both would have known I was lying. Another part wanted to wrap her in my arms and give her the hug Justine hadn't, but she looked too fragile—like the slightest touch would shatter her into a million pieces.

In the end, I did nothing. I stared helplessly out the window and watched her trudge disconsolately to Justine's car.

Tiffany dropped heavily into the chair behind the check-in desk and buried her face in her hands. "This sucks. Big time."

For what was likely the first time in history, I agreed with her. Frustrated dread congealed in my stomach. Rachel's arrest wasn't right. It couldn't possibly be right. My eyes followed Justine's car out of the parking lot, but I spoke to Tiffany. "Go back to Pete's Pets and help Michael. Your studio work can wait."

"What are you going to do?"

I ignored her and rummaged around in my purse until I found Detective Martinez's card. "Nothing. Don't worry about it." I set my purse on the desk and reached for the phone.

Tiffany placed her hand over the receiver and pulled the phone toward her, blocking me. "Seriously, Kate, who are you calling?"

I stopped for a moment, surprised by the determined look on her face. "Detective Martinez. She's one of the detectives working the case."

"Then I'm not going anywhere. I like that kid. I want to help."

I had no idea how Tiffany could help, but I wasn't sure how she could hurt, either. "We only have one phone, and I can't put it on speaker," I told her. "Detective Martinez may not speak freely if she knows someone else is listening."

"I understand."

I held up my index finger. "I mean it. She can't know you're here."

"I'll be quiet, I promise." Tiffany stood and offered me the chair next to the phone.

I took a deep breath before dialing, vowing not to take my frustration out on Detective Martinez. She wasn't the enemy. She was simply a cop—a good one—doing her job. I vowed to keep my voice low, calm, and even. My words, respectful.

Martinez answered on the second ring.

My voice seemed to jump three octaves. "You arrested her? You promised me that you'd look at other suspects!" Tiffany winced and scooted several inches away.

Martinez sighed. "Hey, Kate. I figured you'd call. I promised you that I'd look at the *evidence*. I know you think your friend's innocent, but the evidence disagrees."

I spoke at twice my normal speed, as if by saying the words faster, I'd become more convincing. "Look. I'll agree that what I saw at the hospital was suspicious, but it's far from conclusive. Dr. Jones—"

"Stop right there, Kate," Martinez interrupted. "We didn't arrest Mrs. Jones based on your statement. At least not exclusively."

Tiffany slid a sticky note in front of me. *Slow down.* I closed my eyes and counted to three. "Please, hear me out. Dr. Jones wasn't exactly a Boy Scout. Lots of people might have wanted him dead."

"Maybe so, Kate, but—"

"And the hospital was packed on Saturday." I started to speed up again. "Hundreds of people went to the open house. Not to mention the staff and all the patients who were on site. Any of them could have stabbed Dr. Jones. The murderer could have cleaned up and gone right back to the party."

"So could Mrs. Jones, and she was the only one seen running from the crime scene."

"She left the break room in a hurry, sure. But like I told you, it might not have had anything to do with Dr. Jones's death. She probably didn't even know his body was in the restroom."

I paused and waited for Martinez's reply. After several moments of stress-filled silence, she spoke. "I'm sorry, Kate. Mrs. Jones's fingerprints were on the knife."

"How on earth did you have time to run her prints already?" I asked, surprised. Fingerprint analysis took time. "You only arrested her a few hours ago."

Martinez sighed. "We know how to do our jobs, Kate. Mrs. Jones's prints were already on file. The state did a fingerprint background check when she applied for her nursing license."

"Were hers the only prints on the knife?"

"No, but that's not surprising. Anyone who cut a piece of that cake touched it."

"Then they don't mean anything. Rachel might have used the knife to cut the cake herself. Even if she didn't, that knife is probably kept in the staff room. She could have touched it on an entirely different day. What did she say when you asked her about it?"

"She didn't say anything. She lawyered up and is exercising her right to remain silent."

Tiffany slid me another note. *Nicole said that the police searched her house. Did they find something?*

The search warrant. Martinez had waited until after today's search to arrest Rachel. There had to be a reason beyond Rachel's fingerprints on the knife. She was holding back on me.

I readied myself for bad news. "There's something else. Something you're not telling me."

Martinez paused, as if carefully considering her words. "John O'Connell says you're trustworthy. From what I've seen, I'm inclined to agree with him. Am I wrong?"

"No. Whatever you say will stay between you and me." *And Tiffany. And maybe Michael. And Dale, if he ever gets back from Mexico and returns my phone call.*

"We haven't released this to the press, so I'm counting on you to keep it confidential. The body was moved."

"Moved? From where?"

"Not far. Probably just from the break room. We think Mrs. Jones killed her husband in the break room and dragged his body into the women's restroom, hoping it wouldn't be found right away." I imagined Martinez leaning forward and placing her forearms on one of the police department's cheap metal desks. "Most of the victim's bleeding was internal, but not all of it. Mrs. Jones cleaned up as best she could—likely with some paper towels—and she was careful not to get blood on her clothes. We think she might have worn a lab coat or scrubs."

"I saw her when she ran out of the break room, remember? She was wearing a sundress—the same dress she had on at the party."

I heard Martinez shuffle through paper. "I have a photo from the open house here. When Mrs. Jones ran past you, was she carrying anything?"

Dull pain throbbed behind my eyes. "Yes. A red shoulder bag." *A big one. Big enough to hide bloody clothes, a roll or two of paper towels, and a spare outfit for good measure.*

"That sounds like the purse in the picture." She paused. "So here's the thing. We searched Mrs. Jones's house today. We found that entire outfit. Dress, nylons, jewelry, shoes. Everything except that red shoulder bag. Mrs. Jones isn't answering any questions, but we have a theory. She stabbed her husband, then panicked. She hid the body, cleaned up the blood, and stashed the paper towels, lab coat, and whatever else she used in that bag. Then she ditched it somewhere in the hours it took us to find her."

"That doesn't make any sense. If she was smart enough to move the body and clean up the blood, why didn't she take the knife and dump it with everything else?"

"Like I said, Kate. She panicked. This wouldn't be the first case I've worked on where the killer cleaned up the scene but left the murder weapon behind."

I hated Martinez's theory. Big time. Especially since it made sense.

She continued. "Unfortunately for Mrs. Jones, we don't need the bag to convict her. When she cleaned up the blood, she missed some spots, and she forgot to cover her shoes. We found traces of blood on a sandal in her closet. The shoe is still at the lab, but trust me. The blood came from the murder scene. The marks on the sole match a blood smear we found near the restroom door."

The throbbing behind my eyes amped up to pounding. That damned burgundy smudge. "Anything else?"

"Yes. We found divorce papers in Dr. Jones's desk." She waited a beat. "Kate, I'm sorry. We've arrested the right person."

"What about Dr. Jones's mistress, Mariella?"

"She claims she never left the party until after the police arrived. Besides, what motive would she have had? The victim was about to leave his wife, presumably to be with her."

I tapped a pen against the desktop. "Maybe Mariella didn't know about the divorce papers."

Detective Martinez sighed. "If you were planning to leave your wife, wouldn't your lover be the first person you told?"

I didn't have an answer for that. Not one that would help Rachel, anyway.

Tiffany slid another note across the table. *Bail?*

"Has bail been set?" I asked.

"Mrs. Jones hasn't been arraigned yet, but we've charged her with first-degree murder. I'd be shocked if the judge granted bail."

I met Tiffany's eyes and shook my head no. I added two words to her note and passed it back to her. *Other questions?*

She shrugged.

I had about a million, but I only asked one. "Mariella, the girl-friend. What's her last name?"

Martinez's tone left no room for argument. "I'm not going to connect you with any other witnesses, Kate. I only told you this much so you'd stop feeling guilty. It's time for you to accept that Mrs. Jones killed her husband and move on with your life."

I opened my mouth to tell her I would, but I couldn't bring myself to lie. I settled for avoidance instead. "Thank you for speaking with me. I appreciate your candor."

Tiffany spoke as soon as I hung up the phone. "Was that as bad as it sounded?"

"Worse. Martinez and Henderson are convinced that Rachel's the killer." I frowned. "They won't spend much more time on the case."

My comment wasn't a criticism. The Seattle Police Department was over budget and understaffed. Every case Martinez and Henderson closed allowed them to focus on the backlog they still had open. I didn't blame them, but I couldn't step aside and let Rachel get railroaded, either.

"What do we do now?" Tiffany asked.

"I don't know."

She raised her eyebrows.

"Seriously, I don't." I thought for a moment. "Though I'd sure like to have a chat with the mistress."

"Mariella?"

"Yes, but I don't know how to find her." I flashed on an image of Dr. Dick and Mariella at ABBA. For the first time since walking into the studio, I smiled. "But I think I know someone who does."

TWELVE

THE PERSON I WAS thinking of was Summer. If the saying was true, there were at most six degrees of separation between myself and Dr. Dick's murderer. If Mariella was the killer, I'd only need two. Summer could connect me with Tamara, the nurse Summer apparently "had a history with" at ABBA. Tamara (I hoped) could connect me with Mariella. She'd certainly seemed to know Mariella that night at ABBA.

A few minutes after I hung up the phone with Detective Martinez, I picked it up again. Summer was on her way to a birth, but I convinced her to meet me for a walk at Gasworks Park the next evening, provided she was done supporting the birth by then. I told her I needed to ask some questions about Rene's birth plan. I felt bad about the fib, but I wasn't sure how Summer would react if she knew my real intentions.

Tiffany made me promise to keep her posted about Rachel and Nicole, then left to take over for Michael at Pete's Pets. I led my five o'clock private client through a short movement and breath practice to help ease depression, then turned the studio over to the teacher of our Monday evening Yoga for Round Bodies class. After I put out more pigeon food for Mister Feathers, I joined Bella at my car and headed home, praying that Michael hadn't taken one look at his garden and committed puppicide.

The reality was worse.

He'd decided to cook.

This time, the culinary tornado had touched down on the stovetop. Chopped onions, tomatoes, and green peppers were scattered across the stone kitchen floor. A legume rainbow of red, lima, black, and garbanzo beans colored the countertop. Seitan crumbles peppered the stove like a fine powder of fresh snow. The spicy aroma of simmering onions and chili powder could mean only one thing: Michael was making his famous vegan fire-alarm chili. He stood at the stove, stirring the bubbling concoction with an oversized wooden spoon while belting out an off-tune rendition of "If I were a Rich Man."

Keep dreaming, buddy.

Not an inch of counter space had been spared in this newest culinary disaster. The sink overflowed with pots, pans, plates, and cutting boards. The walls were dotted with greasy spots of red goo. How one man could create such chaos when cooking a supposedly one-dish entrée was truly beyond me. I smiled away my momentary irritation, wrapped my arms around him from behind, and nuzzled his neck.

"I see you're cooking. Smells delicious."

The pups woke up to my voice, spied Bella, and galloped toward her as if they'd been separated for over a decade. Mutt slid to a stop by colliding with Bella's leg. She gripped Bella's tail between twenty-eight puppy-shark teeth and pulled. Jeff leapt for her face, apparently planning to swing from her lower lip. Bella flattened her ears to her skull and begged with her eyes for me to make them stop.

"Come on guys, leave her alone." I scooped a pup in each arm and deposited them in their ex-pen. Bella swished her tail gratefully.

I scratched the top of her head and gave her a cookie for bravery. "You know, I love it that you're so nice to them, but you're allowed to defend yourself."

Michael dipped a clean spoon into the mixture and offered me a taste. The flavor of sweet red tomatoes burst through an instant before my tongue spontaneously ignited.

"What do you think?" he asked. "More habaneros?"

"Nope. It's perfect." I pointed at my two mournful inmates. "I hope those guys start calming down soon. Bella's getting tired of them using her as a teething toy."

"Better her than my tennis shoes," Michael replied. I wasn't so sure.

"Sorry about your plants today," I said. "I know you were looking forward to that garden."

"No worries. It'll give us an excuse to spend more weekends at the Ballard Farmers Market."

"The market is awesome," I replied, "but we still have a problem. How are we going to keep the little monsters from destroying the house the next time they escape?"

"I have a plan."

Michael placed a lid on the kettle and wiped his hands on the *Messy but Cute* apron I'd given him on his birthday. He reached into a bag on the table and pulled out a dark brown teddy bear.

"It's adorable, Michael, but it won't entertain the puppies for long. They'll destroy it in ten seconds flat."

"It's not a toy, it's a nanny cam. It's going to show us how Mutt and Jeff are getting out of their crate. I conned Tiffany into putting in more overtime tomorrow so I can work part of the day from home.

I'll set up the nanny cam, lock them in their crate, and work on ordering and bookkeeping from the office. When they get out..." He pretended to jump out from a corner. "Busted!"

Bella jumped up and scanned the area for evil intruders. Michael tossed her another cookie. "Once I have the little monsters' escape act on tape, I'll figure out how to stop them."

I smiled. "You know, for a dog food store owner, you're pretty smart."

He gathered me in his arms and planted an enthusiastic kiss on my lips. "For a yoga teacher, you have great taste in boyfriends."

My belly—and a few body parts considerably lower—tingled. I glanced at the stairs leading up to the bedroom. "Want to—"

The timer on the stove dinged. Michael kissed the top of my head. "Hold that thought. The cornbread's done. First we have dinner, then dessert."

The chili was mouth-burning delicious, but it was *nothing* compared to dessert. For the first time since the pups' arrival, we even had seconds.

———

The next morning passed in a whirlwind of group classes, private clients, and long-overdue studio paperwork. Before I knew it, the time had arrived for my afternoon yoga sessions at the Lake Washington Medical Center. I took a quick detour home to pick up Bella and give her a break from the puppies who—according to Michael—had made zero prison breaks, filmed or otherwise.

My motives for rescuing Bella were partially selfish. I knew she'd enjoy the alone-time, but I also wanted her present for my evening walk with Summer. Bella was large and imposing, but she put most people at ease—unless they had facial hair, wore a postal uniform, or drove a UPS truck. If Summer was distracted by enough Bella therapy, she might slip out a few extra secrets. Besides, what fun was taking a walk without a dog?

I pulled into the employee parking area on the tenth floor of the hospital's garage, cracked open the windows and sunroof, and filled Bella's water bowl.

"Okay Baby Girl. It's nice and cool in here. Perfect for your nap. I'll be gone a couple of hours. When I'm done, we'll meet Summer and go for a walk." I picked up her leash. "Do you need to take a bathroom break first?"

If Bella understood my words, she chose to ignore them. She stretched her body across the entire back seat of my Honda, nestled her head against the seat back, and started snoring.

"Sweet dreams, Puppy Girl."

My intestines rumbled, still suffering from the after-effects of extra hot chili. Evidently *I* was the one who needed the bio break. I journeyed through the parking garage, took the elevator down, and walked across the lobby of the main hospital building toward the old perinatal unit.

I hesitated outside the employee break room. My stomach felt queasy, and not from the habaneros still making their way through my system. Rationally, I knew that the room was just an empty space with four institutional-beige walls, some utilitarian furniture, and that oh-so-important restroom. Rationally, I knew that Dr. Dick's body was long gone and that the static-electricity-like charge of violence had left with him. Emotionally, however, I still felt an eerie sense of danger—of evil—lurking inside. My overactive imagination whispered, *Don't go in there.*

My intestines spoke louder.

I cracked open the door, glanced inside the break room, and whispered, "Anyone here?"

"Just us caffeine addicts," a male voice replied. The orderly smiled as he pushed past me, holding up a Styrofoam cup. "My fourth cup today. I seriously need to go decaf."

He wasn't the only one fighting a case of the jitters. I released the breath I'd been unconsciously holding and eased through the door. One quick stop and I'd be on my way. I slipped into the ladies' room and entered the stall closest to the door.

A syringe clattered to the floor. A hand in the stall next to me reached down and snatched it up again. Evidently I wasn't as alone as I'd thought.

"Everything okay?" I asked.

"I'm fine."

The voice sounded familiar. "Justine, is that you?"

After a moment's hesitation, the woman on the other side of the metal wall replied. "Yes."

Of course! Justine. Why hadn't I thought of talking to Justine? She'd been at the hospital on Saturday, and she was friends with Rachel. I wasn't sure if she knew anything that would help, but I'd be crazy not to ask.

"Hang on for a minute, would you? I need to talk to you."

When I exited the stall, Justine was standing near the sink. From the glassy sheen of her eyes, I assumed she'd been crying. She glanced at my reflection in the mirror and smiled. "Oh hey, Kate. I didn't realize that was you." She placed the syringe in a sharps container affixed to the wall.

I hesitated, unsure whether I should ask about the tears in her eyes or pretend that I didn't notice them.

She must have misinterpreted my concern. She pointed to the sharps container. "Diabetes. Had it since I was a teen. I can usually keep it under control, but the stress of the last few days has my blood sugar way out of whack."

"Are you upset? You look like you've been crying."

She smiled. "No, but not because I don't want to. I'm exhausted." She rubbed underneath her eyelids. "The watery eyes are courtesy of my allergies. They're going as crazy as my blood sugar."

"I thought you'd be home with Nicole."

"I'd like to be, but I can't. I'm scheduled to work a double shift again today." Justine turned on the faucet and lathered up her hands. "Mom's home-care assistant promised to let me know if Nicole needs anything. They'll be fine, though. Nicole doesn't need a baby-sitter. Rachel doesn't give her nearly enough independence."

"How's she doing? Nicole, I mean."

Justine shrugged. "About as well as can be expected. She's a tough kid." She turned off the tap and shook water droplets from her hands. "You said you wanted to speak with me?"

"Yes, about Rachel, or at least about the mess she's in. I don't believe she killed her husband. Do you?"

Justine pulled two paper towels from the holder and slowly dried her hands as if carefully considering her words. "No. At least I don't think so." She tossed the towels into the trash can without meeting my eyes.

"I'm sensing a 'but' here," I said.

She turned toward me. "How can either of us know for sure? You saw Richard that night at the studio. He claimed he was going to kick Nicole out, and it sure looked to me like he meant it. I can't imagine Rachel harming anyone, but when my daughter was alive, I'd have done anything to protect her. When someone you love is threatened ... " She glanced down at her hands, then back up again. "Let's just say that if Richard was planning to harm Rachel's daughter, I could understand the impulse to strike first."

Unfortunately, so could I.

"I spoke to the police yesterday," I said. "Rachel's case doesn't look good."

"It's early yet," Justine replied. "If Rachel didn't kill Richard, they'll figure out who did."

"I wish I had your confidence. They won't keep looking if they think they've already arrested the murderer."

Justine didn't reply. I continued. "I'm not a cop—or a private investigator, for that matter—but I've helped solve crimes before. I'd like to find the real killer. That's why I need to talk to you."

She frowned and looked pointedly at her watch. "Can we do this later? I'm already late for my shift." She turned and reached for the door.

I shouldn't have been surprised by Justine's hesitation. To her, I was just a yoga teacher. For all she knew, the past "crimes" I'd helped solve were yoga sequencing errors. Justine had a job to do. When nurses were late to their shifts, patient care suffered. I'd have to convince her that talking to me was a good use of her time.

"How about tomorrow morning?" I asked.

Justine's shoulders slumped. When she turned back to face me, her face wore a resigned expression. "I have to take care of my mother tomorrow morning, then I need to get some sleep. After that, I work graveyard. I won't be up and around again until Thursday evening."

Later than I'd hoped, but it would have to do. "That would be perfect," I told her. "I'm hosting a Sound Bath at the studio Thursday night at eight. Why don't you and Nicole come as my guests? You'll love it."

"Sound Bath?"

"It's hard to explain, but it's deeply soothing. I'll treat you and Nicole to the class, and we can talk afterward."

"No guarantees, but I'll see if we can make it." Justine hesitated halfway out the door. "Do me a favor and don't tell anyone about the diabetes, including Nicole. I prefer to keep my health issues private. The last thing Nicole needs is to worry about me being sick."

"Of course. No problem. I'll see you Thursday at eight."

I hoped.

A few minutes later, I pushed all thoughts of murder out of my mind and shifted into yoga teacher mode. I departed the break room and smiled at the blonde nurse seated at the nurse's station.

"Got any customers for me today?"

She handed me a sheet of paper. "Yes, but only two."

"That's actually perfect." Having only two clients would allow me to spend as much time as needed with each student and still easily make my six o'clock meeting with Summer.

She handed me a clipboard. "The first is in 472. She was admitted yesterday. Preterm labor with quadruplets. We're trying to keep her from going into full labor for a few more days—longer if possible.

I felt my face whiten. "Quadruplets? As in four? Baby humans?" I tried to imagine Rene's body with double the babies, but I couldn't. "I take it Sun Salutations are out."

The nurse grinned. "She's confined to bed right now. Stick with one of those meditations everyone raves about."

The second name on the list was familiar.

"Kendra asked for me again? That's awesome."

I'd met with Kendra the prior week, and the session hadn't gone well. She was hospitalized with borderline preeclampsia, a serious pregnancy complication that would cause any mom-to-be stress. In Kendra's case, the stress often escalated to PTSD-like panic. Kendra's first baby had been stillborn eighteen months ago. She was terrified that she was about to lose her second.

I'd taught her a practice designed to help her relax and let go of the past, but if her tense expression and shallow breath had been any indication, she'd experienced fear-laced annoyance instead. I'd left the session convinced that she'd hated our time together. Evidently I'd been wrong.

"How is her blood pressure?" I asked.

"Still higher than we'd like, but it seems to have stabilized."

"Would some gentle arm and leg movements and a relaxing breath practice be safe?"

The nurse smiled. "Sounds great."

Approved plan in place, I went to work.

I taught the quadra-mom a thirty-minute practice designed to create space: in her body, for the four babies growing within; in her mind, so she could remain sane while caring for four needy infants; and in her heart, for the love she already felt for each child.

Our work was more symbolic than physical, but by the time we finished, her face wore a peaceful smile. Proving once again that yoga wasn't really about the body. It was about healing the mind and restoring the spirit.

Kendra was up next.

I planned to lead her through a relaxing sequence that would calm her energy, center her thoughts, and hopefully lower her blood pressure. It wouldn't fix the root cause of her health issues, but it certainly couldn't hurt. At worst, she could use the practice to relax after the baby was born.

I knocked on the door. "Hey, Kendra. It's Kate."

"Come on in."

She sat in a rocking chair facing a large window that overlooked Lake Washington. A bouquet of fragrant yellow roses brightened the windowsill; the sun bathed her face and brought out the auburn highlights of her hair. Mount Rainier stood in the distance, guarding her.

She turned toward me and smiled. "I'm so glad you're here."

"You look great! How are you feeling?"

"Better, actually. I wasn't sure about the meditation you taught me last week, but I practiced it every day for ten minutes like you told me to. It helped with my stress. A lot. I'm feeling quite a bit better emotionally, thanks to you."

I smiled. "I'm happy to hear that." And a little surprised, but I didn't tell her that. I'd take my victories wherever I could find them.

"Now I have a different problem," she said.

I sat in the chair next to her. "What's that?"

"Back pain. The lying around all day is killing me. I swear they're giving me sugar pills instead of Tylenol. I'm ready to go into labor just so I can get the strong stuff."

"How soon will you be able to deliver?"

"They'd like to let the baby's lungs develop for a few more days, but it won't be long. My section of the floor is being transferred to the new building tomorrow, so at least I'll have more interesting surroundings. Hopefully I'll get a room with a view again."

She winced and placed her palm against her low back. "I don't suppose you smuggled in any morphine, did you?"

I smiled. "Sorry. Controlled substances are beyond my scope of practice. But I have a meditation that might help."

I ditched my original plan and taught her a Full Body Scan meditation. The practice was surprisingly effective in reducing chronic pain. It didn't change the pain per se, but it helped practitioners learn how to focus their minds on something else. In essence, it taught people how to disconnect from their pain and lessen their emotional reaction to it.

"Do you want to lie down?" I asked.

"If it's okay, I'd prefer to stay sitting. I love feeling the sun."

As she turned her face to the light, I invited her to close her eyes and deepen her breath. Several minutes of mind-focusing breath practice later, I brought her attention to her feet.

"Inhale and feel your toes … "

By the time we'd gone from toes, to legs, to belly, to back, the lines around Kendra's eyes had softened. As we continued up through arms, hands, chest, neck, and face, her breath became smooth and subtle. Her posture changed. I would have sworn that I felt her low back muscles release.

When we finished, she opened her eyes and smiled. "You know, I think that helped!"

"You seem surprised."

"Honestly, I am. That was great." She winked. "But I won't argue if you smuggle in a few dozen Vicodin next time."

A gruff male voice interrupted from the doorway. "It's about time you got some relief."

I turned toward the sound and froze.

I'd seen the stranger before.

In the chaos of Dr. Dick's murder, I'd forgotten about the angry man with the goatee—who was now standing in Kendra's doorway. Although he'd exchanged his T-shirt and jeans for a jacket and slacks, I'd have recognized those dark, wary eyes anywhere. They belonged to the man who'd glared at Dr. Dick and Mariella. The man who'd been upset enough to drop his plate. The man who'd disappeared from the room when Dr. Dick left to chase after Rachel. Nerve endings tingled up and down my arms. Was this also the man who had killed him?

Kendra waved him inside. "Hey, sweetie. I'm glad you're here. This is the yoga teacher I told you about. Kate, meet my husband, Liam Delaney."

———

Kendra, Liam, and I made small talk while I tried to find a way to smoothly turn the conversation toward murder. I finally segued by bringing up the open house.

"I think I've seen you before. Weren't you at the celebration this past Saturday?"

Liam's eyes, never that friendly to begin with, clouded over. "For a little while."

"Did you hear about the incident that afternoon?"

"You mean the doctor that was killed?" He lowered his voice. "Good riddance."

Kendra gasped. "Liam!"

"What? Do you seriously expect me to act like I care? That SOB killed our son."

Their son? Was he referring to their stillborn baby?

I chose my next words carefully. I didn't want to upset Liam—or Kendra, for that matter—any more than necessary. "Kendra told me about your son's stillbirth. I'm so sorry."

The words, though true, felt entirely inadequate. Then again, how could any words be sufficient? I glanced at Kendra, conflicted.

Should I press Liam for more information? Upsetting Kendra couldn't be good for her blood pressure, which by definition couldn't be good for her baby. Still, Liam was my first solid suspect, and I didn't want to waste the opportunity to question him.

In the end, Kendra decided for me. "Please excuse Liam. I suppress grief with panic. Liam gets angry. Most people think we should be over the loss of our baby by now, but they don't understand." Her eyes grew wet. "How could they? No one knows what it's like to give birth to a stillborn child. Not unless they've gone through it."

"Especially when it could have been prevented," Liam growled.

Kendra reached for his hand. "Honey, we don't know that."

He crossed his arms and walked to the window. "I do."

Kendra stared at his back for a moment, then spoke to me. "The man who was killed—Dr. Jones—was our first fertility doctor."

Dr. Dick was a fertility specialist? That surprised me. I'd assumed he was an OB/GYN. I remained quiet and let her continue.

"Liam never trusted Dr. Jones," Kendra said, "but his clinic came highly recommended, and for good reason. We got pregnant on our first IVF cycle. Everything went like clockwork until the delivery."

Kendra glanced toward her husband, as if waiting for his permission to go on. Liam stared out the window, body as rigid as Mount Rainier.

After several long, uncomfortable moments, I gently prodded them. "You don't have to tell me, but..." My voice trailed off.

Kendra finished my question. "What happened? That's just it. Nobody knows. My labor was slow, but everything seemed to go fine." Her face became blank, as if she was purposefully numbing herself for the end of the story. "When the baby came out, he wouldn't breathe. Dr. Jones tried CPR, but..." She closed her eyes for a breath, then slowly opened them. "We had an autopsy done, but it didn't find anything. The coroner's best theory is that the baby's cord got constricted somehow during the delivery."

The baby's death saddened but didn't shock me. Summer had mentioned a similar case in doula training. Although it was extremely rare, sometimes things went horribly wrong, even in the lowest-risk births. I was, however, surprised that Dr. Jones was present. Since when did reproductive endocrinologists deliver babies?

"The hardest thing for me is that we never got any answers," Kendra continued. "That's why I keep panicking. If they don't know what caused my first baby to die, how can I prevent it from happening again?"

Liam turned away from the window, kneeled, and took his wife's hand. "We *are* preventing it. We're going with a completely different clinic this time. We may not know specifically who's going deliver our baby until the day it's born, but it won't be some high-profile quack."

"Excuse me," I said to Kendra, "but I'm confused. I thought Dr. Jones was your fertility specialist, not your OB/GYN."

"He was both. That's one of the unique selling points of Reproductive Associates. They stay with their clients from pre-conception to birth."

Liam stood up again. "I had a bad feeling about that clinic all along. Reputable fertility docs don't deliver their own babies. We never should have let them and that stupid birth coach talk us into using that new-age birth center. If we'd been in a hospital, our son would still be alive."

"Honey, we don't know that either," Kendra replied.

"Our lawyer thought so. If we'd been here, you would have been consistently hooked up to a fetal heart monitor. It might have shown heart decelerations. Our doctor certainly wouldn't have been drunk."

"Drunk?" I asked.

Kendra frowned. "Please ignore that, Kate. And Liam, stop saying it. Our lawyer warned you. We could get sued for slander. You have absolutely no proof that Dr. Jones was drinking that night."

"Well, something was off about him. We certainly weren't his highest priority."

"What you mean?" I asked.

"Like I said earlier," Kendra replied, "my labor was long. Dr. Jones wanted to hurry things along."

"It was more than that," Liam said. "He acted irritated by the delay, as if our birth somehow inconvenienced him. Believe me, as much money as we paid that SOB, he could have worked a few hours of overtime."

The petty part of me wondered if Dr. Dick had been anxious to meet Mariella in a hotel room somewhere, but I didn't say that. "You mentioned a lawyer. Was there a lawsuit?"

The two spouses shared a veiled look.

"If you can call it that," Liam said. "We tried to sue both the so-called doctor and that birth coach with the hippie name. Spring, or Sunshine, or whatever it was."

The name popped out before I could stop it. "Summer?"

Liam narrowed his eyes. "You know her?"

I backpedaled as fast as I could, hoping I hadn't blown it. "I took a class with her a while ago. I don't know her personally." I neglected to mention a couple of minor details—like that "a while ago" was six weeks ago, Summer had *taught* the class, and I was meeting with her again in a few hours.

Kendra continued the story. "The case never made it to court. Our lawyer told us that a bad outcome didn't equal malpractice. He said if we didn't settle, our case might get tossed out before it ever went to trial." Her chin trembled. "Liam wanted to keep fighting. For our loss to have meaning. But I needed to move on with my life. I couldn't keep talking about that horrible day over and over. All I wanted was enough money to pay for fertility treatments again."

"So we settled for ... well, for not nearly enough," Liam grumbled. "What's the price of a son you'll never have?"

Kendra gave him a wan smile. "Honey, none of this makes sense to me, either. I mourn Liam Jr. every day. Maybe losing him was the price we had to pay for our daughter. Maybe that's our meaning."

We sat silently for several moments, the only sound the soft tick, tick, ticking of the wall clock across the room. I wanted to ask for more specifics about the lawsuit. I could understand Liam's grudge against Dr. Dick, even though it might be factually unfounded. But Summer? How could Summer have been responsible for the baby's death? There was a story there, and I wanted to hear it.

More than that, I wanted to help. To come up with a magic assurance that would make everything better. Some healing phrase that would melt away Kendra and Liam's pain. Of course, there was none. I settled for words that were at least true. "I can't imagine how hard that day must have been for both of you."

"You have no idea," Liam replied. "That's why I almost lost it when I saw that quack at the open house. It felt like some demented version of *Groundhog Day*. Like we couldn't be safe from him, even here."

That was my cue. "Is that why you didn't stay at the party? I noticed you left about the same time Dr. Jones did."

Small muscles on either side of Liam's jaw twitched. "Wait a minute. How do you know when that quack left the party? You knew *him*, too?" He took several steps toward me. "What's going on here?"

I held up my palms and took the same number of steps back. "Nothing. I swear. The birthing community is a small world. I knew who he was, that's all." I wasn't sure my words appeased Liam, but I pressed on anyway. "I'm super curious about what happened on Saturday, though. Aren't you? Did you see anything suspicious or unusual?"

Liam's eye's hardened. "The police asked me the same question. I didn't see anything. I came right back here to Kendra's room the minute I saw that SOB. I didn't leave again until after the police told me he was dead."

Kendra didn't make eye contact. Her hands trembled in her lap. "Liam was here with me all day Saturday, except for the fifteen minutes he went to the party. And that's exactly what I told the police."

Liam marched to the door and held it open. "I don't mean to be rude, but you're upsetting my wife. She needs to rest, not be reminded of death. Please leave. Now."

It wasn't a request. Either I left the room voluntarily or he'd carry me out.

I chose option one.

I paused at the doorway. "I'm sorry if I upset you."

Liam slammed the door so forcefully that—unlike the saying—it actually *did* hit me on my way out.

I rubbed my bruised elbow all the way to the parking garage, feeling paradoxically saddened and re-energized. I was fond of Kendra. I'd hate for her to raise a child alone while Liam spent twenty-to-life in prison. But it might happen. I could easily envision Liam thrusting a knife into Dr. Dick's sternum. Maybe even twisting it a time or two.

They were *both* hiding something. I didn't know what, and I didn't know why, but I was determined to find out.

First, I was going to have a very interesting conversation with Summer.

THIRTEEN

BELLA AND I ARRIVED at Gasworks Park at five-thirty, which left me thirty short minutes to strategize. I felt uneasy about my upcoming meeting with Summer. When I'd called her yesterday, all I'd wanted was to finagle Nurse Tamara's phone number out of her. But my discussion with Liam and Kendra had unearthed new, potentially significant information. Information Summer could help clarify. Was Dr. Dick's murder related to Liam and Kendra's stillborn baby? If so, was Summer an innocent bystander, a suspect in Dr. Dick's murder, or the next victim? And how could I find out without admitting that I was investigating Dr. Dick's death?

Dad's voice echoed inside my head. *Good luck with all that.*

"Come on, Bella. I can think while you walk."

I clipped a leash on Bella's collar and meandered behind her as she followed an invisible scent trail across the parking lot, through the trees, and onto the large grassy field. As I took in the green space around me, I was awed—as always—by the park's junkyard-meets-playground vibe. A short walking distance from the University of

Washington's main campus, Gasworks Park had been dubbed "one of the strangest parks in the world."

I could understand why. The nineteen-acre, waterfront recreational area was built on the grounds of an abandoned coal gasification plant. Rusted distillation columns towered over a backdrop of emerald green grass, Lake Union's sparkling blue water, and the distant gray skyscrapers of downtown Seattle. Dark relics of Seattle's industrial past shadowing its metropolitan future.

The boiler house to my left had been converted into a children's play barn filled with a maze of brightly painted machinery. To my right stood a steep, man-made grassy hill that was bisected by a zigzag white path and dotted with evening sun worshippers. At least fifty Canada geese waddled around the hill, herding their teenage goslings toward its top. I said a quick prayer to the universe that the Seattle City Council wouldn't gas them this year. Unattractive—and supposedly unhygienic—droppings or not, I loved the majestic creatures.

"Come on Bella, let's hike up to the top."

I followed the uphill pathway, enjoying the sun on my shoulders and the cool evening breeze on my cheeks. Bella tugged at the end of her leash, playfully teasing the geese into flight.

A large, surprisingly grumpy-looking goose stood in our path, away from his gaggle. Bella glared at him, giving a clear, silent message:

Move.

The goose ignored her.

Bella added a single, loud bark and a halfhearted lunge.

I said, move.

The goose lifted his wings and replied with a fierce-sounding hiss.

I wrapped Bella's leash tightly around my wrist. "Bella, leave it." I punctuated the command by stepping off the path. Bella planted her paws, assumed the stance of a hundred-pound statue, and growled.

The feathered menace—who apparently had a death wish—glared at Bella, flapped his wings, and marched toward her, hissing. Bella erupted.

She lunged, she jumped, she snarled, she growled. Cujo on meth would have been friendlier. I dug my heels into the earth and held on, mentally translating her vocalizations into English:

I said move! And I mean now! Or I'll crush your hollow-boned body between my jaws and shake until every one of those ugly black feathers falls out. I'll—

The goose took the hint. Sort of. He slooooowly waddled away, down the hill, one grumpy step at a time. Bella followed, barking and lunging at his tail feathers.

I desperately waved my free arm, trying to prevent the impending nosedive, but it was no use. Bella and I each weighed a little over a hundred pounds. Since dogs can pull two-and-a-half times their weight, Bella could easily drag two-point-five yoga teachers. The best I could do was hang on for the ride.

Five steps later, I fell. Bella charged after the feathered creature, pulling me down the hill like a kite behind her. The goose finally took flight. He soared overhead, dropping a parting gift on my forehead.

Gross!

Bella stopped pulling, happier than I'd seen her in days. She pranced. She play-bowed. She nibbled my chin. She jumped up and down at the end of her leash, tongue lolling out in a clear doggy grin: *Did you see? Did you see? I chased him away!* She stopped, suddenly transfixed, and took three quick sniffs. *What is that delicious-smelling morsel dripping down your nose?*

I muttered words likely banned in most Bible Belt states and pulled myself up to standing. No injuries, at least not that I felt so far. But I was seriously reconsidering my pro-waterfowl position. I wiped my forehead with one of Bella's dog-waste bags and cleaned my fingers on the grass.

"Come on, Bella. We're going to the beach."

Bella reversed course and pulled me toward the water.

I stopped her at the edge of the embankment. "Not so fast, sweetie. The sign says no swimming."

Dogs weren't allowed on Seattle beaches, a ridiculous law that most dog owners—myself included—ignored with impunity. In this case, however, the warning was important. In spite of multiple cleanups, the sludge along the shore was still polluted with toxic chemicals. Much too toxic for Bella's paws.

I kneeled at the edge of the cement embankment, reached my hand into the water, and rinsed my forehead with the hopefully-not-too-health-threatening water. A voice came from behind me.

"That water's toxic, you know."

Bella whipped toward Summer, gave a single, loud warning bark, and stepped between us, blocking her. I knew Summer, of course, but to Bella, she was a stranger. Any stranger who approached me, especially from behind, was automatically suspect. Bella's actions put Summer on notice: if she planned to harm me, she'd have to go through a hundred-pound German shepherd first.

I placed my hand between Bella's shoulder blades and gave her the canine version of a "stand down" order. "Bella, this is Summer. Summer is our friend. Say hello."

Exactly the words Bella had been hoping to hear. Her ears relaxed. Her tail lowered and slowly swished back and forth. She eased up to Summer, sat, and lifted her paw. Summer cringed but gave it a cautious shake.

"Oh my goodness! Look at the size of that paw!" Summer backed away. "Are you sure it won't eat me?"

I understood her reaction, but it still caught me by surprise. After living with Bella for almost a year and a half, I sometimes forgot how truly imposing she appeared, especially to strangers.

"You'll be fine," I assured her. "Bella's friendly to women and kids, especially if they give her a treat."

At the sound of the T-word, Bella's ears pricked forward with interest. I pulled a dog cookie out of my pocket and handed it to Summer, who awkwardly held the treat at the end of her fingertips, as far from her body as possible. A position I secretly called the please-amputate-my-fingers mudra. Bella gingerly grasped the treat between her teeth without touching skin.

Good girl.

Summer snatched her hand back and buried her fists underneath crossed arms. "That animal's huge. How much does it weigh?"

I smiled. "Almost as much as a five-foot-three-inch yoga teacher. Don't worry, though. She's truly a big teddy bear." I thought back to her most recent adventure. "Unless you're a goose."

Summer stepped out of striking range, still clearly skeptical. I wanted to assure her that Bella would never bite, but the truth was, I couldn't. Bella hadn't used her teeth on a human so far, but any dog would bite given sufficient provocation. Especially if people acted afraid of them.

Time for a little distraction. "Mind if we walk?"

I followed the winding trail back up the hill, Summer and Bella both panting heavily behind me. We sat on a relatively goose-dung-free spot and I stalled for time by digging through my handbag, pretending to search for a chew toy for Bella. I still hadn't come up with a good strategy for questioning Summer, so I decided to stick with the truth. Sort of.

I flipped my hands back and forth to show Bella they were empty. "Sorry, girl. No treats." Bella sneezed in frustration, then lay down and rested her head between her paws. Dreaming of goose poop pâté, no doubt.

I massaged her neck and spoke to Summer. "I'm still exhausted from Miracle's birth. How do you do it?"

She shrugged. "Believe me, it's not easy. The hardest part is the unpredictability. Babies come when they want to come. They don't care if their mom's doula hasn't slept in twenty-six hours, if she has concert tickets, or if she's come down with food poisoning. Sometimes I think the little buggers mess with my life on purpose. Their first practical joke." She grinned. "Still, I wouldn't give it up for anything. Nothing's better than helping bring babies into this world. Nothing."

"I'm a little nervous about attending a birth by myself, and I'll have to do it soon. Rene's at thirty-four weeks. We're meeting to discuss her birth plan on Saturday."

"That late?" Summer chided. "I thought your friend was having twins."

"She is."

"Then you should've met weeks ago. Twins are usually early."

"I know, but Rene's superstitious. First she refused to talk about the birth until she was far enough along to deliver safely, then she insisted on waiting until Lake Washington Medical Center's new birthing center opened. She won't even pack a suitcase. She claims the girls will crawl out of her va—" I stopped, reconsidering my words. Summer might not appreciate Rene's warped sense of humor.

"She thinks she'll go into labor as soon as the twins hear us planning their birth."

Summer scowled. "That's ridiculous."

"I agree, but there's no convincing her. Believe me, I tried. She said she'd only talk to me before this weekend if I sewed her lady parts shut. Anyway, she's ready now, and I want to seem professional. I have that list of questions you handed out in class, but I'm not sure what to do with them. How much do I guide her in the answers?"

"You don't guide her at all. Once we've accepted a client, our role is to help them figure out what *they* want, not tell them what we think is best."

"Even if we think they're making bad choices?"

"Yes, even then." Summer picked a dandelion from the grass and idly twirled it between her fingers. "Which can be tough if you have strong opinions, like I do. That's why I only take clients who want a natural childbirth. There's no way I could keep my trap shut if a woman planned on having an epidural or, God forbid, an elective C-section. I prefer assisting with home births, though I work at ABBA when necessary. But I draw the line at hospital births. It's a woman's choice to have her baby wherever she wants to. It's my choice whether or not to be part of it."

I knew my next comment might torque Summer off, but she had provided the inroad I'd been hoping for.

"Aren't hospital births safer?"

Summer flicked the dandelion to the ground. "For who? The doctor's insurance company? Birthing babies is natural." She pointed at Bella. "If that dog of yours were having puppies, would she want to be trapped in bed with a gazillion tubes poked into her? No way."

"Maybe not, but if something goes wrong, a hospital is better equipped to deal with it. In fact, I had that very conversation with two of your prior clients today."

Summer frowned. "Who would that be?"

"Kendra and Liam Delaney."

Summer's entire body tensed for a moment, then her shoulders sagged. "They still think that baby would have lived if they hadn't been at ABBA?" She slowly shook her head. "I suppose they have to blame someone. It's a coping mechanism."

Bella groaned and flopped onto her side, closer to Summer. Summer scooted several inches away. "That baby's death wasn't anyone's fault. It was an anomaly. A horrible, tragic anomaly. Being at a hospital wouldn't have changed anything. Even the coroner said that."

"The baby's father thinks that the doctor was compromised."

"Compromised? How?"

"Liam says he was drunk."

Summer stared off to the side for a moment. "I only worked with Dr. Jones that one time, but he wasn't drunk, just impatient. The labor was slow, and he was in an awful big hurry to get it going. Like the baby was holding him up from his golf game or something. Practically bullied Kendra into having Pitocin."

"What was his rush?"

"Who knows? Using Pitocin's not all that uncommon, actually. He was simply more vocal about it than most doctors. Slow or fast, it wouldn't have made a difference. Which is exactly what I told the parents. Weird thing is, he got them to blame me."

"You?"

"Crazy, isn't it? He wanted me to strong-arm Kendra into going to a hospital for a C-section." She scowled. "I wouldn't do it. Kendra didn't want a C-section, and he couldn't give me a reason why it was medically necessary."

"What did you do?"

"I told Kendra the truth: that it was her decision, but it wasn't part of her birth plan. I also told her to make sure that she understood the risks of a surgical birth before agreeing to one. Dr. Jones clearly didn't make his case. Still, our disagreement gave him a reason to throw me under the bus when the parents started talking lawsuit. He claimed Kendra would have gone to the hospital but I talked her out of it. Ridiculous."

I thought back to Miracle's birth and how Summer had chastised Nurse Tamara for offering Rhonda an epidural. I had a feeling she was underestimating her influence on Kendra—and the heat of her confrontation with Dr. Dick. Biases were tricky that way. In a sense, Summer was color blind. She could only see what her mind allowed her to see.

"Could they really have sued you? You were the doula, not the nurse or doctor."

"Honey, we live in the USA. You can sue anyone. It would've been hard to make it stick, since I don't make any medical decisions. I think Dr. Jones was hoping that if the parents got mad enough at me, they'd forget about him."

"What happened? With the lawsuit, I mean." I knew, of course, but I wanted to hear Summer's version of the story.

"It ended in a settlement, thank goodness. The doctor's malpractice insurance covered most of it. Mine paid the rest. Then we all moved on with our lives. Some better than others, I guess."

I listened for bitterness in Summer's tone, but I couldn't find any. She was clearly over any anger she once felt.

Or very good at hiding it.

"You know Dr. Jones was killed on Saturday, don't you?" I asked.

"How could I not? It's been all over the news. He was a jerk for trying to set me up, but I still feel bad for him. He didn't deserve to be murdered."

I pretended to think for a minute. "The baby's father was at the hospital on Saturday."

Summer didn't reply.

"He still seems pretty angry," I continued. "And not just at Dr. Jones. At you, too."

Summer gave me a questioning look. "What are you getting at, Kate?"

"Aren't you worried? If Liam killed Dr. Jones, you might be in danger, too."

Summer leaned over, picked another dandelion, and pulled off teeny, tiny petals one by one, as if playing a new childhood game: *He hates me. He hates me not.*

When less than half of the petals remained, she spoke. "I'm not in any danger, Kate. I was named in the lawsuit, but the doctor was Liam's real target. Besides, Liam's not the killer. I heard on the radio that the police arrested Dr. Jones's wife."

I shook my head. "I don't think Rachel killed him."

"What makes you say that?"

"She's a friend of sorts. I can't believe she'd commit murder. You've met her, too. I introduced you to her at the party."

"That nurse from the hospital? Huh. She's a lot more attractive than I'd imagined," Summer said slowly. "Dr. Jones always described her as sort of mousey."

Nerve endings tingled up and down my spine. "I thought you only worked with him once."

"That's true, but the birthing industry is like a small town. People gossip. Especially about cheaters."

I pretended to be surprised. "Dr. Jones cheated on his wife?"

"Yes, at least twice that I know of. Remember Tamara, the first nurse at Miracle's birth?"

I nodded, trying not to seem excited. The conversation, for once, was going exactly as I'd hoped.

"She and Dr. Jones were an item when she was an IVF nurse at Reproductive Associates."

Tamara had worked with Dr. Dick? And they'd had an affair? No wonder she got upset when she saw him making out with Mariella. I didn't share my new insight with Summer, though. Instead, I asked, "If Tamara's an IVF nurse, what's she doing delivering babies at ABBA?"

Summer shrugged. "It's not unusual. Lots of nurses change specialties. Anyway, Dr. Jones convinced Tamara that the baby's death was my fault. That's why she was so testy with me the other night. You'd think she'd be less cranky about it now that Dr. Jones dumped her for that tech at his clinic. Turns out she likes to hold a grudge."

"Was he still having an affair with the tech when he died?" I asked. If the answer was yes, the tech Summer was talking about was probably Mariella. And I now knew where to find her: Reproductive Associates.

"Yes, and that little dalliance caused him some trouble. Tamara got so mad that she quit Reproductive Associates and filed a sexual harassment lawsuit."

"Another lawsuit for him? That couldn't have been pretty."

Summer shrugged. "Like I said. USA. You can sue anyone."

"Is that why Tamara started working for ABBA?"

"She's doesn't. Work for ABBA, that is. At least not technically. She's employed by Sound Nursing, one of those contract nursing agencies. She temps at ABBA when they need extra help."

I gave myself a mental high five. I now knew how to find Tamara, too. Through Sound Nursing.

A buzzing sound came from Summer's pocket. She glanced at her cell phone. "Sorry, Kate. That was a text from one of my moms. She thinks she's in early labor. We're doing a home water birth, so I should stop by and make sure everything's ready to go. You'll do fine with your friend this weekend. If you have more questions, shoot me an email. For now, duty calls."

She slowly pushed herself to her feet and lumbered down the hill.

I led Bella back to my car and drove home, feeling both victorious and frustrated. On the plus side, I'd gotten everything I'd wanted from my meeting, and for once without blowing my cover. I now knew how to find both Mariella and Tamara, provided neither of them had changed employers. I'd also heard Summer's side of the stillbirth story. On the minus side, only two days into my sleuthing and I already had three new suspects to eliminate: Liam, Mariella, and now Nurse Tamara.

Make that four. As much as I wanted to, I couldn't eliminate Summer.

Summer didn't strike me as a killer, but she might be good at hiding resentment. She had motive. Dr. Dick had tried to make her the scapegoat in a potentially career-ending lawsuit. The knife was in plain sight, so like everyone else at the hospital that day, she had means. And although I hadn't tracked her movements at the party, I suspected she had opportunity, too.

Summer made her living helping bring life into the world.

Was she also capable of ending it?

FOURTEEN

I ARRIVED HOME TO a surprisingly clean kitchen and a take-out order of vegetarian Pad Thai from Fit to be Thai'd, my favorite Ballard restaurant. Michael had been too busy catching up on paperwork and spying on puppies to cook. In spite of his video-capturing protocol—or perhaps because of it—the little monsters hadn't escaped from their crate once.

He kept me company in the kitchen while I slurped noodles covered in spicy peanut sauce. "Whatever the issue with the crate was, we must have fixed it," he said. "Maybe I was more careless with the latches than I thought."

"Maybe … " I didn't want to jinx today's good luck, but Michael's assumption seemed an awful lot like wishful thinking.

"Either way, I'm going back to work at the store tomorrow."

"I have to work a full day tomorrow, too." I glanced at the gold and black fur balls, who were curled up with Bella, twitching and snoring. Dreaming about their next adventure, no doubt. "Leaving them at home alone for a full day seems pretty risky."

"I know, but we don't have a choice. Tiffany's been a champ this past week, but I can't expect her to work without breaks forever. I'll come home to check on them at lunch. Can you stop by in the afternoon?"

I mentally thought through my next day's calendar. "I can take a break around three, but if we're leaving them unattended, we need to lock Bella's dog door, just in case."

Michael stubbornly shook his head. "No. If we start locking it, Bella will never learn how to use it."

I was feeling pretty stubborn myself. "We can't risk it. If the puppies *do* manage to get out of their crate, they'll hightail it straight for the yard and dig a hole under the fence again. They could run out into the street and get hit."

Michael opened a drawer and pulled out a collar that was at least three sizes too big—for both puppies, combined. "That's what this is for."

"You're going to make a noose and strangle them?"

He grinned. "No—this is the ultrasonic collar that came with Bella's dog door. We'll put it on her and activate it. Bella will be able to go in and out, but Mutt and Jeff won't. That way, if they get out of their crate again, they'll only destroy all of our earthly possessions."

I wasn't fond of the idea, but I didn't have a better one, either. I agreed.

We cleaned up the dinner and relaxed in the living room. Michael opened a Guinness while I sipped on a home-brewed soy latte. I would have preferred a glass of Merlot, but I needed to be mentally astute for our upcoming conversation. I'd formulated a plan to "accidentally" run into Mariella, but it required Michael's help. I had a feeling he wasn't going to like it.

I cuddled against Michael's chest and started with what I thought was a safe topic.

"Any news on the pups' origins yet?"

Michael grumpily set his beer on the end table. "No, and I'm beginning to think that we'll never know who dumped them. I've talked to all of the business owners on the block. The residents of the apartments, too. Tiffany grilled every customer. No one saw anything."

"Did you ever talk to Momma Bird?"

"Nobody's seen her lately. Have you?"

I shook my head no.

"Momma Bird must have dumped them," Michael said. "Why else would she have disappeared?"

"She doesn't work in Greenwood every day. Maybe she's at another location."

"Maybe. Then again, maybe she left town. I called *Dollars for Change* today to see if they knew how to contact her."

"You did?" Michael was taking this whole dog situation much more seriously than I'd thought.

"Yeah, for what good it did me. The woman who answered the phone wouldn't tell me a thing. She said it was against company policy to share information about their vendors."

I'd gotten the same answer when I was investigating George's murder. Momma Bird had been my one willing source.

"So what now?" I asked.

Michael shrugged. "I don't know. I'm still trying to figure that out. Maybe I should go to the *Dollars for Change* office in person."

"You can try, but it won't do any good. You'd be better off giving up and looking for a new owner."

Michael took a deep swig of his beer, but he didn't reply. I decided to let the subject of rehoming the puppies go for the time being. I leaned away from his embrace, set my espresso cup on the end table, and turned to face him.

"Speaking of workplace visits, I have one you can help me with."

I filled him in on my afternoon's activities, starting with my conversation with Liam and ending with my meeting with Summer.

"That's all interesting information, Kate, but what do you plan to do with it? The police know about Dr. Jones's affair. From what you just told me, they already questioned the baby's parents, so I assume they know about their lawsuit, too." He shrugged. "I guess you could call Detective Martinez and make sure she has all of the relevant details…"

"Not yet. She and Henderson are convinced that they have the right killer. I haven't learned anything so far that will change their minds."

"What else can you do?" Michael asked.

"Go back to my original plan."

"Which was?"

"To question Mariella. Now that I know she works at Reproductive Associates, I can go there, look around, and ask her some questions."

Michael drained the last of his beer. "What do you think she'll tell you? If Mariella isn't the killer, she probably thinks Rachel is. Why would she help you prove otherwise?"

I kept my voice carefully neutral. "I'm not going to tell her that I'm investigating the murder."

"What other excuse will you have for visiting her at a fertility center?"

I made my eyes wide and smiled at him alluringly. "Want to make a baby?"

Michael leaped to his feet and held up his hands. The beer bottle dropped to the floor with a loud thump. "Uh uh, Kate. No way."

"I thought you wanted kids?"

"Don't try to play me. That's not what this is about, and you know it. If we wanted to, we could get pregnant tonight. You're talking about setting up a medical appointment under false pretenses. Count me out. I'm not about to help you commit insurance fraud. That's a federal offense."

He had a point.

"You're right. No insurance claims." I mentally balanced my checkbook. "I wonder how much a consultation costs? Maybe I can pay out of pocket."

Michael shook his head adamantly. "I know you want to help your friend, Kate, and I promise not to stand in your way. But I am *not* going to a medical clinic under false pretenses, and you shouldn't, either. Please promise me you won't make an appointment and go there alone." He stared at me, refusing to break eye contact.

I didn't want to lie to him, but I wasn't sure I could be completely truthful, either. I hedged my bets by surreptitiously crossing my fingers.

"I won't." *Unless it's absolutely necessary.*

Time to come up with a plan B.

FIFTEEN

WHEN I LEFT HOME at eight the next morning, Michael was living up to the Boy Scouts motto: *Be Prepared.* He obsessively tinkered with the dog door, fitted Bella's new collar, and tested the nanny cam setup. If the pups successfully performed their Houdini act again, he'd be ready.

I arrived at the studio at eight-fifteen. Enough time to say a quick hello to Mister Feathers and a quicker goodbye to the Morning Yoga Immersion teacher, who'd finished up late and had to run straight to her full-time job. That left me with a full hour to work before the students of my nine-thirty All Levels class started arriving.

I'd barely started typing Serenity Yoga's monthly newsletter when the chime clanged against the front door. Tiffany backed through it, carrying two white cardboard cups printed with Mocha Mia's logo.

The smell of caffeine was so overpoweringly tantalizing that I almost didn't notice her skintight hot pink yoga pants and her *I'm just here for the Savasana* tank top. Almost.

"You brought coffee." I hungrily reached for the cup labeled *Kate.*

"I asked the barista if you had a favorite drink, and she made this. A triple soy macchiato." Tiffany emphasized the word "triple." "I thought yoga teachers were supposed to be Zen. Shouldn't at least one of those shots be decaf?"

Every cell in my body hungered for stimulants, so I didn't reply. I drowned my snarky thoughts in hot, bitter deliciousness and reached into the desk for my billfold.

Tiffany held up her hand. "Don't worry about it. It's on me."

I set the cup on the desk and eyed her suspiciously. "You brought me a present?"

"It's not a gift; it's a bribe. I brought you coffee. Now tell me everything you learned from that Summer person yesterday, and hurry. I have to be at work in thirty minutes. Michael has a hissy fit when I'm late."

I gave her an abbreviated version of yesterday's events, focusing mainly on Mariella, Tamara's sexual harassment lawsuit, and my dilemma about snooping around at Reproductive Associates.

"I thought I had the perfect cover story, but Michael won't go for it."

"Maybe you could pretend that you want to offer a fertility yoga class. You know, one of those Tantric Yoga things."

"Tantric Yoga isn't ... oh, never mind." I thought for a moment. "Telling them I want to offer a class isn't a bad idea, though. Yoga can help improve reproductive health." I walked to the bookshelf, pulled out a yoga therapy text, and thumbed through it. "I haven't been trained in those techniques, though. I'll have to do some research." I thumped into the chair behind the desk and started reading.

Tiffany wrinkled her brow. "Oh for goodness sake. You're making it too complicated. I have a better idea." She pointed to the computer. "Scoot over and let me look something up on that thing." She sat at the keyboard and started typing. "Reproductive Associates, you said?"

"Yes."

She leaned forward and stared at the screen. "Good lord, look at this cheesy tagline. *Let our family help create yours.* Gag me." Three mouse clicks later, she pumped her fist through the air. "Ha! I'm so good. It says here that the first consultation is free. You won't have any insurance problems at all."

"Free?" I moved behind her and glanced over her shoulder. She was right. "Why didn't I think to check that last night?" Hope ballooned in my chest. Then I flashed on Michael's obstinate face and it quickly deflated. "Michael still won't go for it. He vetoed the idea last night, even after I said that I would pay for the appointment myself."

"So, go without him."

"I can't. I promised him that I wouldn't go there alone. I can't even drag Rene along this time."

A Cheshire Cat grin spread across Tiffany's face. Her eyes sparkled. I would have sworn that her pupils dilated.

"I can do it!"

"Do what?" I asked.

"I can go with you to the clinic." Her grin turned into a smirk. "We'll tell them you're my mother."

I ignored the intentional jab at my age. Thirty-three wasn't exactly grandmother material. I gave her a not-quite-fake scowl. "No way."

"Fine. My life partner then. We'll say we want to select a sperm donor." She picked up the phone and started dialing.

"What are you doing?" I asked.

She held her index finger against her lips, shushing me.

"Hi. My name's Kate Davidson. I've been looking at your website and I'd like to schedule an appointment for a free consultation." She reached across the table and grabbed a pen and a notepad. "My fabulous life partner, Tiffany, will be coming with me. We'd like to get pregnant. I want to carry the baby, but we're afraid I might have trouble conceiving." She listened for a moment. "No, I haven't seen any other fertility doctors, but I'm quite a bit older than she is. My ovaries have probably shriveled up."

I leaned across the table and slugged her.

She winked. "I see." She jotted a line of dollar signs across the middle of the page. "I'd heard your clinic was more expensive than some, but money's no object." I opened my mouth to argue, but she shoved her palm in my face. "All that matters is that we end up with a healthy baby." I waited through what seemed like a century before Tiffany spoke again. When she did, her voice sounded depressed.

"Next Wednesday? Seriously? That's the soonest?" She drew a frowny face next to the dollar signs. "Gosh, we both have tomorrow and the next day off. We don't want to wait that long." She frowned and made several mouse clicks. "I understand. I guess we'll have to go with Bellevue Fertility then. You were our first choice, but…" She smiled and gave me the thumbs-up sign. "Tomorrow? At eleven? That would be fabulous. Thanks so much for squeezing us in." She wrote down a name and an address. "We look forward to meeting you, too."

Tiffany hung up the phone. Her smile showed more teeth than a crocodile readying to chomp on a muskrat. "We have an appointment with a Dr. Steinman tomorrow at eleven. Evidently they're squeezing us in during his research time. I really *do* have the next two days off. Can you make it?"

Unfortunately, I could.

"Why didn't you at least call under your own name?" I asked. "Now they think I'm some crazy loon with shriveled ovaries."

"It's supposed to just be a consultation, but I couldn't be sure." She pointed below her navel. "Murder or not, no doctor is getting anywhere near *my* Reproductive Associates. You're going to be the patient." She glanced at her watch. "I have to go. It's time for my shift at Pete's Pets. I'll meet you here at ten-fifteen tomorrow. Don't forget to wear clean underwear." She stopped at the door. "Kate, what should we tell Michael about this?"

"Absolutely nothing. He'll try to talk us out of it."

Tiffany winked. "I was hoping you'd say that. But remember, if he finds out, this was all your idea." She did a happy skip and bounced out the door.

I shook my head in amazement. Who would have guessed? Tiffany. The new Thelma to my Louise. I could only hope our adventure had a happier ending.

————

The rest of the day was blissfully uneventful, filled with prenatal classes, private sessions, and studio paperwork. The weirdest part of my afternoon was the hour-long break I took to check on the puppies. As Michael had predicted, they were firmly imprisoned in their crate. That was unusual all by itself. More surprising still was the almost-impossible-to-unknot necktie Michael had used to tie the crate door shut. Who knew Michael owned a tie?

He'd left me a note taped to the kitchen door: *I couldn't find a padlock, but if you have one somewhere, use it. Until then, the tie will have to do. Wait until you see what I caught on the video.*

I let the pups out for a few minutes of playtime, took Bella for a fifteen-minute walk, then headed back to the studio. I would have stopped by the pet store to ask Michael about his cryptic note, but I had back-to-back private clients scheduled all afternoon. Before I knew it, it was six p.m. The Yoga for Men teacher had arrived and it was time to go home. I tossed more birdseed to Mister Feathers and headed to my car. I hadn't heard any complaints from Michael, so I assumed his day had been as uneventful as mine.

I assumed wrong.

The back yard was littered with the severed branches of Michael's prized blueberry bushes. The casualties, I assumed, of an afternoon's worth of puppy teething. Bella greeted me in the kitchen with her tail tucked between her legs and her ears flattened against her skull. A deep rumble emanated from her belly.

"You feeling all right, sweetie?"

Hopefully Bella wasn't about to suffer an EPI setback. Setbacks with EPI were common, but thus far the only one Bella had endured had been caused by human error. Specifically, mine, during a two-day stretch of vacation when I'd forgotten to add enzymes to her food. But I'd been out of my element then. We were home now, and my food-making routines were intact. If Bella had a setback today, it might prove to be more complicated.

I reached down and rubbed her ears. "What's the matter, girl?"

Michael's grumpy voice came from the office. "Kate, is that you? Come in here."

I hesitantly tiptoed into the office. Bella slinked in behind me. The puppies snoozed in an ex-pen next to Michael's desk. Michael stopped typing and faced me. He didn't look happy.

"I see the puppies escaped again," I said. "I'm sorry. I don't know how that keeps happening. I tied the door shut after their playtime, exactly like you asked me to."

"You used a slip knot." Michael reached into the garbage can next to his desk and held up the shredded remains of his necktie.

Oops.

"Sorry, hon. The knot you used earlier was impossible to get undone."

Michael dropped the tie back into the trash can. "That was the point, Kate. To make it hard to untie. Besides, the puppies aren't the problem." He frowned sternly at Bella. "She is."

Irritable defensiveness prickled the back of my neck. Michael loved Bella as much as I did, but that didn't give him the right to criticize her. "What exactly do you mean?"

He winced at my clipped tone. "Sorry, Kate. I'm a little cranky, but you'll see why in a minute." He gestured to my desk chair. "Bring that over here and have a seat. You need to see this." A couple of mouse clicks later, he pointed at the screen. "This recorded this morning."

As I watched the screen, a video-recorded Michael placed each wiggling puppy inside the crate, carefully closed the top and bottom lock bars, and walked out of the camera's view. Four unbearably sad puppy eyes followed him out of camera range. About a minute later, I heard a door close.

"That was me leaving for work," Michael explained.

Video Mutt went into a sloppy sit and stared mournfully through the crate's wire bars. Video Jeff nudged the door with his nose. Michael fast forwarded.

"This is about five minutes later," he said.

Five minutes was evidently five centuries in puppy time. The two now-desolate, obviously-abandoned-forever puppies started their prison break. Jeff tried to dig a tunnel through the crate's bottom while Mutt cried for help, in the highest-pitched, most annoying series of yelps I'd ever heard.

"Good Lord, that's irritating," I said. "It's a wonder the neighbors haven't complained."

"I'm sure they would, but it doesn't last long."

By the end of his sentence, Video Bella had slinked into the camera's view, ears flattened against her head, tail tucked between her legs. I reached down and scratched her neck.

"Poor baby," I said. "Does the crying hurt your ears?"

Meanwhile, back on the video, Jeff spied Bella and joined in the chorus. The yipping grew louder. Real Bella jumped up from her spot next to me and scurried out of the office. I covered my ears with my palms.

"They're louder than the fire alarm." I continued to watch, half convinced that I was about to watch one of my neighbors break into the house to strangle the dogs. Video Bella slinked to the front of the crate. She nudged the top metal rod with her nose until it flipped to the open position. Then she pawed it to the side, disengaging the lock. She repeated the process, albeit with much greater difficulty, on the bottom. The second lock unfastened; the crate door swung open.

The puppies finally stopped screaming. They scrambled outside the crate and attacked their rescuer, biting at her ears, her feet, her belly, and her tail. Bella drag-walked both pups out of camera range.

"So that's how they got out. Unbeliev—"

Michael held up his finger "Shhh. You have to listen."

Nothing came into the camera's view, but I heard a distinct flop.

"What was that?"

"The dog door."

Less than thirty seconds later I heard a second flop, which indicated that at least one of the creatures had come back inside. I had a feeling I knew which one. Video Bella trotted back into camera range, ears relaxed, tail swishing back and forth. She entered the crate, turned a quick circle, and lay down. The lone sound was her contented sigh.

I bit my bottom lip to keep from laughing. "She trapped them outside, didn't she?"

"Yes. I put them back when I came home at noon, but then she did the same thing after you locked them in the crate. She figured out how to untie your slipknot in less than a minute."

I affected chagrin, but inside I felt an odd mixture of frustration (at the situation) and pride (in my dog). One more example of the obvious: Bella was smarter than Michael and me—combined.

"Well, at least we know what's happening now," I said.

Michael frowned. "I hate to do it, but we're going to have to padlock the crate shut."

"We can't do that. The neighbors will have a fit if the puppies scream all day. Old Lady Schuman across the street almost had a stroke when Bella used to howl, and that was a lot less annoying. Besides, it's not fair to Bella. The puppies obviously drive her batty when we're not at home."

"It's not their fault. They're just babies!"

Arguing about which animal to blame was useless. Michael was right, anyway. Mutt and Jeff *were* babies. They'd been separated from their mother much too early, and lord knew what their lives had been like before that. They could be forgiven a little neurosis. We humans—who supposedly had the bigger brains—would have to come up with the solution.

"Maybe this is a good thing," I said.

Michael frowned. "How's that?"

"It's forcing us to face the truth. We have to come up with a better arrangement for the puppies."

Michael's jaw hardened.

"Hear me out," I said. "You need to start working regularly at the store again, and neither of us can afford to come home every two hours to take care of Mutt and Jeff. It's pretty obvious that leaving the puppies home all day in the crate isn't going to work."

Michael threw up his hands. "Exactly what do you expect me to do? You know they can't be exposed to other dogs yet, and I'm not going to send them to a rescue. Not this young."

I had a feeling he actually meant "not ever," but that was a battle best fought later, over a fifth of tequila.

"I know, Michael, you've already told me. They aren't vaccinated."

"Well then, what's your bright idea?"

"Calm down, Mr. Cranky Pants. I know someone who'll help, at least for a few days. She owes me."

"Tiffany's already paying off her debt to you, Kate. It wouldn't be fair to ask her to watch the pups on her two days off."

"Not Tiffany. Someone else. Someone who could use a little practice taking care of twins."

Michael's face lost its scowl. "You wouldn't…"

"I most certainly would. The puppies are going to daycare at Aunt Rene's."

SIXTEEN

After Michael left for Pete's Pets the next morning, I filled my car with an assortment of dog toys, blankets, crates, and treats and drove Bella and the pups over to Rene's. Sam quickly made friends with the two six-pound fur balls and submitted himself to Bella's cool, not-quite-friendly greeting. Bella had never warmed up to Sam, likely due to his caterpillar-like mustache. On the plus side, at least she didn't snarl at him anymore.

Sam was skeptical about babysitting all three dogs at once, but Rene, as always, was confident. She was already Bella's designated dog-sitter, so how much trouble could two tiny puppies be? A true friend would have warned her, but these were extenuating circumstances. I vowed I'd make it up to her. Someday.

With a hundred and twelve pounds of canine chaos unloaded on my best friend, I headed to the studio to pick up Tiffany for our eleven o'clock appointment at Reproductive Associates.

She stood outside Serenity Yoga's front entrance wearing an impatient scowl—and not nearly enough else.

"At least she's not dressed in yoga clothes this time," I muttered to no one in particular.

Tiffany wore a deep burgundy miniskirt that ended a mere four inches below her lady parts—about the same measurement her black platform shoes added to her 5'4" frame. The matching, midriff-bearing bra-top exposed more skin than it covered, and its open back hinted that she wore no undergarment beneath it. She carried a black jacket draped over her left forearm, though why she chose to cover that part of her anatomy was beyond me.

She opened the door and hopped into the passenger seat. "No Bella?"

"It's too hot to leave her in the car today. She's at Rene's."

Tiffany stared from my shirt to my shoes and back again, frowning at my loose cotton slacks and conservative white blouse. "I thought you'd dress up a little. You practically look like a nun. They'll never believe we're a couple."

"You're the one who doesn't know how to dress for an appointment. Where do you think we're going? A strip club?"

"It's hot out! Besides, this outfit is a lot dressier when I put on the jacket." She latched her seat belt. "Come on, let's get going. We don't want to be late."

After thirty minutes spent navigating Seattle's famously slow traffic, we arrived at the fertility clinic's main office, which was located in one of downtown Seattle's newer glass skyscrapers. Twenty floors later, I stopped outside the elevator and fastened all three buttons of Tiffany's waist-length, three-quarter-sleeve jacket. She responded by unbuttoning the top two of my blouse.

"I'm clearly the more feminine partner in this relationship," she quipped.

"Fine. Whatever. But remember, I ask the questions. You listen and say nothing. I don't *think* we're breaking any laws with this little deceit, but I'm not positive. The last thing you need is another arrest on your record."

"Stop worrying. I'll be as quiet as a little church mouse." Tiffany grabbed my arm and pulled me down the hall. "Let's go!"

She sauntered through the double-glass doors and whistled. "Oooooh … swanky."

And it was.

A huge saltwater aquarium spanned the reception area's entire back wall. Water cascaded down tall stone fountains, filling the room with nature's most soothing lullaby. The room even smelled tropical, thanks to huge floral bouquets scented with jasmine and tuberose.

But in spite of the soothing, gorgeous atmosphere, a single phrase reverberated through my mind. *Trying too hard.* The room's energy felt conflicted, empty somehow. As if it couldn't decide whether to be relaxing, hopeful, depressing, or tragic. Pamphlets advertising infertility support groups were artfully arranged on one set of tables. Photos of smiling infants decorated another. A tense-looking, middle-aged couple filled out forms while avoiding eye contact with each other. I unconsciously placed my hand on my belly. I'd recently told Michael that we should wait a few years before starting a family. Was that a mistake I'd later regret?

"Can I help you?"

An olive-skinned woman behind a large reception desk motioned me toward her. Her name tag read *Daria Martelli*.

I curled my lips up into a fake smile. "Oh, sorry. I got distracted looking at the space. It's beautiful. I'm Kate Davidson. I'm here for an eleven o'clock appointment."

Tiffany sidled next to me and spoke in a much louder voice than I would have preferred. "I'm here for moral support. I'm her partner, Tiffany."

"It's wonderful to meet you both. I'm Daria. We work with a lot of same-sex couples." She smiled at me. "I'll need your driver's license and insurance card please."

Nervous uncertainty tickled my belly. "Sorry, I left my insurance card at home. I thought the first appointment was free."

"It is, but we like to get everything photocopied for your chart."

Daria shrugged. "No worries. I can make a copy of it the next time you come in. I *will* need your driver's license, though."

I reluctantly handed her my ID. She photocopied it, then returned it along with a multi-page form attached to a clipboard. "Fill this out, both front and back, and be sure to sign at the bottom. The doctor's assistant will call you back shortly."

I slinked across the lobby to the chair farthest from the desk.

Tiffany chastised me every step. "You didn't ask her any questions!"

"She's not the person I want to talk to."

"So? You want to know more about the guy who got killed, right? Who better to ask than the receptionist! Receptionists talk to *everybody*. I'll bet she knows more about that doctor than he knew about himself."

She was right.

"Let me fill out the new patient forms first. Then I'll have an excuse to go back and talk to her."

"Fine," Tiffany grumbled. "But you're a much better patient than you are detective."

She had a point about that, too.

Tiffany curled next to me in a comfy blue loveseat while I answered page after page of embarrassing questions. When I'd had my first period (age twelve), how regular my cycles were (like clockwork), if I'd ever been pregnant before (no, thank goodness), and the number of abortions I'd had (zero).

I flipped over the page and stared at a long list of sexually transmitted diseases. The form asked me to indicate whether or not I'd ever acquired each disease by circling the word *yes* or *no* next to it.

Tiffany peered over my shoulder and pointed to one in the middle. "Pick that one."

I yanked the form out of her reach and hissed, "Are you nuts? I am *not* falsifying my own medical records. How rude are you, anyway? What if the answer really *was* yes."

Tiffany rolled her snooping, prying, beady little eyes. "Puh-lease, Kate. You're much too boring to have contracted a social disease."

I turned my back to her and completed the form in private. Ten minutes later, a middle-aged blonde woman entered the waiting room.

"Kate Davidson? We're ready for you now."

I leaned over and whispered to Tiffany, "Keep your eyes open for a pretty Hispanic woman. It might be Mariella."

The nurse led us down a long hallway while we dawdled and stalled and glanced in every open doorway, hoping to glimpse Mariella. No success. The blonde ushered us into a tastefully decorated office and pointed to two guest chairs.

"Dr. Steinman is finishing up with a guest. He should be with you shortly. Would you like a bottle of water or an espresso?"

"Seriously?" Tiffany replied. "I would kill for a latte."

"I'll have the receptionist bring one in for both of you."

She exited the office and closed the door behind her. Tiffany leaned toward me and whispered, "What kind of ritzy doctor's office is this? When I go to the free women's health clinic, I'm lucky if the water fountain works."

I ignored her question and asked one of my own. "How much time do you think we have? I'd like to snoop around a little."

"Go for it. If anyone comes, I'll tell them you went to the bathroom."

I cracked open the door and peered up and down the empty hallway. I'd already checked out the exam rooms to the right, so I turned left and glanced into the larger room across the hall. It was filled with an assortment of lab equipment, microscopes, and computers. A woman in plum-colored scrubs eyed me curiously.

I smiled, then quickly turned away. "Sorry, wrong room."

Next to the lab, I hit pay dirt: a closed door with Dr. Jones's name on it. His office, I assumed. I tried the handle. Locked.

The receptionist's voice sounded behind me. "Can I help you?"

I pasted on a confused expression. "I'm sorry. I went to the restroom and got turned around. Isn't this the office I was waiting in?"

She smiled. "No. Dr. S's office is two doors down. Come on, I'll show you." She gestured with her chin to the tray of porcelain mugs she was carrying. "These are for you."

When we entered the office, Tiffany stood at the wall, pretending to examine Dr. Steinman's many diplomas. I had a feeling she'd been doing some snooping herself.

Daria set a cup on the desk in front of each guest chair. "I make a fabulous latte, if I do say so myself."

"Thanks," I said. "We're not used to such great service in a medical facility. Do you treat all of your patients this well?"

"You're more than patients to us," Daria replied. "You're part of our professional family." She smiled. "We like to make all of our guests feel welcome." She pointed to a silver container. "We have sugar, honey, brown sugar, and artificial sweeteners if you need them." She tucked the tray under her arm and turned to leave. Tiffany poked me in the ribs and mouthed, *Ask her something.*

I resisted the urge to poke Tiffany back and asked the first question that came to my mind. "Hey, were you the person I spoke with on the phone yesterday?" Tiffany had made the phone call, of course, but hopefully Daria hadn't figured that out.

She stopped at the door. "No, I don't answer the phones. Dr. S wants me free to focus on guest hospitality. You spoke to our scheduling assistant. She makes all of his appointments."

"Well, please tell her how grateful I am that she fit us in so quickly, given the circumstances."

"Circumstances?"

I lowered my voice to a whisper. "The doctor who was killed."

"Dr. Jones." Daria's smile disappeared. "You know about his death? Is that why you were poking around outside his office?"

I pretended to be surprised. "Was that his name on the door in the hallway?" I shuddered. "Creepy." I put my hand on Tiffany's shoulder. "Hon, can you believe that? I almost walked into a dead man's office." I looked back at Daria. "I don't know why I didn't remember his name from the newspaper. I must be more nervous than I thought."

Daria narrowed her eyes suspiciously. I widened mine in pretend innocence.

"Don't worry about it," she said. "This is a big day for you." She turned toward the door again, clearly trying to end the conversation.

Tiffany spoke. "It must suck to have your boss murdered. Unless he was a jerk, that is."

Daria stiffened. "Dr. *Steinman* is my boss. But yes, Dr. Jones's death is a terrible loss to his patients. Now if you'll excuse me—"

Tiffany interrupted. "What will happen with them? His patients, I mean."

Daria frowned but didn't answer.

I reached over and interlaced my fingers with Tiffany's. "I'm sorry. All of these questions must seem terribly rude. Please understand, this baby is important to us. We don't want our case to get lost in the transition."

Daria glanced behind her, then eased back into the room. "You won't have to worry about that. Dr. S held a staff meeting this morning. The clinic's future is secure. He has a long list of fertility specialists vying to get on staff here, and he plans to have two new doctors on board within the next month. He's wanted to bring on additional physicians for some time. Now that he's the sole owner, he can."

"Wow," Tiffany replied. "Sounds like the clinic may be better off without Dr. Jones."

Daria stared at her feet for a moment. When her eyes met Tiffany's, they seemed conflicted. "I wouldn't say that. Not exactly. Dr. Jones was a great doctor. His patients loved him. But he was complex. He didn't have good—"

A stern voice interrupted from the doorway.

"Daria! Shouldn't you be at your desk?"

I gasped, and not simply because I'd been startled. I recognized the man scolding Daria. It was the silver-haired man I'd seen standing with Dr. Dick and Mariella at Lake Washington Medical Center's open house.

Dr. Steinman, I presume.

Daria flinched. "Sorry, Dr. S. I was just telling these two ladies how much they'll enjoy being clients here. I'm headed back to my desk now." She scurried out of the office.

He closed the door behind her and smiled at us through impossibly white teeth. "I'm Dr. Charles Steinman. Which one of you is the patient?" I wiggled my fingers. He reached out and shook my hand. "It's a pleasure to meet you, Ms. . . . ." He glanced down at my chart. "Ms. Davidson." He tilted his head toward Tiffany. "And you are?"

"I'm Tiffany Davidson. At least I will be, after we get married." She wrapped her arm around my waist and rested her head on my shoulder. "We got engaged last week."

Dr. Steinman kept smiling, but his brow furrowed. "Well, that's wonderful. Congratulations." He sat behind the desk, laid my chart face-down on its surface, and laced his fingers together. "So, you two ladies are ready to start a family. How can I help?"

I pointed at the paperwork I'd spent twenty minutes completing. "Don't you want to read my chart first?"

He gazed across the wide walnut desk, unblinking, as if preparing to deliver a well-rehearsed speech. "Here at Reproductive Associates, our relationship with your family is more than writing on a clipboard. More, even, than the process of uniting sperm and egg. We like to think of ourselves as your extended family. If you've read our website, you know that we stay with our clients from pre-conception through birth. If you're a good fit for our clinic, the three of us will spend significant time together for well over a year. There will be plenty of time to discuss your patient forms. For now, tell me about you."

I froze, my mind suddenly blank. A professional detective would have already come up with a detailed backstory. But a professional detective wouldn't have spent the last week teaching yoga and wrangling six-pound fur demons. I stalled by asking a question. "What would you like to know?"

"Why don't you start by telling me your goals?"

"Goals?"

"Yes. Why do you want to start a family now, and what made you choose Reproductive Associates?"

Tiffany chewed on her bottom lip and pointed to me. "Kate's the one who made the appointment. Go on, Kate. Tell him."

They both stared at me expectantly. I was afraid I'd stumble over a lie, so I opted to tell the truth. Or at least a version of it. I spent the next fifteen minutes talking about Michael and me, though I substituted Tiffany's name for Michael's. How we'd met when I was trying to find a home for Bella, how we'd fallen in love almost instantly, how I'd stupidly tried to throw our relationship away, and how after six months of living together, our relationship seemed more solid than ever.

To my surprise, I actually believed the words I spoke next. "I'm thirty-three now. I know my biological clock isn't ticking very loudly—at least not yet—but I might want to have multiple children. I probably shouldn't wait much longer."

Dr. Steinman pushed my file to the edge of his desk. "Our scheduler told me that you seemed to be in a hurry." He looked at his desktop for several beats, then back up at me. "I understand your concern, and I make my living helping people create babies. So believe me, I don't say this lightly. Starting a family should never be a rushed decision. The beauty of practicing reproductive medicine in a fertility clinic is that there are no accidental pregnancies. My clients are, by definition, *choosing* to have a child."

He leaned forward, put his elbows on the desk, and laced his fingers together. "You should choose to have children when you are truly ready, Ms. Davidson. Not one minute before. Same-sex couples like you actually have an advantage, timing-wise. You can always wait and have the younger partner conceive."

Tiffany, the smart-ass, nudged me under the table.

The doctor continued. "Barring that, we could retrieve some eggs and freeze them for later."

"Thirty-three's not too old, though, right? I mean, women give birth in their forties all the time."

He smiled. "Thirty-three isn't close to being too old. Many women wait until their late thirties or even their early forties to start having children. With an egg donor, you can wait longer than that. Relatively speaking, getting pregnant in your early forties isn't the hard part. The challenge of starting a family later in life comes as both you and the child get older. When you're fifty-five, do you want to be saving for retirement or your child's college tuition?"

Gulp.

"On the flip side, having a child changes your life dramatically. Are there things you'd like to do before you start raising a family?"

Answer? Absolutely. I just didn't know what they were yet.

Dr. Steinman leaned back in his chair. "Ms. Davidson, I have to be honest. You seem hesitant to me. I can't predict your future, but unless you have fertility issues we haven't discovered yet—other than needing a sperm donor, of course—we have no reason to rush. I suggest that you wait to conceive until you know that you're ready."

His points were all valid, and ones I hadn't considered before. I sensed a serious conversation in Michael's and my future. For the moment, though, it was time to shift the conversation toward Dr. Dick—and hopefully Mariella.

"I appreciate your candor, but Tiffany and I *have* thought about it, and we want to start our family now."

"Excellent." He reached into a file folder and pulled out a pamphlet. "This has information about choosing a sperm donor."

I picked up the pamphlet, then laid it back on the desk again. "Before we sign on the dotted line, I have a couple of concerns."

"Concerns?"

"About your clinic."

Dr. Steinman's smile thinned.

"She means about that doctor who was killed," Tiffany added.

The thinned smile turned into a scowl. "You mean Dr. Jones. Is that why you asked Daria about him?"

"Yes. He was the doctor we planned to use when we first learned about Reproductive Associates. A friend told us he was the managing physician here. The real star of the practice." I'd heard no such thing, but I hoped the comment would annoy Dr. Steinman into saying something he might otherwise keep quiet.

It worked. At least the annoyed part. Droplets of spittle spewed from his lips. "I don't know where you heard that, but it's a lie. Richard and I were equal partners in the business, and we shared the same vision. But I was the more experienced physician. I was helping create families before Richard started med school. Trust me. We can give you excellent care now that he's gone."

"Are you going to be financially stable without him?" I asked. "I mean, IVF is expensive, and I know it can take multiple attempts. I don't want to waste my money on a clinic that may not be around for the long term."

Dr. Steinman's jaw hardened. His eyes shifted warily from me to Tiffany and back again. "I have a feeling you've been misleading me, Ms. Davidson. I was told that you'd researched Reproductive Associates before making this appointment. If you truly had, you'd know we're the highest-ranked fertility center in the Pacific Northwest.

Trust me, we're more than financially solvent. I'm a doctor, but I'm also an astute business person. The business was protected should either Dr. Jones or I become permanently disabled or die. Dr. Jones's death is a tragedy, but it will not impact the longevity of this practice or the quality of our care."

"So you had an insurance policy on him?"

"It's none of your business, but yes, we did."

Tiffany jumped in. "What about the lawsuit?"

Dr. Steinman's energy changed. From guardedly annoyed to piercingly defensive—like a porcupine cornered by a mountain lion. "What lawsuit?"

She opened her eyes wide, pretending surprise. "Why, the sexual harassment one, of course. Were there others?"

"I don't know how you heard about that, but that lawsuit died when Richard did. I'll admit, my ex-business partner didn't follow appropriate boundaries with his employees, and part of that was my fault. I should have insisted on no-fraternization policies. But that simply points out flaws in our employment practices, not in our quality of care."

Tiffany placed her palms on the desk and leaned toward him. "So in a way, you're better off now that Dr. Jones is dead, aren't you?"

Dr. Steinman leaped to his feet, smashing his chair into the wall behind him. "I don't know what kind of scam you're pulling, but you're obviously not here to become our clients. You're wasting my time. I have *real* patients to attend to."

He stormed from behind the desk, grabbed Tiffany and me by our upper arms, and marched us to the door.

"Leave my clinic. Now. Tell whoever sent you that if they harass me again, I'm calling my lawyer." He shoved us into the hallway and slammed the door behind us.

I rubbed my bruised triceps and gaped at Tiffany, a little shell-shocked.

She cringed. "Sorry, Kate. That didn't go well, and it's my fault. You told me not to talk."

"You're right, I did. But I'm glad you ignored me. Your questions worked." I nodded toward Dr. Steinman's closed door. "He transitioned from Dr. Jekyll to Mr. Hyde pretty darned quickly. I think we just found another suspect."

Tiffany looked confused. "Dr. Jekyll? Is he on *Grey's Anatomy*?"

"Geez, Tiffany. Do you even read?"

Daria appeared before Tiffany could answer, looking significantly less friendly than when she'd delivered our lattes. "I've been asked to escort you two ladies out of the building. Let's go." She walked us through the waiting room, out the door, and onto the elevator, like two unwelcome crashers of an elite baby-making party.

Which, come to think of it, we were.

She pressed "L" as the elevator doors closed. "You two aren't even gay, are you?"

Tiffany backed into the corner, seeming to have lost the ability to speak.

I shook my head no.

"Why were you really here?"

I had a feeling Daria wouldn't accept anything other than the truth, so I gave it to her. "I'm a friend of Rachel Jones. I'm trying to prove that she didn't kill her husband."

Daria's eyes widened. "And you think Dr. S did?"

"No. I don't know. I mean ... "

Daria held up her hand. "Save it. We don't have much time. I don't appreciate being lied to, but I'm not your enemy. I wasn't a huge fan of Dr. Jones, but he didn't deserve to die." The elevator door dinged open. She ushered us out and walked us across the expansive marble lobby. "If Dr. Jones's wife didn't kill him, I'd like to know who did. But if I tick Dr. S off, he'll fire me for sure. I can't afford to lose this job."

We continued through the revolving door and out to the sidewalk. "I have about five minutes before he starts wondering why I'm not back. You have that long to ask me your questions."

I got right to the point. "Do you know anyone who wanted to hurt Dr. Jones?"

Daria shrugged. "He and Dr. S had been fighting a lot lately, that's for sure. Dr. S would never have hurt him, though."

"Why had they been fighting? Over the sexual harassment lawsuit?"

"You asked Dr. S about that? No wonder he kicked you out. That's a touchy subject around here. Dr. S was especially pissed because Dr. Jones was doing it again."

"Doing what?" I asked.

"Having an affair with a staff member."

"You mean Mariella?"

"The one and only. You know her?"

"No. At least not yet."

"You're not missing much. Dr. S wanted to get rid of both of them, but he couldn't afford to buy out Dr. Jones, and he was afraid Mariella would sue." She shrugged. "He was probably right. That woman is cold. She hasn't missed a single day of work since Dr. Jones died. Frankly, she doesn't seem all that heartbroken."

"I was hoping to talk to her today."

"You'll never get back in the office, at least not while Dr. S is there." Daria looked at her watch. "You might have another option, though. Mariella's lunch break started five minutes ago. If you hurry, you can catch her."

"Where?"

"The same place she goes every day from noon to two." She pointed to a storefront across the street: *Some Like It Hot Yoga.*

"She takes yoga?" I asked.

"Yes. But if you go inside, prepare to sweat. That place makes Hell feel like a ski resort."

Tiffany finally spoke. "Well, how about that, Kate? Looks like I'm finally going to try yoga."

SEVENTEEN

As Tiffany and I dawdled outside Some Like It Hot Yoga's entrance, I only knew one thing for certain: "some" didn't include me. Sweat already poured down my neck and pooled under my armpits, and I hadn't opened the door yet.

A herd of scantily clad Barbie and Ken dolls filtered around us and drifted through the door. I planted my heels and did my best impersonation of a yoga teacher statue. "We don't actually have to attend the class, Tiffany. Why don't we wait out here and ambush Mariella as she leaves?"

Tiffany waved aside my suggestion. "You're a terrible detective, Kate. It's a wonder you've solved any crimes at all. If we ambush her outside, she'll know we're up to something. It's much better cover to take the class and strike up a conversation with her there." She placed her hand on the door handle.

I grabbed her wrist and pulled it away. "I really don't think this is a good idea."

"What are you afraid of? That I'll show you up in my first yoga class?"

Tiffany was more right than she knew. I wasn't *afraid* that I'd look stupid in a Hot Yoga class, I *knew* it. I had survived (barely) my one and hopefully only Hot Yoga class with Rene over five years ago. The memory still made me shudder. At ten minutes in, I'd been reduced to a sweaty, stinky puddle of goo. By twenty, my skin had semi-permanently melted to my mat. At thirty, I'd fled from the room and vomited in the parking lot.

But I could never admit that to Tiffany.

"This isn't a class for beginners, Tiffany. You might get hurt." I pointed to the burgundy Band-Aid covering her backside. "Besides, you can't practice yoga in a miniskirt."

"Nonsense. I hear you tell students all the time: you can wear anything to yoga class. Besides, this isn't a skirt; it's a *skort*. It's designed specifically for yoga classes!" She lifted the front of her hem to reveal burgundy shorts so tiny, they made the four-inch piece of cloth covering them seem modest. "Until I started working at Serenity Yoga, I never paid attention to yoga clothes. I had no idea they were so stylin'!"

She was right. Yoga was a multibillion dollar industry, and much of that money was spent purchasing outfits so tight and revealing they would have made Patanjali blush. The whole yoga clothing industry was silly, really. As Tiffany pointed out, a student could wear anything—including pajamas—to practice yoga, as long as the outfit allowed her body to move freely.

Except slacks and a long-sleeved blouse in a 105-degree room.

I gestured from my collarbones to my ankles. "I'll broil in this outfit, Tiffany."

"Good lord, Kate. Have you ever been to a yoga studio other than Serenity Yoga? You really need to check out the competition. They'll have clothes for sale inside."

She grabbed my hand and pulled me into the blissfully air-conditioned lobby, which contained a huge retail area. Unlike Serenity Yoga—which sold a small collection of yoga books, blankets, blocks, and yoga mats—this studio sold everything an aspiring yogi could need—and lots of things she didn't. Racks and racks of designer clothing, towels, straps, jewelry, headbands, water bottles, super-absorbent towels, and aroma-therapeutic map wipes. They even sold small spray bottles labeled Pure Oxygen, evidently for those times when your pranayama practice needed that little extra boost.

Tiffany paid for our class while I rummaged through the sale rack until I found the cheapest items in my size: a sixty-dollar tank top with a purple lotus flower on the front and a pair of supposedly extra large Spandex shorts so tiny, I sincerely doubted they'd cover my privates.

Tiffany pointed at the tiny swatch of fabric. "Those are cute, but they're way too big for you." She pulled out a pair half their size and handed them to me. "Try these instead. Class is about to start. I'm going in. I'll see you inside."

I shoved Tiffany's recommendation back onto the rack, paid for the world's most mortifying outfit, and slipped it on in the women's locker room. Five dollars for a rental mat later, I eased into the practice space ten minutes after class had already started.

I'm not sure which hit me first. The heat—which sucked every molecule of oxygen out of my lungs—or the stench—which was a disgusting mixture of underarm odor, gym socks, and recently burned sage. Space heaters blasted from every corner, which seemed like overkill considering the amount of body heat radiating from the sixty or so people jammed into the forty-person room. Despite the crowd, I spotted Mariella near the back.

The instructor—a twenty-something Adonis wearing a black Speedo and a headset—gave me the stink eye from an elevated stage. I nodded to Tiffany in the front row, mouthed the word "sorry" to the instructor, and squeezed into an almost-space next to Mariella. She scooted her mat six inches in the opposite direction.

The first drop of sweat oozed down my nose before I'd finished unwinding my yoga mat. The next five hundred joined thirty seconds later. I closed my eyes and prayed for lightning to strike me dead. Five seconds later, I opened them again.

Still breathing. Bummer.

I gave that abominable class my most valiant effort. Truly, I did.

I raised my arms in Warrior I, only to notice that my wringing-wet armpit hairs were long enough to braid. A minute later, I gratefully lowered my arms and pressed my rear to the sky in Downward Facing Dog. Both of my calves cramped at the same time. I reached back with my right hand to rub the knots out of my muscles; my left hand slid forward on the sweat-drenched surface. I tumbled, face-first, onto my mat. I would have burst into tears, but I couldn't spare the hydration.

As I lay drowning in a lake of my own bodily fluids, I assured myself that I still had one consolation. If I was suffering this much, Tiffany must be in agony. I rolled to my side, pressed myself up to sitting, and peeked around the fifty-nine Barbie Dolls bending in front of me.

Tiffany looked …

Beautiful.

Sure, her form was atrocious. Embarrassing, even. But her face seemed to glow. A few feminine-looking beads of moisture dotted her brow. Her yoga skort magically draped around all of her flaws while wicking away every embarrassing sweat drop.

I glanced down at my own supposedly hot-yoga-approved outfit. The hem of my shorts dug into my thighs like rubber bands around five-pound hams. My tank top was soaked; the lotus flower, wilted. An embarrassing stench radiated from my fur-covered armpits. I gritted my teeth and glared at Tiffany.

She lowered her knees to her mat, opened her eyes, and flashed a thousand-watt smile at Adonis. He flashed an even friendlier smile back at her, then noticed my glare.

"If class is too difficult for you, close your eyes and rest in Savasana."

He didn't have to tell me twice. I lowered what was left of my body to the floor, where it had to be cooler. Heat rises, right?

If anything, I felt hotter.

I closed my eyes and prayed for a heart attack.

The teacher spoke. "I think we should try something a little different today. Let's finish with some partner poses."

My entire body constricted. Except for my lips, which lifted into a grin.

Partner Yoga might be the one thing I loathed more than Hot Yoga. On most days. I'd rather practice nude yoga while skydiving through acid.

But not today.

Partnering with Mariella would give me the perfect opportunity to connect with her. I couldn't ask her about her lover's death during superheated gymnastics, but a few paired poses would at least allow me to get a feel for her—literally. I turned toward her mat ...

And came face-to-face with the sweatiest, hairiest man I'd ever encountered. His grisly, wiry brown beard was just the beginning. Hair was everywhere. His chest, his uncovered shoulders, his back.

All the way down past his navel, to parts never meant to be exposed in yoga class.

I'd been working with a counselor to overcome my aversion to beards, although with limited success. If she'd been in the room, she'd have assured me that this was a perfect, real-world opportunity to practice the techniques that she'd shown me.

She'd have been wrong.

The only reasonable strategy was retreat.

I searched desperately for someone else—anyone else—with whom I could partner. Mariella had moved her mat to the other side of the room and was paired with a blonde woman. Tiffany had climbed onto the stage, where she was demonstrating the moves-to-come with Adonis. Everyone else in the room had already found their partner and was preparing to begin.

Hairy Guy (who was undoubtedly mentally calling me Stinky Girl) shrugged.

"Looks like it's you and me."

Gulp.

"Umm. I guess so."

The experience didn't start out too badly, all things considered. In the first paired pose, Hairy Guy stayed in Downward Facing Dog while I did a weird L-shaped handstand with my palms on the floor and my feet on his lower back. I can't say I enjoyed the feet-to-rear-end experience, but I could live with it. At least I didn't have to stare at his facial hair. He lifted his head and smiled at me—the perfect position for an upside-down kiss. His beard came within two inches of my lips.

Aack!

I tumbled to the floor. My heel connected solidly with his forehead; it was like an advanced move in a blend of yoga and karate.

Yogarate? Was that a thing?

I lifted myself off the floor, rubbed imaginary beard cooties off my cheeks, apologized to Hairy Guy for giving him a concussion, and prayed for Savasana.

God wasn't listening. Or if he was, he was too busy laughing to answer.

The instructor directed each pair to stand back to sweaty back, link elbows, and lower down into Half Squats. Bodily fluids squished from Hairy Guy's shirt into mine.

I vowed to bathe in hand sanitizer and tried not to vomit.

When the instructor placed us in an oddly perverted rear-to-rear Child's Pose and asked us to hold hands, I cried uncle. I stood up, put my hands on my hips, and gave him my fiercest *no freaking way* glare.

He released hands with Tiffany (who I now hated again) and spoke into his microphone. "That's enough asana for today. Let's finish with some partner yogassage."

Yoga *what?*

I would have bet Bella's enzymes that *The Yoga Sutras* never mentioned the term "yogassage." Not once. Patanjali would have flipped over in his two-thousand-year-old grave at the thought.

The instructor continued. "We'll spend about five minutes per person." He glanced at my fiercely scowling face. "I can see that yogassage makes some of you uncomfortable, which is why it's such a good practice." He made eye contact with me and continued lecturing. "Yoga on the mat is practice for your life off of it. In yogassage, you practice asking for what you want. If you learn to ask for what you want, the universe will give you what you need."

A laudable sentiment, but what I wanted and what I needed were in direct opposition. I *wanted* to run screaming out of this ten-thousand-degree room. I *needed* to stay put and keep an eye on Mariella.

Hairy Guy lifted his eyebrows and said, "Do you want to go first or should I?"

The answer, of course, was neither. There was only one man on earth allowed to grope my sweat-covered, scantily-clad body, and he wasn't in the room.

Hairy Guy shrugged.

"That's cool. You massage me first."

He knelt on the floor in Child's Pose, his ribs touching his thighs and his forehead resting on his forearms.

"Start with my back."

Start with?

I placed my hands on the least furry part of his shoulders and halfheartedly rubbed.

"Could you go a little deeper?"

I silenced my grossed-out thoughts by giving myself a mental pep talk.

Okay, Kate. You can do this. Think of it as an anatomy lesson.

I made my hands into fists and pressed my knuckles firmly into the space between his shoulder blades.

Upper trapezius.

He groaned. "That's perfect. A little lower."

I moved my thumbs down to his lower ribs.

The upper attachment of quadratus lumborum, near the kidneys. Which is precisely where I will slug him if he tries to get frisky.

He glanced over his shoulder. "Wow. You're good at this. Are you a masseuse? Move a little lower. My low back is super tight."

I had a feeling I knew where this was going, and I didn't like it. I unclenched my fists, pushed my thumbs into his erector spinae muscles, and moved my wrists in small circles down the muscles of his low back. He groaned again, more loudly this time.

"A little lower—down to my hips."

The words "erector" and "hips" hit my mind at the same time, creating a horrifying, way-too-anatomically-correct image. I jumped up and vigorously wiped my hands on my destined-for-the-trash tank top. No clue on earth was worth rubbing Hairy Guy south of the Mason-Dixon Line.

I swiped my hands through the air. "That's it. I'm outta here."

I peeled my mat off the floor and marched up to Tiffany, who was currently receiving a shoulder rub from Adonis. The expression she wore was so sensuous, it would have made a porn videographer blush.

"I'll be outside," I said.

I tossed my disgusting, wet, smelly mat onto a pile labeled *used mats for cleaning,* futilely tried to dry myself with my sopping wet hand towel, and retreated into the women's locker room for the world's quickest shower. I'd endured indignity, dehydration, quasi sexual harassment, and physical torture to get to Mariella. I wasn't about to let her scoot out of the building without talking to me.

Less than three minutes after storming out of the yoga room, I hurried outside to wait for Mariella. Exactly how I'd planned to before Tiffany talked me into taking that class from hell. I had no idea how to convince Mariella to open up to me, but at this point I would do anything.

Except attend another Hot Yoga class.

Fifteen minutes later, there was no sign of Tiffany, but Mariella emerged from the studio with a crowd of students. She looked showered, blissful, and—believe it or not—fresh. I pasted on a bright smile and strode toward her. As soon as she spied me, her lips flattened. Her muscles tensed. She stomped my direction, waving her mat like an organic rubber battle flag.

"Who are you and why are you stalking me?" she yelled.

"Stalking you?"

"Yes. First you spied on me and my boyfriend at ABBA, then you followed us to the party on Saturday."

"I never followed—"

She didn't let me finish. "I thought you were some PI that Richard's whack-job wife hired to follow us, but he's dead, and you're still sniffing around. I don't know whether to be terrified or just pissed."

She'd obviously chosen pissed, but I didn't point that out to her.

She looped her mat strap over her shoulder and placed her hands on her hips. "I don't know what you want, but it had better be good or I'm calling the cops." She glared at me in silence.

I held my hands up in surrender. "I'm not stalking you, I promise. The first two times you saw me were coincidences. I just happened to be at the same place you were."

"And today?"

"Today I came looking for you." I closed the gap between us. "I get why you're upset, but I swear, I mean you no harm."

She narrowed her eyes. "How did you find me?"

"I went to see you at work. They sent me here." The statement wasn't a lie; more of a misdirection. After all, Daria *was* one of her coworkers. I continued. "All I want is some information." I gestured to a nearby bench. "Please, can we sit down and talk? It will only take a few minutes."

Mariella stared at me for what felt like an eternity, then marched to the bench. "Fine. I have to be back at work in ten minutes. You've got five of them. Not one more."

I sat next to her and told her the truth. I started with who I was and why we kept running into each other. Then I moved on to why I'd sought her out today. "I'm Rachel Jones's friend. I doubt that you know her very well, but I do. She didn't kill her husband."

Mariella crossed her arms and huffed. "I wouldn't be so sure about that. According to Richard, she's got quite the temper. And they'd been fighting a lot lately."

"Fighting? About what?"

She shrugged. "I didn't ask the specifics. Believe me, we had better things to do than talk about his wife." She paused for a moment. "Though he did complain a lot about that daughter of hers. Said the kid was nothing but trouble. Always giving him lip, even after he'd spent a fortune on her rehab. Richard claimed the best thing about leaving his wife would be getting away from that kid."

"Forgive me, but did you believe him? That he'd leave his wife?"

"Not at first. I'm not stupid. But after a few months, he changed. Making more promises. Wanting more. He said he was going to leave his wife and marry me, but he couldn't. At least not yet. He was in the middle of a sexual harassment lawsuit. He had to play house until it got settled. His lawyers wanted him and his wife to look stable."

"Tamara's lawsuit, you mean."

She lifted her eyebrows. "Someone's been doing her homework."

"Like I said, I'm convinced Rachel is innocent. I can't let her go to prison. Did she know about Richard's affairs?"

"She knew about Tamara, but Richard swore to her that he'd never cheat again." Mariella shook her head. "I can't believe Rachel stayed with him. No way I'd have put up with that crap. Richard thought she might be getting suspicious about me, too." She smirked. "If she wasn't, my little demonstration at the party should have convinced her."

"You groped Dr. Jones in front of Rachel on purpose. Why?"

Mariella's expression was deadpan. "I was tired of sharing. Richard was mine."

Warring emotions vied inside me for dominance. Anger at Mariella's cruelty to Rachel, disgust at her underdeveloped conscience, and sheer incredulousness that so many woman—three that I knew of—wanted Dr. Dick. Incredulousness won.

"You knew he was a cheater. You'd never be able to trust him. Why would you want to be with him?"

Mariella draped her arm across the back of the bench. "Look. I'm a lab tech. I make decent money, but in this city it's nothing. Richard could be *very* generous. In the time we were together, I netted two diamond necklaces, a tennis bracelet, and the down payment for a new Audi. Another month or two and he'd have been paying my rent."

She picked up her mat and stood. "I'm not nearly as dumb as you think. You want to get your friend off by proving that her husband's slut is the killer. Good luck with that. I liked Richard. I even miss him a little. But for me, Richard was a meal ticket. I was much better off with him alive. There's no way I would've killed him."

"Do you have any idea who would have?"

"Yeah. She's sitting in the King County Jail. If it's not her, it's that creepy daughter of hers." She pointed at her watch. "I gave you two more minutes than I promised, and this had better be the last time I see you. You come sniffing around me again, I'm calling the cops."

Mariella took two steps toward the street, then turned around and came back. "But if you're harassing everyone who might have wanted Richard dead, don't forget about Tamara. You saw her that night at ABBA. The woman was pissed."

She jaywalked across the street and headed for her building.

I watched until the revolving door swallowed her, then turned around to see Tiffany and a fully dressed Adonis walking toward me.

"See, Chad?" Tiffany said. "I told you she'd wait for me." She gave him a kiss on the cheek and wiggled her fingers. "See you tomorrow night. I'll text you my address."

I gave her a questioning look.

"We're meeting for smoothies." Her smile brightened. "By the way, he's looking for more teaching gigs, so I told him to call you. He was surprised to hear that you're a yoga teacher."

After today's class, the feeling was mutual. "I don't offer Hot Yoga at Serenity Yoga."

"I know, but maybe you should." She winked. "Chad says practicing Hot Yoga would loosen you right up."

Touché.

I ignored her jab and gestured toward the parking garage. "Let's get going."

Tiffany giggled and texted Adonis until downtown Seattle's skyline had disappeared in my rearview mirror. I stared quietly at the roadway, oddly disappointed in my conversation with Mariella. I disliked her. She was a user. I wanted her to be guilty.

And she was.

But of murder?

Her energy toward Dr. Dick was flat, indifferent. Not bereaved. Certainly not murderous. I couldn't imagine her drumming up the passion to bury a knife in Dr. Dick's heart. She simply didn't care about him enough.

Tiffany interrupted my musing. "Kate. Can I ask you a question?"

I nodded. "Sure. What is it?"

"I know we were play-acting in that meeting with Dr. Steinman, but for a minute there, you seemed like you were telling the truth. About wanting to have kids soon, that is." She paused. "Did you mean it? Michael told me you two weren't planning to have kids for a while. Maybe years."

I didn't want to answer. The question made me feel vulnerable, and Tiffany and I didn't have a serious-girl-talk kind of relationship. I opened my mouth, fully intending to deflect the conversation with a smart-assed retort. To my surprise, the words that came out were the truth.

"We're not planning for kids yet. At least we weren't. Being in that clinic sort of freaked me out, though. I'm beginning to think that Michael and I shouldn't wait much longer." After a few seconds of uncomfortable silence, I nudged her with my elbow. "I'm a lot older than you are, after all."

Tiffany's eyes became serious. "Kate, you know I don't really think you're old, right?"

I didn't reply.

"Seriously, I don't. I just get a kick out of harassing you."

A surprising sensation tickled my throat.

Affection?

For *Tiffany?*

"I *do* know that," I replied. "But thanks for saying it."

She smiled.

"Can you do me a favor?" I asked. Tiffany nodded. "Don't say anything to Michael about this. I'd like to sit with my new insight for a while before I bring it up with him. It might be a passing phase. Before I get Michael excited about kids, I need to make sure that I'm serious."

Tiffany flashed the Scout's Honor sign. "I won't tell him a thing."

I gave her a stern look. "I mean it."

Tiffany turned sideways in her car seat. The tone of her voice matched her earnest expression. "Kate, I know we didn't get along at first, but you did me a solid after that incident with your car. I'd have gone back to jail if you'd reported me to the police."

"Don't give me too much credit. I wanted to call them. Michael talked me out of it."

She shook her head. "Nobody talks you out of anything. Not unless you want them to."

She was right.

She lowered her eyes and examined the skin around her thumbnail. "I know we're not friends. I'm pretty sure you don't even like me. But I owe you. I promise, I won't let you down."

I glanced over at Tiffany, surprised by the lump in my throat. "You're only partially right. I *didn't* like you at first, but that was because of my own petty jealousy. We've both grown up a lot in the past year." I shrugged. "Besides, Michael was right. You're growing on me." I reached over and touched her hand. "I'm sorry you don't think we're friends, because I do."

A slow smile spread across Tiffany's face. "Well, if you say we're friends, we must be friends. And that makes you pretty darned lucky."

I smiled back. "Oh yeah? Why's that?"

Her smile morphed into a smirk. "Because I'm a heck of a lot cooler than you are. Kate Davidson, you just worked your way up to the in-crowd."

EIGHTEEN

I DROPPED TIFFANY OFF at her apartment over the studio and headed to Rene's to pick up the dogs. It was only three-thirty, but Michael would be home by six and I had a feeling that Rene and Sam would appreciate a short shift the first day. When I called to tell Rene I was on my way, she said to use my key and come directly inside. I found her ensconced on the living room couch thumbing through baby magazines.

"Where is everyone?"

"Sam's out giving Mutt and Jeff their millionth potty break. He's determined to housebreak the little suckers."

"We've been trying, but we haven't made much progress. We have at least four accidents per puppy every day."

Rene tossed the magazine on the end table. "You neglected to share that little tidbit when you asked us to watch them. Gee, I wonder why?"

I exercised my right to remain silent.

She gave me a chastising look. "We've had two potty incidents so far, but they were both first thing this morning. Sam has been on those little fur-monsters like white on rice since then. He says they've already done all the damage they're allowed for one day."

I cringed. "Oh no, what did they do?"

She pointed to a large box near the front door.

"Go see for yourself. Sam hasn't taken it outside yet."

I slinked to the half-refrigerator-sized box and picked through its contents. Torn baby photos, crumpled catalogs, computer print-outs that smelled suspiciously of dog urine, and a stack of shredded patterns.

"Oh Rene, I'm so sorry."

"Eh." She waved her hand through the air. "Could've been worse. I'd already tossed most of that stuff in a reject pile. That's how they got hold of it in the first place. Sam didn't get grumpy until the second potty accident. I'm not sure which little monster did it, but they have remarkable aim. They made the deposit in Sam's tennis shoe." She stifled a giggle. "You should have seen the look on his face when he put it on."

"Oh no!"

"Yep. Priceless. I wish I'd gotten a video. It totally would've gone viral. Anyway, now he's the potty Nazi. The pups go out every hour, on the hour. Bella goes out every two."

I glanced around the room, looking for my canine best friend. "Is she outside now?"

"Nope. She's locked in the twins' room in a time-out." Rene paused, as if carefully considering her words. "Don't freak out, but she snapped at Sam's face when he tried to pet her."

"Snapped at him?" My stomach twisted. Bella had never taken to Sam, but she had never once threatened to use her teeth on him. "Was Sam hurt?"

"I told you not to freak out. Sam's fine. Bella didn't actually bite him. She just air-snapped about three inches from his nose. But her teeth made this super loud crack when they hit together, and it scared the bejeesus out of him. I decided to give them both a break for a while. She seems happier by herself."

"I'm sorry, Rene. Maybe she doesn't feel well."

"Her digestion's whacked out, that's for sure. Did you forget to add enzymes to her food again? I wasn't outside when she went to the bathroom, but Sam was pretty alarmed. He described it to me. It sounded like that setback she had at Elysian Springs."

I sank into the guest chair. "Darn it. I was afraid of that. Her stomach's been making those rumbling noises again. I think she might have SIBO." SIBO—Small Intestinal Bacterial Overgrowth—was a common complication of Bella's digestive condition. It could be managed, but it would require a thirty-day course of antibiotics. "That settles it. I'm calling her vet."

Sam hobbled into the living room, a play-growling puppy attached to each pant leg.

"Knock it off, you little sharks. Let go already. This isn't fun for me."

I flew next to Sam and wrestled with Mutt until she released. Sam extricated Jeff and handed him to me. Both puppies covered my face in sweet little kisses.

"Sorry about that, Sam. Did they tear your jeans?"

He scratched Mutt's ear. "I doubt it, but it wasn't for lack of trying. They're tough for a couple of munchkins."

"Rene told me that you guys had a rough day. Don't worry about watching them the rest of the week. Michael and I will figure something else out."

Though I have no idea what.

Sam shrugged. "Don't worry about it. They're a handful, but at least they don't hate me. Bella almost took my face off today."

"She's stressed, honey," Rene replied. "Taking care of babies is hard work. Wait till the twins are born. I'll probably saw your ears off with a kitchen knife."

Sam stared at her, deadpan. "Something to look forward to."

He lifted Mutt out of my arms, snuggled her up to his cheek, and crooned, "You don't want to stay home alone in Kate's icky crate. You want to hang out with your Uncle Sam, don't you?"

If it weren't for Sam's mustache, I would have kissed him. "Thanks for offering, Sam. It means the world. But I can't take advantage of you guys that way."

"Seriously, Kate," he replied. "It's fine. Watching the puppies will help ease my conscience. You won't let us pay for your doula services, and that training you took couldn't have been cheap."

"I told you, that's my baby present. You guys already have everything else."

Sam didn't give up. "Let us do this for you. I'm working from home again tomorrow. I'd enjoy hanging out with the little dudes."

"Don't forget Bella," Rene added.

Sam didn't reply, but his expression wasn't exactly enthusiastic.

"Thanks, Rene," I said. "But I'll keep Bella with me tomorrow. That way she'll get a break from the puppies and I can squeeze in a vet visit. But if you're serious and can provide puppy daycare for a few more days, it would be awesome."

That settled, I loaded the puppies into the car, then went back inside and released Bella from the twins' nursery. She slinked up to Sam, slowly swished her tail back and forth, and licked his hand. He flinched, then tentatively reached out and scratched her throat with the tips of his fingers, keeping as much distance between Bella's teeth and the rest of his body as possible. Whatever had happened between them, all was forgiven, at least from Bella's perspective. I wasn't so sure about Sam.

I dropped the pups off at home and securely locked them inside their crate with some toys to destroy. The whining started as soon as I turned to walk away.

"Sorry, guys, the whining won't work this time. I'm taking Bella to the studio with me, so she won't be here to assist in your prison break. Michael will come home from work and let you out in an hour or so."

Their howling yelps serenaded me all the way to the car.

I turned the key in the ignition and grumbled to Bella, "The neighbors are going to *love* that. How long before they get laryngitis?"

She didn't reply.

They were still screaming when I pulled out of the driveway.

———

I spent the next several hours catching up on paperwork, checking in students for our drop-in classes, and taking Bella on a week's worth of bio breaks. Rene was right. Bella was experiencing a flare in her EPI symptoms—the worst I'd seen since we'd gotten her stable over a year ago. I called her vet, who said to keep monitoring her, make sure she drank plenty of water, and bring her in the next morning at ten. I hoped we wouldn't need to make a late-night trip to the emergency vet before then.

Before I knew it, students had started lining up for the studio's eight o'clock Sound Bath. Sound Baths were a concert of sorts, in which the sounds—in this case drums, chimes, bamboo sticks, and vocalizations—caressed students' bodies while they rested in Corpse Pose. I'd tried to describe the powerfully soothing effect of the practice multiple times with little success. Suffice it to say, once someone tried their first Sound Bath, they were invariably hooked.

The instructor set up her instruments in a small semicircle and lit tea candles around the room's perimeter, filling the space with soft, flickering light. I left her to center herself while I checked in students.

I was sitting behind the desk preparing to run the next credit card when a flash of pink caught my eye. *Momma Bird!* Or, more specifically, her pink flamingo hat bobbing past my window. The first time I'd seen her since the puppies arrived.

I stood and stared out the window. Did I dare go outside and talk to her now?

On the one hand, class started in five minutes, and I still had at least a dozen students waiting in line. On the other, I was the boss. If I abandoned my post, no one would fire me.

An annoyed voice interrupted my musing.

"Excuse me, Miss." The elderly woman stared pointedly at my hand, which still held her Visa card. "Can I have my credit card back?"

"Sorry, I haven't run the charge yet."

The students behind her shuffled and grumbled. A man near the back of the line looked pointedly at his watch. I might not get fired if I left the desk now, but I would certainly lose customers. Quizzing Momma Bird would have to wait.

Two minutes after class was scheduled to begin, Nicole and a haggard-looking Justine rushed through the door.

"I'd almost given up on you two. I'm glad you made it."

"Barely," Justine replied. "Do you still have room for us?"

The honest answer was no. When I'd last checked the yoga room, the mats were packed three inches apart. Still, I couldn't bring myself to turn them away. Not only did I want to talk to Justine, but more than that, I wanted to help her. If her sallow skin and drawn expression were any indication, she could use every moment of soothing tonight's class would provide. Luckily, Sound Baths didn't require movement, so crowding the mats together wouldn't put anyone at risk. I could always move my personal mat into the storage room.

I stood and gestured toward the yoga room. "I won't be able to get you two together, but we'll find space. Follow me."

Justine took three steps, then suddenly stopped and grabbed on to a shelf. Her body swayed; her skin paled. For a moment, I thought she might pass out.

I grabbed her arm and guided her to the bench. "Have a seat. Are you hypoglycemic?"

She glanced at Nicole. "Sweetie, would you please bring me a glass of water?"

Nicole moved to the water cooler, grabbed a glass, and started filling it.

"I'm not sick," Justine said. "I'm tired. I had a rough night last night."

"Bad night at the hospital?"

"I wish. I never went to work. My mom got out of the house and wandered off, so I had to stay home and look for her. We searched the neighborhood for hours. I finally found her asleep in the garage at four this morning."

"Is she okay?"

"She was scared, but she's a heck of a lot better than I am." Justine's eyes grew wet. "It will kill me to put Mom in a nursing home, but I think it's inevitable. I'm not sure how much longer I can keep her safe."

Nicole handed Justine the water. "What she's not telling you is that it was my fault. I forgot to set the alarm." Her lower lip trembled. "I'm sorry, Justine. I let you down."

Justine took a deep breath, then wrapped Nicole in a one-armed hug. "Don't be silly. It could happen to anyone."

"Your dizziness concerns me," I said. "Stress can play havoc on blood sugar levels—especially in diabetics. I have juice boxes in the supply room. Do you want one?"

Nicole gave Justine a questioning look. Justine's shoulders grew tense. She spoke in clipped tones. "Nicole, I need to talk to Kate alone for a second. Go grab mats for us, would you?"

Oh no. I felt like an idiot, which was appropriate given the circumstances. Justine had expressly asked me to keep her condition confidential.

I lowered my voice and whispered, "I'm so sorry. I forgot that you didn't want Nicole to know about the diabetes. I was trying to be helpful, but I blew it, big time."

"It's okay." Her facial expression clearly implied that it wasn't. "But please don't mention it again. Let's forget about it and go inside."

I shuffled mats around to make room for two more, mentally kicking myself. Yoga teachers weren't bound by medical privacy laws, at least not yet. That didn't get me off the hook ethically, though. Referring to Justine's confidential health condition in front of Nicole was an unacceptable mistake. I vowed to be more careful in the future.

I was still chastising myself when I laid my mat at the edge of the practice space, partially in the storage closet. I should have skipped class and spent the time chasing down Momma Bird, but I was too upset with myself. I'd look for her after class.

I covered up with a purple Thunderbird blanket and closed my eyes, determined to reconnect with my center. The first deep chimes from the vertical gong loosened the fingers of tension gripping my shoulders. The cherub-like sounds of crystal singing bowls filled the room next, oddly soothing my ears and stimulating my throat at the same time. A few minutes later, the instructor began walking around the space while rhythmically beating a large drum. She paused for about thirty seconds directly above me, creating a vibrational wind that caressed my entire body, relaxing every nerve ending, purifying every cell. Hot Yoga be damned. I'd choose this over sweating out my neuroses every time.

As she continued around the room, I allowed my mind to wander, hoping that the drum's vibrations would shake loose some insights about Dr. Dick's murder.

Who could have killed him, and why? Anyone near the perinatal unit that day had opportunity. The break room knife gave them all means. So I prioritized my suspects based on motive.

My first two suspects were Dr. Dick's lovers, Mariella and Tamara. When I'd spoken with Mariella, her energy had seemed flat, almost cold, and I'd thought she hadn't cared enough about her lover to kill him. Now I wasn't so sure. Weren't psychopaths known for their lack of emotional connection? Mariella claimed that she was better off with Dr. Dick alive, but that excuse fell flat if he'd been planning to leave her. Maybe the divorce papers were still in his desk for a reason. I tapped my fingertips lightly on my mat. I didn't know

Mariella's motive, but she might still have one. I put her solidly in the "medium likelihood" bucket.

As for Tamara, wasn't the jilted lover always a suspect? She was angry enough about the breakup to sue Dr. Dick. What if she was going to lose the lawsuit? But a year had passed since the affair ended, so that motive seemed flimsy. Besides, as far as I knew, she hadn't even been at the hospital on Saturday. I put her in the "low likelihood" bucket, but mentally put a check mark next to her name. She had information I wanted, and I hadn't spoken to her yet. If nothing else, she could weigh in on my Mariella-as-psychopath theory.

The drum beat ceased, and the instructor filled the silence with a sound remarkably like deep, resonant birdsong. She punctuated each vocalization by striking a mallet against hollow bamboo. I allowed myself a moment to listen, then continued making my list.

Liam and Kendra, the parents of the stillborn baby. Kendra was definitely low on my suspect list. She was at the hospital the day of the murder, but she was also on bed rest. It seemed highly unlikely that she could have overpowered Dr. Dick.

Not true for her husband.

Liam went solidly into the "high likelihood" category. Kendra claimed that Liam was in her hospital room at the time of Dr. Dick's death, but I didn't believe her. The couple was hiding something. I simply needed to figure out what.

The birdsong faded away, replaced by a flute's soothing lilt.

I couldn't eliminate Dr. Steinman, either. Dr. Dick's murder erased a sexual harassment lawsuit and provided a likely significant insurance payout. Reproductive Associates' upscale facilities couldn't possibly be cheap. Defending two separate lawsuits—that I knew of—in the past year couldn't be any cheaper. How much did Dr.

Steinman need that insurance money? I put him solidly in the "medium likelihood" category.

I wanted the list to end there. I wanted the killer to be one of those five people. People I didn't know. People I didn't care about. People I could help put in prison and still walk away whole. But if I was honest with myself, I had to add three more: Summer (in the "low" bucket), Nicole ("medium"), and, as much as I hated to admit it, Rachel. Each of them had been harmed by Dr. Dick. Each of them was on site the day of the killing. Each of them was physically capable of the murder. I put Rachel in the "low" category, mainly to make myself feel better. Martinez was right. The evidence against Rachel was compelling.

That left me with eight viable suspects. Seven too many.

I rolled to my side and sat up, much too frustrated to rest on my back anymore. The instructor frowned. I closed my eyes and pretended to meditate.

I was overlooking something. I could feel it, just like Bella sensed when the UPS truck turned onto our block. It tickled the edge of my awareness, bringing with it a heavy sense of foreboding. Was I subconsciously overlooking a clue to protect someone I cared about? Was my inner self helping me hide from the truth?

With my luck, Rene was the killer.

When the music stopped playing, I'd come to a single conclusion: I had way too many suspects, and way too little information. I'd corner Justine tonight. Tamara was next on my hit list. I'd find a way to speak with her soon.

As the students rolled up their mats, I whispered to Justine. "I need to say goodbye to the instructor, but I'll see you in the reception area."

I thanked the instructor for her time and met Justine and Nicole in the lobby.

"How's your mom doing, Nicole?" I asked.

"Not good. She calls me from jail every night, but I can't see her again until Tuesday." She avoided meeting my gaze. "Is Tiffany here? Justine bought me the makeup she recommended, but I can't get it to look right. Maybe Tiffany can show me how to put it on again."

"Sorry, she's not working tonight."

Nicole glanced at Justine. "Can I check her apartment?"

"Go ahead, but be quick."

Justine didn't speak again until the door closed behind Nicole. "I hope your friend doesn't mind. The poor kid's having a tough time today. She's been talking about seeing Tiffany ever since I told her we were coming here. I didn't have the heart to say no."

"It might be best if you and I spoke alone, anyway."

She shrugged. "I doubt I have anything useful to tell you."

"Maybe not, but even if you don't, you might know someone who does. There were people all over the hospital on Saturday. Somebody had to have seen the real murderer."

"There weren't as many people as you think, at least not in the old building. Everyone who wasn't actively working a birth was at the party. The unit was practically a ghost town."

"You didn't see anything unusual?"

Justine walked to the cooler, poured a glass of water, and took several long drinks before replying. "I've asked myself that question dozens of times. I keep replaying that day over and over and over again. Wishing I'd seen something that could help Rachel." She shrugged. "I didn't. My patient entered transition shortly after I saw you. She was in a lot of pain, so I didn't leave her side. All I saw around the time Richard was killed was the inside of a birthing suite." She shuddered. "It sounds selfish, but I'm glad. I've dealt with more than enough death in my life."

She crumpled the paper cup and tossed it in the trash. "Sorry, Kate. I wish I could help. If you'd like, I can quiz the other nurses."

"It might be more productive if we spoke to them together."

Justine frowned. "I'm happy to help, but there's only so much I can realistically do. I'll talk to the other staff members when I see them, but I don't have time to coordinate group meetings. If anyone knows something, I'll give them your contact information and ask them to call you."

"Fair enough."

Nicole knocked on the window and waved. Justine picked up her purse. "Sorry, Kate, but I need to head home. I'm exhausted. I'll let you know if I learn anything useful."

I watched the two of them walk across the dark parking lot until they were safely inside Justine's car. Then I took a quick walk around the block, hoping to find Momma Bird. Not surprisingly, she was gone. I went back inside, quickly swept the yoga room floor, straightened the mats, and performed the plethora of other duties required to close up for the night. A half hour later, I double-checked the lock on the front door, went out the back, and added more seeds for Mister Feathers.

"'Night, buddy."

I climbed the three steps to the parking garage and froze.

What now?

Someone had tucked a note under my windshield wiper.

When I unfolded the page, the hairs on the back of my neck tingled. By the time I finished reading, my entire body was quivering.

It was an address on Bainbridge Island. I read and re-read the cryptic lines underneath it:

Check the yellow shed. You'll find your answer there.

NINETEEN

I SQUINTED MY EYES and leaned toward the windshield, trying to safely maneuver through downtown Seattle's impenetrable fog. My mind felt hazy; my body, woozy. I didn't feel drunk, exactly; more like I'd been drugged.

The taillights in front of me swirled hypnotically. A second later, the rest of the world started spinning. I closed my eyes, trying to fight off a nauseating attack of vertigo. When I opened them, Dr. Dick stood in the road, wearing nothing but underwear. I yanked on the steering wheel and swerved, barely missing him.

I slammed on the breaks, pressed my forehead against the steering wheel, and gulped in deep, hiccupping breaths. My head throbbed; frenzied heartbeats pummeled my chest. But my mind still felt dulled. I wasn't safe to drive.

And I wasn't alone.

Bella crawled into the front seat and rested her chin in my lap. I couldn't drive anymore, but we couldn't stay here, either. I abandoned the car next to the curb, gathered her into my arms, and trudged through the streets, hoping to flag down a taxi. The fog swallowed us and my car vanished.

We were lost.

I kept lurching forward, feet pushing through hardening cement. At last, to my left. A landmark I recognized. Pike Place Market.

I staggered down the unlit hallways, desperately trying to find something familiar, but even Pike Place felt foreign. Every storefront was dark. My legs burned. My back ached. Every muscle screamed. Each time I found a new hallway, I stumbled onto a dead end.

I turned right and continued searching.

Finally, a person. An old man selling newspapers.

I staggered up to the *Dollars for Change* vendor, trying to hold back the tears threatening my eyes. "How do I get to Greenwood Avenue?"

He pointed toward a steep, spiral staircase. "Up there."

I stared up through the center of the tornado-like vortex. "Isn't there another way?"

"Lady, in this line of work, I try not to see too much. Not safe, you know?"

I stood at the bottom step, terrified. I couldn't climb it—not while carrying Bella—but I didn't have a choice. This was the only way home.

You can do this, Kate.

I hugged Bella close and tentatively climbed the first step.

Then the second.

When my foot touched the third, Bella panicked and kicked out her legs, knocking me off balance. We crashed to the bottom. My tailbone hit the cement floor—hard. Electric pain jolted up my spine.

I curled into a ball and sobbed.

I can't do it. I have to find another way.

I gathered Bella into my arms again and dragged us both down the hallway, each step a torment. I had no idea where we were going anymore, but it didn't matter. Wherever it was, we weren't going to make it.

I looked down at my dog. "I'm sorry, sweetie. You have to walk on your own."

The moment her feet touched the ground, my whole body lightened. The electric jolts ceased. Without Bella, I was free.

Then I realized why I'd carried her in the first place.

Bella wore no collar. No leash. No mechanism to tether us together. No tool to keep her from running into the street. I couldn't prevent Bella from getting lost. From attacking another dog. I couldn't protect Bella from herself.

I gathered her up again, muscles screaming. But this time, the fiery burning didn't bother me. The pain, the heaviness, the inevitability of being lost forever ... none of it mattered. All I wanted—all I needed—was to hold Bella close.

I finally understood.

Carrying Bella wasn't a sacrifice; it was a gift. I'd rather stay lost with my dog than find my way home alone.

I slowly opened my eyes, disoriented. Still hovering on the nebulous edge between dream and reality, I took in the darkness, breathed into my pillow. Gazed at the puppies, still asleep in their crate. I reached over and touched my sleeping boyfriend, then stroked my softly snoring dog.

This. This was reality. This was my life.

Thank God.

What was that about?

I was no stranger to powerful dreams. Dreams were my subconscious's way of solving life's problems. This time especially, I had a feeling the answer was important. But like a frustrating, REM-sleep version of *Jeopardy!*, my mind gave the answer but refused to provide the question.

Was my dream about Bella, or was it about Dr. Dick?

Bella stirred beside me. She moaned, hopped off the bed, and tried to nudge the bedroom door open.

"I'm coming, sweetie."

Bella needed her five-hundredth bathroom break, and after that, I needed rest. Whatever my subconscious was telling me, it would have to wait until morning.

Or so I thought.

I spent an interminable sleepless night trying to decipher my dream, agonizing over the note and who could have left it on my car, and taking Bella outside for all-too-frequent bathroom breaks. I hadn't told Michael about the note yet; by the time I'd gotten home, he'd been frustrated, grumpy, and distracted. Like me, he'd glimpsed Momma Bird outside of Pete's Pets, but by the time he'd finished up with his customer, she'd vanished.

I kidded myself that telling Michael about the note would simply fuel his frustration, but the truth was, I didn't *want* to tell him. Keeping it secret was the easiest way to avoid conflict. Michael would inevitably order me to give the note to Martinez, then issue a mandate forbidding me from checking out the address by myself.

So I decided to skip the argument and follow the mandate. I wouldn't go alone. I called Tiffany as soon as Michael left for work the next morning and asked her to go to Bainbridge Island to check out the address with me. We arranged to meet at the studio after Bella's vet appointment. I knew Michael would make me pay for the infraction later, but I chose to vacation in the land of self-righteous denial. I was simply protecting Michael from his own over-protectiveness. Right?

I fed Bella her enzyme-rich, finely blended gruel, then scooted off to her ten o'clock vet appointment. Bella made herself comfortable on the exam room's large, well-worn dog bed while her veterinarian spent a few minutes giving ear rubs and receiving dog kisses. After the requisite bonding, she started the examination.

"So, tell me what's going on with our girl?"

I listed Bella's symptoms: grumpiness, general malaise, rumbling stomach noises, excess gas, and digestive by-products so disgusting that only the owner of a dog with EPI could describe them without gagging.

As the veterinarian moved Bella's joints and looked in her ears, eyes, and mouth, she went over a list of potential triggers for an EPI flare-up: new food, untreated snacks, expired enzymes, insufficient food incubation, garbage can raids. The answer to each possible indiscretion was no, which wasn't surprising. If the trigger was one of the usual suspects, I would have figured it out already.

She jotted a few notes on a clipboard, then honed in on the symptom that had terrified me the most.

"I'm concerned that Bella snapped at your friend. You say that's unusual for her?"

"Bella is often reactive with strangers, but snapping at Sam? Yes. It's unheard of."

"Unusual aggression often indicates pain, but I didn't see any signs of pain in my examination."

Bella relaxed on her side and rested her chin on my thighs. "That's good, right?" I asked.

"Maybe. If it's not pain, it may be stress, which makes a lot of sense, considering the digestive upset. In my experience, dogs with EPI don't do well under stress. Could something be upsetting Bella? Maybe some changes to her environment?"

Two adorable fur-monsters scampered across my mind. I didn't reply, as if not uttering their names would magically make them irrelevant.

The vet furrowed her brow. "Kate?"

I knew she wouldn't approve, so I avoided eye contact and mumbled, "Michael and I are fostering two puppies."

The vet's furrowed brow disappeared, replaced by wide, horrified eyes. "Puppies?" Bella sat up and pricked her ears forward at the word. "What made you do a crazy thing like that? A dog-aggressive dog like Bella could easily hurt them."

"But she loves Mutt and Jeff!" I argued. "She hasn't so much as growled at them. In fact, they're the first dogs she's gotten along with."

The vet slowly shook her head. "That may well be true—for now. But dogs like Bella usually don't do well with canine siblings, especially puppies."

"Bella will adjust, right?"

The vet didn't reply, at least not at first. When she finally spoke, I wished she hadn't. "Kate, I might be wrong. You can certainly give the arrangement more time. I'll give you medicine for Bella's diarrhea and an herbal remedy for stress. I'm worried about the future, though. Puppy license doesn't last forever. Once the puppies become adolescents, the rules change pretty drastically."

"You don't think Bella would hurt them?"

She patted Bella's head, then slowly stood. "Honestly, I don't know. But I have to tell you, I've stitched up a lot of dogs in my time—many of whom were attacked by another dog in the same household. How big do you think the puppies will get?"

"Michael thinks they're medium-sized labradoodles."

She lifted her eyes toward the ceiling, calculating. "So when they're adults, they'll be thirty to forty-five pounds. Less than half of Bella's size." She shook her head. "That makes the risk significantly higher. Bella could hurt them without intending to."

I hid my tears by burying my face in Bella's fur.

"Kate, I'm sorry. I know this is hard to hear, but I have to be honest with you. Bella is not an ordinary dog. When those puppies hit adolescence, it might not be pretty. At the very least, you'll need to train them to have appropriate boundaries with her."

"So basically, you're saying we should give them away."

She didn't reply.

I felt my chin tremble. "I can't do that. Michael loves them. It would break his heart."

She hugged the clipboard against her chest. "Look, it's not my business to tell you what to do. Frankly, there are no easy answers. Why don't we see how things go for the next few weeks? In the meantime, we should assume that Bella has SIBO and get her started on antibiotics. She should start to improve in a day or two. If she doesn't, bring her back in. Keep her stress as low as possible."

I forced myself to smile as I paid for our visit, but by the time I reached my car, the tears I'd been hiding streamed down my cheeks. The vet was right. Bella was a good dog—a good mother. She'd suppressed her own needs to care for the puppies, and the effort had taken a toll.

Bella was miserable.

That's what my dream had been trying to tell me. Her metaphorical muscles were screaming, begging for someone to help her.

That someone had to be me.

Achy sadness gripped my throat. Michael had always planned to keep Mutt and Jeff. He was simply waiting for me to come around to the idea.

And I would have.

Now, I couldn't.

Bella's wellbeing had to come first. I loathed the thought of breaking Michael's heart almost as much as I loathed Bella's suffering. Hopefully Michael would see that. Hopefully he would agree. Hopefully, together, we'd find the puppies a fabulous home.

Hopefully.

Either way, it was time—past time—for Michael and I to be honest with each other. We had to figure out what to do with the pups.

I kneeled next to Bella, touched her nose with my own, and made her a promise.

"Don't worry, sweetie. I'll carry you anywhere."

TWENTY

TIFFANY WAS IMPATIENTLY WAITING in front of Serenity Yoga when I arrived. She hopped into the passenger seat wearing black yoga pants, a skin-tight solid black T-shirt, black Birkenstocks, and a black head band. The yoga equivalent of a cat burglar.

"You know it's daytime, right?" I asked.

"The camouflage yoga pants I ordered haven't come in yet."

"We're not burglars, Tiffany. We're just going to check out the address."

She rolled her eyes. "Whatever." She reached over the seat back and tossed Bella a cookie.

"Don't feed her without my permission," I snapped. "Bella already has enough stomach troubles."

Tiffany jolted as if I'd slapped her. "I always give her these cookies." She stared out the passenger-side window. "Sheesh. Someone's in a bad mood today."

I felt like a jerk—which made sense, since I'd just acted like one. "I'm sorry, Tiffany. I'm having a bad day, but I shouldn't take it out on you." I told her about Bella's recent illness, our vet visit, and what it meant for Mutt and Jeff. "I don't suppose you'd like to adopt two puppies…"

"I wish. I can't have pets in my apartment." She nibbled on a black-lacquered thumbnail. "You probably don't want to hear this right now, but Michael's planning to keep those dogs. He's been waiting for the right time to tell you."

I closed my eyes and rubbed my forehead. "I know." My eyes welled up again. "Honestly? I thought we'd end up keeping them, too."

We drove in silence the rest of the way to the downtown Seattle ferry terminal. I paid for our car at the ticket window and parked in the crowded waiting area.

"Did that ticket seriously cost thirty-five dollars?" Tiffany exclaimed. "How do people afford to ride the ferry to work every day?"

"I assume they buy commuter cards, but it's still expensive." I shrugged. "At least the ticket was round-trip."

Twenty minutes later, we drove onto the car deck and parked. I rolled the windows down a few inches and filled Bella's water bowl. "We'll take you for another walk when we get to the island, sweetie."

Bella's ears briefly perked up at the W-word, but they relaxed to bored-dog level when I didn't clip on her leash. She placed her head between her paws and settled in for a nap.

"We've got twenty-five minutes," I said to Tiffany. "Let's go upstairs." We grabbed coffee in the galley, went outside to the viewing deck, and watched the downtown Seattle skyline fade into the distance.

"Is it always this exciting?" Tiffany asked.

"Riding the ferry?"

"No! Following clues to a murderer!" Tiffany gesticulated wildly, sprinkling bitter, caffeinated raindrops across the deck. She tossed the cup in a garbage can and kept talking. "Today's excursion may be no big deal to you, but I'm a sleuthing virgin. I'm so pumped I'm about to crawl out of my skin. The only thing more exciting is my six o'clock smoothie date with Chad."

I would have assured Tiffany that there was no such thing as "always" for me when it came to sniffing out murderers, but I'd have been lying. This was, after all, the fourth time I'd found myself trailing a killer.

"This isn't exciting for me at all, Tiffany. It's nerve-racking. Frankly, I wish you weren't excited, either. Excitement makes people reckless. If we get into trouble, the next murder you'll be solving is mine. Michael's going to be mad enough as it is."

"So what's the plan?"

"Honestly, I'm not sure. We'll drive to the address and see if we can find this mysterious shed."

"Maybe the person who left the note will be there."

The thought sent chills from my scalp to my toenails. I was convinced the note was a clue, but I had no idea who'd placed it on my windshield. For all I knew it had been left by the murderer, trying to lead me off track.

"I doubt it," I replied. "Whoever wrote the note obviously wants to remain anonymous. If someone's at the address when we get there, don't mention the shed. I'll come up with a cover story."

Tiffany grinned. "We're like an improv duo. Cool!"

"Trio," I corrected. "Whatever we do, Bella's coming with us. She'll keep us safe."

"It's too bad they don't allow dogs off the car deck. Bella would love it up here."

Tiffany and I breathed in the cool, mist-sprinkled breeze and gazed at the horizon until Seattle's gray skyscrapers disappeared, replaced by the emerald green forests of Bainbridge Island. A disembodied voice announced over the PA system that it was time to return to our vehicles. Ten minutes later, Tiffany programmed the mystery address into her smart phone's GPS as I drove off the ferry. Before I knew it, we'd driven past the outskirts of the island's main town of Winslow and were headed down Highway 305 toward West Port Madison.

Expensive ferry rides notwithstanding, I could see why many of Bainbridge Island's twenty-three thousand residents endured the hour-long commute to and from Seattle each day. The two-lane highway wound through walls of evergreen trees so dense, you could easily forget you were in civilization. I felt isolated—in a good way. From stress, from violence, from the constant buzz of Seattle's urban energy. By the time the voice on Tiffany's GPS announced that we had arrived at our destination, I wished I could call this place home.

Not that I could have afforded it.

Every room of the address's huge, single-story house had an unobstructed Puget Sound view. The nearest neighbor (at least a city block away) was hidden by dense vegetation, and the four-car garage had twice the footprint of my tiny two-story home.

I drove to a turnout half a mile past the property and turned off the ignition. Bella whined and pressed her nose to the window. After clipping the leash to her collar, I folded down the front seat. "Come on out, sweetie." She immediately relieved herself next to the tire, replacing the resinous, woody scent of pine with something significantly less pleasant.

Tiffany plugged her nose with her thumb and her index finger. "Ewwwww."

"I know. It's pretty disgusting, poor thing. Hopefully the antibiotics will kick in soon." I cleaned up the mess and started walking.

"Come on. Let's check out the property. If we see someone, tell them we're searching for a lost dog. That way we'll have an excuse for looking around."

"Gretel."

"What?"

"The missing dog's name is Gretel. She's a German shepherd with the same coloring as Bella, only she's normal size." Tiffany gestured to her shirt. "She's wearing a black collar, to match my outfit."

I pointed at Tiffany's fingernails. "Did you paint her claws black, too?"

She pursed her lips and peered at the sky, thinking. "I wonder … " She glanced at Bella's feet and scowled. "You're messing with me. Their toenails are already black!"

I grinned. "Just checking. You seem to know a lot of details."

"You're not a very good liar. Details are important!" Her face turned red. "Not that I've had any practice."

"Uh huh. Let me do the talking, okay?"

The three of us hiked along the road until we reached the home's long, curved driveway. Tiffany pressed her face up to one of the garage's half-moon-shaped windows. "I see a bunch of tools and a big riding lawn mower, but no cars. Maybe no one's home."

"We should knock, just in case." I handed Tiffany the leash. "Keep Bella back here, out of striking range. She's grumpier than normal. If someone answers, she might give them a nose-ectomy."

I climbed the three steps to the front entrance, rang the doorbell, and counted to thirty. Then I rang it again. No answer. "You're right. No one's home. Let's check out the yard. Act worried. Remember, we're looking for your lost dog."

"Gretel. She's wearing a black collar. No tags 'cuz she's micro-chipped."

"Whatever."

We meandered around the property, trying to act like we belonged there. Bella sniffed every bush while Tiffany pretended to search for her imaginary dog. The back side of the partially fenced yard was bordered by a cliff with a stunning ocean view. A steep path led from the cliff to the beach. The rest of the multi-acre property contained a cleared area of green space with a swimming pool, a tennis court, and a small yellow outbuilding.

"That must be the shed," Tiffany said. "What do you think's in there?"

"I have no idea, but I'd sure like to find out." I pointed to the shed's entrance. "I'll see if the door is locked. Why don't you check out the back?"

While Tiffany tiptoed around back, I tried—unsuccessfully—to peer through the closed blinds in front. I jiggled the doorknob. Locked.

"Psssst! Kate!" Tiffany peeked around the corner. "The window back here is partially open. I think I can crawl through it. Want me to give it a try?"

The trio of disapproving men in my head yelled in unison, *Absolutely not!*

John ordered me to stay out of trouble.

Dad reminded me that breaking and entering was illegal, and that the last time I'd done it, I'd almost been killed.

Michael added that Tiffany had a record. A new offense would land her in prison.

Rene's voice vetoed all of them. *Go for it!*

"Do it," I answered. "I'll keep watch."

Sorry, guys.

Bella stood guard while I nervously scanned for nosy neighbors and returning homeowners. I heard a soft grunt, then a swear word. Then the sound of breaking glass.

I yelled in a whisper, "What happened? Are you all right?"

"I'm fine," Tiffany whisper-yelled back. "I couldn't fit through the opening. It was stuck, so I had to break the window."

All three men in my head groaned.

"You weren't supposed to ... oh, never mind."

Less than a minute later, Tiffany cracked open the door. Her face was pale; her expression, grim. "You need to come in here, Kate, but you can't bring Bella." She pointed to a water faucet. "Tie her to the spigot." Her eyes begged me not to argue.

I fastened Bella's leash to the water faucet, ordered her to stay, and prayed for her to obey. Tiffany pushed open the door. "I'll look for a light switch." She swallowed hard. "Prepare yourself."

The smell that hit me when I entered the shed was so foul, it felt like a physical blow. The dark building was filled with cages. Filthy cages. Empty, thank goodness. Any animals that had once been inside them were gone.

Tiffany turned on the light.

Except one.

An emaciated yellow dog cowered in the cage farthest from the door. She was disheveled and terrified; likely covered in fleas. A week's worth of feces piled in the cage around her. From the size of the dog's mammary glands, she'd recently nursed puppies.

The note was from Momma Bird.

We'd followed a clue, all right. To the wrong crime. Momma Bird had left directions to Mutt and Jeff's mother.

Tiffany kneeled in front of the cage and whispered, "It's okay, baby. Don't be scared. We won't hurt you." Her eyes met mine. "I saw her when I was messing with the window. I had to break in."

"I would have done the same thing." I lifted the padlock attached to the cage. "I don't think we can get her out."

Tears pooled behind Tiffany's lashes. "Kate, we can't leave her here."

I pulled out my cell phone. "We're not going to. I'm calling in reinforcements."

"Michael?"

"No. Better."

If anybody knew how to kidnap a dog from a puppy mill, it would be Betty from Fido's Last Chance. She'd devoted most of her six-decade life to saving dogs in distress.

Fortunately, I had her number programmed on speed dial.

TWENTY-ONE

AT FOUR O'CLOCK, TIFFANY started to get restless. By four-thirty, she was positively agitated. She paced back and forth. She looked at her watch at least five times a minute. She tapped her fingers on my car's hood and kicked at the bumper. "How much longer until your friend gets here?"

"I don't know. When I called her, she said she'd leave right away, but Maple Valley is an hour from Seattle, and then she has to catch the ferry."

"What if she drove by already and we missed her?"

"I don't see how that could happen. I told her where we were parked and she knows my car." My Honda was the only vehicle parked on the abandoned road. "We're not exactly inconspicuous." I consulted the ferry schedule. "You need to learn patience. If Betty made the 3:45 sailing, she should be here any time. Otherwise it could be another hour."

Tiffany groaned.

"Got someplace better to be?"

She lowered her chin, then gazed up at me through her lashes. "My smoothie date with Chad."

I should have guessed. With Tiffany, drama was always about a boy. She went through more boyfriends than Rene did peanut butter cups. This time, though, she seemed truly bereft. Could Chad be different?

I shaded my eyes with my hand and peered down the street for the five-hundredth time. Betty's white, 1990s-era Toyota 4Runner finally rounded the corner. I handed Tiffany my car keys.

"That's Betty now. Load Bella into my car and take her back to the studio. If you hurry, you should be back in Seattle in plenty of time for your date. Tell Michael the truth about what happened, but if anyone else asks—including Chad—you didn't break into the shed. I did. In fact, you tried to talk me out of it."

"You seriously want Michael to know that we did this?"

"Not really, but I'll have to tell him eventually anyway." I motioned for Betty to pull over, then turned back to Tiffany. "I don't know how long I'll be stuck here, so tell Michael to pick up the puppies from Rene and take Bella home."

"How will *you* get home?"

"Hopefully I'll be able to catch a ride with Betty to the studio. Worst case, I'll take a taxi home from her rescue in Maple Valley."

Tiffany looked conflicted. "I feel bad stranding you here."

"I'm not stranded, I'm with Betty. Now go." I squeezed her arm. "You did a good thing here today."

Tiffany trotted to my car looking so happy, I was surprised she didn't belt out a show tune. She quickly loaded Bella into the back seat of my Honda and peeled off for the ferry. I strode over to Betty's SUV, pointed down the road, and spoke into her open window.

"The shed with the dog is about a half-mile that way."

I nodded to the mid-thirties African-American man seated in the passenger seat. His biceps bulged underneath a white, untucked T-shirt, and his muscular body looked uncomfortably crowded even in the large passenger space. I couldn't be sure, but I suspected his height topped six feet by several inches.

Betty tilted her head his direction.

"This is Jamar. He's our muscle today."

I reached through the window and offered my hand. "Thanks for helping. It's nice to meet you." He replied with a firm shake but said nothing. I gave Betty a questioning look.

"Jamar doesn't say much. Hop in and take us to the dog."

I climbed into the seat behind Betty and directed them to the house's curved driveway. Betty stopped in front of the garage and set the parking break.

"Shouldn't we hide the vehicle somewhere?" I asked.

"Absolutely not," Betty replied.

"What if someone comes back?"

She pointed her thumb at her friend. "That's what Jamar is for."

Betty was running this show, so I didn't argue. Still, parking in plain sight didn't seem like the best shed-prowling strategy, even for a not-always-competent sleuth like me. Jamar opened the back of Betty's SUV and retrieved a metal water bowl and a large bolt cutter. The three of us strode purposefully to the shed.

"Prepare yourselves," I said. "The smell's pretty bad in there."

Jamar opened the door and muttered a string of swear words under his breath. Muscles on both sides of Betty's jaw twitched. She kneeled in front of the dog's cage.

"Hey there, Mama. Don't you worry, we'll have you out of there in no time." She gestured toward the lock and spoke to Jamar without inflection. "Do it." She handed me the water bowl. "Go fill this from the faucet outside."

By the time I returned, Betty had coaxed the ultra-thin animal out of her cage. She cautiously sniffed Betty's outstretched fingers. Betty pulled a piece of jerky from her pocket and reached toward her. The dog flinched, then slinked forward and snatched the food from Betty's hand. I set the water bowl on the ground and slid it in the animal's direction. She buried her face in it and began drinking thirstily.

"The cretin didn't even have water in that cage." Betty's tone held no possibility of forgiveness. "Jamar, take the dog back to my truck and make sure that she's safe to travel."

Jamar gently gathered the dog in his thick arms and carried her across the yard, replacing his earlier swear words with whispered assurances. The dog responded by licking his face and nibbling treats from his huge fingers.

Betty stared around the filthy room, as if memorizing it and trying to forget it at the same time.

I placed my hand on her arm. "We should get out of here."

She picked up the bolt cutter, dumped the water out of the bowl, and motioned for me to follow. She grumbled as we crossed the wide expanse of grass. "I don't understand people. All this beauty, all this space, and they locked her up in a stinking three-by-five cage. This place should have been a dog paradise, not a torture chamber."

"How many animals do you think they had in there?"

"I counted thirty cages, but I'm betting there were more dogs than that. I don't want to think about what happened to the rest."

Neither did I.

By the time we reached the house, Jamar had placed the dog in a shady spot near the driveway and was gently palpating her abdomen.

Betty said something to him that I couldn't hear, then nodded and walked back to her SUV. Jamar didn't follow.

"What do we do now?" I asked.

She opened the driver's side door. "We wait."

"Shouldn't we leave before the owners come home? I'd like to be somewhere else before they find out that I broke into their shed. Like Alaska."

"We're not leaving until I talk to the sad excuse for a human being who's responsible for that hellhole." The look she gave me was clear. There would be no further discussion.

I joined her in the front seat of the 4Runner and watched out the window as Jamar fed and examined the timid animal. I turned to Betty. "That dog's a yellow lab, right?" I asked.

"Yep. A small one."

"The puppies Michael and I are fostering are medium-size labradoodles. Could she be their mother?"

"Labradoodles." Betty grunted. "Figures. Every backyard breeder in Washington produces designer mutts these days. They mate pet-quality labs like that one with a small poodle and sell the pups for twenty-five hundred dollars a pop."

"Twenty-five hundred dollars? Apiece?"

"You think that's expensive? That's just the start of the money people spend when they buy designer puppy-mill dogs. Lord knows what kind of health problems those animals will have. You can bet the so-called breeder didn't do any genetic screening. Sad how easy it is for them to take advantage of people. The breed's not recognized by the AKC, so there's no paper trail."

I shook my head. "That's not what I meant. If the puppies are worth twenty-five hundred dollars apiece, it shouldn't be hard to find them a home." I filled Betty in on Bella's digestive upset and my newest puppy dilemma. "I know you usually work with hard-to-place dogs, but you'll have the mother. Can you keep the puppies with her and rehome them through Fido's Last Chance?"

"How old did you say they were?"

"We don't know for sure, but we suspect around seven weeks now. Michael doesn't want to send them to a shelter for adoption because they're not vaccinated yet, but I don't think we have another option."

Betty frowned. "He's right to be worried. I wouldn't put puppies that age in a shelter, either." She stared at Jamar and the lab for several seconds, seemingly conflicted. After what felt like a century, she looked back at me. "My foster homes are all full, but we sometimes make exceptions for puppies. I'm sure we can help you out if you need us to."

I didn't realize how worried I'd been until I felt my body relax. I slumped back into the seat and released a deep breath. "Thank you, Betty. You have no idea how much that would mean to us. Hopefully it won't take long to find a permanent home that wants both puppies."

The muscles around Betty's eyes tightened. "Sorry, Kate. If I take them in, I'll adopt them out separately."

"Separately?" Separating Mutt and Jeff seemed inconceivable. "Why? Would it be that much harder to find a home for both of them together?"

"Yes, but that's not the problem. I only place a dog if I'm sure it's not coming back."

"I don't get it."

Betty sat up straight and turned ninety degrees to face me. "I could find a home for the two puppies together without that much difficulty. *Keeping* them in it—that's the challenge. How much trouble have those puppies given you already?"

I flashed on destroyed gardens, shredded pillows, and puppy-pellet-filled tennis shoes.

"A little."

"Believe me, it's going to get a lot worse when they hit adolescence. Trainers have a term for it: littermate syndrome."

"Littermate syndrome?"

"Littermates adopted out together bond more with each other than they do with their owners. They can be downright impossible to train." She frowned. "I'm not saying it can't be done. The owner has to spend time with each puppy individually and take them to separate obedience classes. With a lot of work, they can end up being downright great dogs."

"So what's the problem? We just need to find someone willing to train them."

"Honey, that's a big 'just.' Most people don't adequately train *one* dog, let alone two. People see cute little puppies like yours and their brains shut right off. They con themselves into believing that two dogs will be easier than one." She snorted. "Tell that to your friend a few weeks after those twins of hers are born. When the dogs reach adolescence or start being destructive, their so-called families slap them with an invisible 'return to sender' label and bring them right back. Then the dogs have one strike against them and are even harder to place the next time."

"So you won't help?" The distressed expression I wore was genuine.

"Guilt trips don't work with me, Kate. If you want to place those dogs together, I'll help you evaluate potential homes. But I will not adopt out puppy littermates through Fido's Last Chance. Not unless I personally know the family and am certain that they'll stick it out through the tough times. You shouldn't either. It's not in the puppies' best interests."

"You don't know anyone who would qualify?"

"Other than you? No one that doesn't already own more dogs than are legally allowed." She placed her hand on my shoulder. "I'm sorry, Kate. Truly, I am. When you've been in this business as long as I have, you know when to make the tough decisions."

I didn't like her words. I didn't like them one bit. But I had to admit, she might be right. The puppies had been a handful, even for Michael and me.

Jamar knocked on Betty's window and gestured with his chin toward the road. Then he opened the SUV's side door and gently placed the dog on the back seat.

Betty glanced in her rearview mirror. "Heads up, Kate. The prison warden is home."

We opened our doors and joined Jamar outside.

A black BMW with the vanity plates *INVITRO* parked next to the SUV. I glanced at the driver, then did a double take.

It can't be.

Dr. Steinman—Dr. Dick's business partner at Reproductive Associates—eased out from behind the wheel. He approached Betty wearing a curious expression. "Can I help you?"

His eyes shifted toward Jamar. Curiosity shrank to wariness.

Then his gaze landed on me.

Wariness exploded in fury. His face turned so red it was practically purple. He charged toward me, yelling. "What kind of a scam are you pulling? First you show up at my clinic under false pretenses. Now you're at my home? I ought to call the police."

Jamar stepped between us, wearing the same fierce expression Bella wore when she blocked me from danger.

"I'd back off if I were you," Betty said. A small vein throbbed in Dr. Steinman's forehead, but he took three steps back.

Betty continued. "If anybody's calling the police, it's us."

"About what?" he snarled.

Betty pointed toward her car. "About your dog."

Dr. Steinman edged next to Betty's SUV and glanced into the back seat. His hands formed tight fists. "What are you doing with my property?"

I opened my mouth to reply, but Betty shoved her palm in my face. "I've got this, Kate." She turned back to Dr. Steinman. "The more important question is, what are *you* doing with your so-called property?" She made finger quotes around the last word. "That dog was locked in a cage, covered in her own filth, without any food or water. That's animal abuse. I could get you tossed in jail."

I had a feeling that Betty was overstating her position. If his home was any indication, Dr. Steinman could hire a bevy of attorneys. As disgusting as his crime was, I doubted he'd ever get within a thousand feet of a jail cell.

"You're the ones who should be tossed in jail," he hissed. "You obviously trespassed on my property and broke into my shed. Lord knows what else you've stolen from me." He pointed at me. "Before I call the police, tell me: who are you, really, and why are you harassing me?"

Betty stood tall, taking full advantage of her five-foot-four-inch frame. "Kate's not the one harassing you. *I* am. I'm an animal welfare advocate. Kate learned that a dog was being abused at this address and asked me to investigate. I did. Lo and behold, she was right. Wasn't she, Jamar?"

Jamar grunted.

"We saw that the animal was starving and had no access to water. It was in imminent danger, so we broke into your shed to take care of it. After giving it the care it needed, we waited for you." She pointed to her friend. "Jamar and I, we're not thieves. We don't steal anything—not even abused animals—no matter how much we want to." She smiled, but the expression looked more threatening than friendly. "Which is why you're going to *give* us this dog. Then we'll call it good."

"It's not my dog. It belongs to my son."

Betty planted her feet wide. "Then I guess we'll have to wait for him."

"You'll be here awhile," Dr. Steinman scoffed. "The idiot got arrested for dealing drugs again. No way am I bailing him out this time. He can rot in prison for all I care."

"He left you his dog?" Betty asked.

"You could say that. The fool convinced me a few months ago that he could make easy money breeding designer mutts. All I needed to do was lend him my shed. I thought he was showing some initiative for once, so I said yes. I should have known better."

I didn't say it, but torturing and breeding unhealthy dogs didn't sound like the kind of initiative that should be encouraged—or enabled, for that matter.

Dr. Steinman continued. "I hired someone to dump the mangy things at the pound two weeks ago, but my son's crack-head girlfriend called and begged me to keep the one with the puppies. She said she was going sell them for bail money as soon as they were old enough."

Betty didn't say anything, but her body was so rigid, it could have been carved from ice. Dr. Steinman kept talking. "Too bad for her, she OD'd again and is stuck in rehab. I was going to sell the puppies anyway, but someone stole them last week." He gestured toward Betty's SUV. "That one was headed for the pound tomorrow." He narrowed his eyes for a moment, then widened them again in sudden understanding. "Wait a minute . . . " He grabbed my wrist and snarled, "*You* stole those puppies, didn't you?"

I yanked it away. "No. I didn't."

Betty stepped between us. "It doesn't matter who took them. They're gone, and you're not getting them back."

"This is ridiculous. I'm calling the police." Dr. Steinman spun toward the house and stomped away.

Crap.

I wanted to chase after him, but my feet were super-glued to the driveway. My heart, on the other hand, did back flips. If Dr. Steinman made that call, I'd spend the night in a jail cell for sure. Which would be significantly more pleasant than facing Michael after he bailed me out in the morning.

I had to stop him, but how? Begging for mercy would be useless. Having Jamar tackle him while I ripped out the property's phone lines wouldn't work much better. I finally leveled the one threat I thought Dr. Steinman might understand.

"I wonder what your patients—your so-called *extended family*—will do when they find out you're an animal abuser?"

He froze.

"Especially when we start posting the pictures," Betty added.

Pictures?

Taking photographs would have been brilliant. And brilliant, I wasn't. The only pictures I had were the ones indelibly seared in my memory. Betty was a better con artist than I'd realized.

Dr. Steinman slowly turned around. "I told you, the dogs weren't mine. They belonged to my son."

"I doubt your clients will see much of a difference," I replied. "You allowed the abuse to happen, and on your property. Besides, your son is in jail now. That poor lab's condition is solely on you."

"The newspapers won't see a difference, either," Betty added. "Frankly, I'd like nothing better than to report you to the ASPCA and let you deal with the fallout." She shrugged. "I still may." Her lips pressed into a thin line. "Problem is, they'll just slap you with a fine. You've got too much money for that to be a deterrent. You'll pay up. You'll hire someone to deal with the PR disaster. Then you'll forget all about it. Someday your son will get out of jail. He might even convince you to try something like this again..."

She stared at Dr. Steinman for several long seconds, then lowered her voice menacingly. "Nope. There's only one way to deal with scumbags like you."

My heart stopped back flipping and dropped to my stomach. Betty's threats were making me distinctly uneasy. I grabbed her arm. "Betty, he won't call the police. He won't risk ruining his practice. We've got the dog. Let's go."

She yanked her arm back, never taking her eyes off Dr. Steinman. "Not yet, Kate. I'm talking to this..." She paused a beat. "Gentleman." She took several slow, menacing steps forward until her nose was inches from his. "Let me make myself clear. Breeding dogs again would be a *very* bad idea."

She pointed to Jamar, who still leaned against the SUV, glowering. "My buddy Jamar doesn't talk much, so I'll do it for him. We go way back, to when I helped run a dog training program at Monroe." I assumed she meant the Monroe Correctional Complex, a Washington State prison that housed violent inmates. She cocked her head to the side, as if thinking. "I forget now, Jamar. What were you in for? Assault? Robbery?"

Jamar's voice contained no inflection. "Attempted murder."

"That's right, attempted murder. Nearly ripped a man's head right off his shoulders."

Dr. Steinman winced. Then again, so did I.

"You're still in touch with your friends from the old days, right Jamar?" Betty asked.

"Yep."

My uneasiness deepened to dread. "Betty, this has gone far—"

"Quiet!" she snapped. "I'm having a conversation here." Her eyes were so cold, I almost didn't recognize her. "Back. Off."

I stopped talking, but I wasn't happy. I wanted to save the dog as much as anybody. But not at the expense of getting someone—even an animal abusing jerk like Dr. Steinman—hurt.

Betty continued. "Here's the thing about ex-cons, especially the ones who've graduated from my program. The only people they hate worse than child rapists are animal abusers. Isn't that right Jamar?"

"Yep." His upper lip twitched.

"And now, they'll be watching you. So when you or that loser son of yours get to thinking that you might want to make a quick buck selling puppies—heck, even if you get a hankering to adopt some cute little mutt of your very own—you might want to reconsider. Jamar and his friends will be checking on you. If they find out that you have a dog—any dog—they might not take it too kindly."

Dr. Steinman's voice sounded fierce, but his hands trembled. "Are you threatening me?"

"Threatening you?" Betty placed her hand flat on her chest. "A little old lady like me threatening a big, powerful, rich man like you?" She scoffed. "That's preposterous."

She lowered her voice to almost a whisper. "Jamar, though, he's sensitive. Hates it when I get upset. And nothing gets my granny panties in a bunch faster than arguing with greedy puppy-mill breeders."

Dr. Steinman shrank.

Betty seemed to grow three inches taller. "Now, Jamar and I are gonna take this dog, and we're gonna do right by her. We'll make sure she never sees your scummy face again. In exchange, you're going to make a huge donation to the Humane Society. I'd ask you to donate to my rescue, but I don't want your filthy money."

Jamar stepped next to Betty. "You'd best be believing the lady. You will *not* be getting any more dogs. You hearing me?" He cracked the knuckles on both hands. "'Cuz I'd hate to have to come back here and remind you."

Dr. Steinman gave a single nod yes.

Betty gave him a not-all-that-friendly slap on the back. "Well, that's just peachy. It's good to have everybody on the same page." She winked. "So glad we had this little talk." As she sauntered back to the 4Runner, she called, "Come along, Kate. We're done here."

Dr. Steinman's skin was still green when we pulled out of the driveway, which wasn't surprising. I felt like I'd been sucker punched, too. Betty, Jamar, and I drove in silence for about five minutes before I found the courage to speak.

"Betty, you weren't serious back there, were you? I don't like Dr. Steinman either, but I don't want him hurt."

"Settle down, Kate. You worry too much. No one's going to hurt that SOB. They won't have to." Betty made eye contact with Jamar in the rear view mirror and winked.

I narrowed my eyes at her, then leaned over to look in the back seat.

Jamar tenderly rubbed the Labrador's ears, wearing a huge grin. "We sure had him going though, didn't we?" he said. "That guy totally bought that I was an ex-con."

Now *I* was confused. "Wait a minute. You mean you're not?"

Betty chastised me. "Kate! I'm surprised at you. Do you think every black man is some sort of criminal?"

Only when you tell me they are.

Betty continued talking. "I babysat Jamie here from the time he was six. Helping me nurse my foster dogs is probably what made him want to go to vet school. He's never gotten so much as a parking ticket."

"Jamie?" I gave her a droll look.

Jamie reached through the bucket seats and handed me a business card. *Puget Sound Mobile Veterinary Services. Jamie Butler, DVM.*

"Jamar's my given name," he said, "but I go by Jamie. Betty thought Jamar would work better today." He lowered his voice and put on a tough expression. "Sound's more gangsta." He chuckled. "You totally bought it, didn't you?"

My cheeks grew warm. "You two could have filled me in on your little charade. Now I feel like an idiot."

"Sorry about that," Betty said. "Our Punch and Judy routine works better if we're the only ones in on it. Adds to the authenticity."

"You've done this before?"

"Let's just say this isn't the first dog I've grabbed from a puppy-mill operator. Jamie pretty much always comes with me. Cowardly scumbags respond best to intimidation. And Jamie here's a darned good actor."

He sure fooled me.

I addressed Jamie directly. "What about your supposed friends?"

"Most of my buddies love animals as much as I do. I'll get a couple of guys to drive by the property every now and again. Maybe park across the street, smile and wave. It's a sad fact of our country, Kate, but being black is often all it takes to intimidate. If my friends *do* see dogs on the property, Betty and I will call Animal Control."

I looked at the Labrador, who was now sleeping with her head in Jamie's lap. "So you're a veterinarian. That explains why you were looking at her so carefully. Do you think she's going to be okay?"

He gently rubbed her neck. "I'll do a more thorough examination when we get her to Betty's, but I think so. She's dehydrated, malnourished, and infested with fleas, and she desperately needs a good grooming. I suspect she's got a reasonable skin infection brewing underneath all of that filth, but I haven't seen anything too alarming so far."

I wasn't sure how to feel about Betty's deception: angry, impressed, shocked, or disturbed. I settled on grateful.

"Thank you—both of you—for coming all the way out here to help me." I nodded toward the lab. "And especially for helping her."

"Not a problem," Betty replied. "Any time."

"Hopefully there won't be another time," I replied. "I don't think my heart can take it."

Betty replied in a matter-of-fact tone. "Of course there will be. Face it, Kate. You find needy animals almost as often as you stumble over dead bodies."

I couldn't bring myself to admit she was right.

TWENTY-TWO

BETTY AND JAMIE CHATTED amiably the rest of the hour-long trip back to the studio. I slumped silently in the passenger seat, second-guessing myself. When I'd first seen the dog inside Dr. Steinman's shed, I'd immediately assumed Momma Bird was the one who'd left the note on my car, hoping that I'd be curious enough to go to Bainbridge Island, find the yellow lab, and rescue her.

Now I wasn't so sure.

Momma Bird taking a trip to Bainbridge Island, that I could believe. She was homeless, but she still might own a car. If not, a bus ride and a walk-on ferry ticket would have gotten her there. I could imagine her learning about the backyard breeding operation some-how—maybe through Dr. Steinman's drug-dealing son or his girl-friend—though that was more of a stretch. I could even imagine her rescuing the puppies.

But she'd never skulk around leaving notes on parked cars. Momma Bird wasn't one for subterfuge. If she'd wanted to sic me on

Dr. Steinman, she'd have told me about him face-to-face, likely conning me out of at least twenty dollars in the process.

So who'd really left the note? Michael had canvassed the neighborhood trying to find Mutt and Jeff's owner. I'd asked most of my yoga students about them as well. Did someone we'd spoken to leave the note on my car? If so, why not simply talk to us?

Then again, maybe the note had nothing to do with the dogs. Betty and I assumed that the Labrador was Mutt and Jeff's mother, but that was pure conjecture. Maybe my original assumption had been correct—maybe the note pointed to evidence about Dr. Dick's murder. If so, I'd totally blown it. The instant Tiffany and I found the dog, we shifted into rescue mode. Signed confessions could have wallpapered the shed and we wouldn't have noticed.

One thing was certain: I wouldn't win sleuth of the year any time soon. I couldn't go back and search the shed now, at least not without risking arrest. My next best option was to grill Momma Bird, though at the rate I was going, I'd have to hire a *real* detective to find her.

Luckily it didn't come to that.

When Betty dropped me off at the studio, Momma Bird was standing in front of the PhinneyWood Market selling the *Dollars for Change* newspaper. I said a quick goodbye to Betty and Jamie, asked them to keep me posted on the dog, and strode directly toward her.

Momma Bird wore one of her usual quirky outfits: neon green Crocs, a bright yellow muumuu with purple daisies, and a hat shaped like a pink flamingo. She held a stack of papers in one hand and a cup of coffee in the other. When she glanced my direction, her bright eyes sparkled with humor.

"Well hey there, Yogi Kate. Care to buy a *Dollars for Change* today?"

I handed her a dollar and took the paper.

"There's a great article on page two about Seattle's shortage of low-income housing," she said.

"Thanks. I'll read it later. I've been looking for you. Where have you been?"

Momma Bird tilted her head and peered at me shrewdly. "What are you, my parole officer?"

"No, but I've missed seeing you." The statement was true. "And I need to ask you some questions about something that happened last Thursday."

Her eyes shifted toward Pete's Pets, so quickly that I almost missed it. "What happened?"

"You left a box of puppies outside my boyfriend's store."

Momma Bird's jaw tightened. "I didn't leave nothing nowhere. Now if you'll excuse me, I have papers to sell." She turned her back to me and approached a woman pushing an empty shopping cart. "Care to buy a *Dollars for Change* today?" The woman rolled the cart past her without responding.

I kept talking. "My boyfriend saw you with the box in front of his store. So if you didn't leave it, you probably saw who did. We're not trying to get anyone in trouble. We just want to find out where the dogs came from."

She whipped back around, suddenly interested. "Ah, so you're solving a mystery again then, are you? The last time I helped you with a case, you paid me fifty dollars."

"It was forty dollars, and that was a murder, not a puppy dumping."

She waved a paper through the air. "Murder, abandonment, it's all the same to me. Time is money. If you can't afford to pay me, I have to get back to work." She walked toward an outdoor display of dark green watermelons, preparing to accost another shopper.

I pulled a ten-dollar bill from my pocket. "You win. I'll give you ten dollars for five minutes of your time." The pretend negotiation was part of Momma Bird's and my game. We both knew I'd always planned to give her the money.

She tucked the bill inside her bra and pointed to a bench near the bicycle rack. "Let's have a seat." Setting the papers on the ground, she slowly lowered herself onto the bench. "Don't know how much help I'll be. Like I told you last time, I try not to see too much in my line of work. It's not safe, you know?"

Déjà vu prickled the back of my neck. Momma Bird *had* said those words to me, a year ago when we spoke about George's murder. The exact same words that the *Dollars for Change* vendor had said in my dream about Bella. Had my subconscious channeled the phrase for a reason?

I let her continue without interruption.

She pointed to Pete's Pets. "I did, however, happen to notice a woman—at least I think it was a woman—setting a box outside the pet store."

"What did she look like?"

"I didn't pay much attention. She wasn't thin like you, but she wasn't round like me, either. She wore black sweats and a hoodie pulled over her head. That's what made me notice her."

"Could you see her face?"

"Nah, like I said, the hood was up. It covered most of her face."

A child toddled up to the bench and handed Momma Bird a dollar. She gave him a paper and said, "Tell your mama thanks for me." He ran back to his mother, who smiled and waved.

"Anyway," Momma Bird continued, "I didn't think much of it at first. Figured she was making a delivery of some kind. But she started acting suspicious, looking over her shoulder like she was afraid someone was watching. She set the box down and scurried away."

Momma Bird took a swig of her coffee. "Now *that* got me curious. This is an okay neighborhood and all, but if you leave something valuable outside, it's gonna walk away. So I watched to see what would happen, you know?"

I nodded my head yes.

"I wasn't gonna steal that box, no matter what that boyfriend of yours thinks. But when I heard the whining, I figured there was something alive inside." She lifted her chin. "I had to open it. I couldn't leave it there knowing there were animals inside that might suffocate."

"I'd have done the same thing. So would Michael."

"I barely got it open before your boyfriend started eyeballing me through the window. I didn't want no trouble, so I took off."

"Why didn't you stay?"

She shrugged. "I was afraid he'd accuse me of stealing. Not everyone takes kindly to a homeless woman digging through a box on their doorstep. Besides, the theater around the corner was about to let out. I make good money there."

"You sell papers in front of the theater?"

"You didn't think I came all the way from the U District to see you, did you?"

Embarrassingly enough, I had.

"Do you remember anything else that might identify the woman you saw?" I asked.

Momma Bird shook her head. "Sorry hon, I don't. And I'm not trying to shake you down for more money, either. I've got a soft spot for animals. Terrible thing to abandon them like that. Just terrible."

She picked up her papers, drained her coffee, and prepared to leave.

"I don't think I was all that much help to you, Yogi Kate."

I pulled another ten-dollar bill out of my pocket. "Before you go, I have one more question. Did you leave a note on my car yesterday?"

Momma Bird seemed confused. "A note? No. Why would I leave you a note when I can come talk to you?"

Why indeed.

I gave her the money. "It's not important. Thanks for your time."

She tucked the bill next to its twin, shuffled three steps away, then changed her mind. "You know, there *is* one more thing, now that I think about it. Probably doesn't mean anything…"

"What is it?"

"The woman who left the box was smoking one of those fake cigarettes."

An electricity-like jolt zapped down my spine.

An e-vape. Nicole.

Nicole was the puppy snatcher. She had to be.

It explained everything. Why she'd been late for the Yoga to Overcome Grief class, where she'd been with her mother's car, even why she'd stolen money from her stepfather's wallet. She needed cash to buy ferry tickets. It explained her actions last night, too. She hadn't gone to Tiffany's apartment after the Sound Bath—she'd finagled some alone-time to put a note on my car.

"She was smoking an e-vape?" I asked. "Are you sure?"

"Hon, I'm an ex-smoker. I can sniff out a *real* death stick a block away." She looked at me shrewdly. "That mean something to you?"

"I'm not positive, but I think the woman you saw was one of my students."

"Well, give her hell for me. Leaving those babies alone like that ain't right." She mumbled under her breath and shuffled away. "Ain't right at all."

I stared after Momma Bird, unsure how many mysteries my new insight had solved. Nicole left the puppies in front of Pete's Pets. I was sure of it. But why did she leave the note on my car? Was she trying to lead me to the puppies' mother or to a clue about her step-father's death?

Or were they one and the same?

Were the puppies and Dr. Dick's murder somehow connected? I asked myself the same questions over and over again, but I couldn't come up with an answer. The clues I'd uncovered about the two crimes were woven together like a poorly knitted sweater. I'd need to unlock the pattern before I could tease the strands apart.

The first step was to corner Nicole. I called and left a message on her cell phone, then hustled back to my car. The evening yoga teacher could close up shop without me. I needed to discuss this new information with Michael. I was so distracted, I'd already inserted my key into the ignition before I noticed the paper on my windshield.

Another note.

I slowly unfolded the creases. A lead weight dropped on my stomach.

Tiffany told me about your recent escapades. I've had enough. We need to talk.

It was signed *Michael.*

TWENTY-THREE

MICHAEL PACED BACK AND forth across the living room floor, so angry I was surprised he didn't spontaneously sprout a beard just to torment me. "It wasn't enough for you to break the law and put yourself in danger? You had to corrupt Tiffany, too?"

I flashed him my cutest, most mischievous grin. "Come on, Michael. That's not fair. Tiffany was corrupted long before I met her."

Suffice it to say, he wasn't amused.

"This isn't funny, Kate. You went to a medical clinic under false pretenses—which you promised me you wouldn't—then you broke into someone's property and stole a dog? Tiffany could do serious jail time with another offense." He stopped pacing and jabbed my chest with his index finger. "As for you … if you get arrested, I might not even bail you out. At least if you're locked in a jail cell, I'll know what you're up to." He recommenced pacing. "I'm not sure what to be maddest about: that you put yourself in danger, or that you broke your promise to me about going to the fertility clinic. Seriously, Kate. I've had enough."

I didn't blame Michael for being angry, but I was starting to get a little testy myself. My voice competed for volume with his. "Hold on there, mister, and cut back on the threats. Tiffany and I weren't in danger, and I didn't break any promises. I told you that I wouldn't go to the clinic alone, and I didn't. I didn't even make the appointment. Tiffany did." I crossed my arms and planted my feet wide. "You're the one who wanted me to spend more time with her. Well, I did. Deal with it."

"And I suppose it was an oversight that you didn't tell me about it."

"Not an oversight. Conflict avoidance. I was trying to avoid the very fight we're having now."

Michael and I glared at each other, each refusing to give ground. Each stupidly trying to prove who was alpha. The puppies cowered in the farthest corner of their ex-pen. Bella stepped between us and whined.

I took a deep breath and consciously lowered my volume. "We need to stop yelling. We're scaring the dogs." My voice quavered. "Are we breaking up?"

"Geez, Kate! No!" Michael's voice softened. "No." He took my hands. "Honey, couples fight. We'll fight. You can't be ready to jump ship every time we have an argument."

My eyes watered. "You said you'd had enough."

"I meant that I'd had enough of you sneaking around and doing stupid things behind my back. Not of you. Definitely not of us."

I bristled at the word "stupid," but I let it go. "Then can we please stop yelling at each other and talk? I need your help."

Michael closed his eyes for a long moment, then slowly relaxed his shoulders. "Let's sit." He led me to the couch, where we sat next to each other, knees touching.

"For the record," I said, "I didn't know Tiffany was going to break the shed's window until it was already done. And no one stole the dog. Dr. Steinman gave it to Betty."

"Why would he do that?"

I paused before answering. Michael would be furious if he learned about Betty and Jamie's ruse. "If I tell you what happened, you'll get mad. Can I just say it wasn't my idea and move on?"

Michael's shoulders tensed again, but he nodded his head yes.

"The good news is, I talked to Momma Bird and I think I know where the puppies came from." I filled him in on everything Momma Bird had told me and the semi-firm conclusions I'd reached. "I left a message on Nicole's cell, asking about the note, but she hasn't called back yet. I think she wanted me to find Mutt and Jeff's mother. But if I'm wrong and she was leading me to a clue about Dr. Dick's murder, Tiffany and I blew it. Once we saw the dog, all we thought about was saving her."

"Tell Martinez."

"Tell her what? That I broke into someone's private property, but I was too stupid to look for unspecified evidence that might not even exist? Come on, even *I* don't expect her to act on that information."

"You are *not* going back to that shed, Kate," Michael ordered.

I lifted my eyebrows and frowned.

"Fine," he replied. "How about you're not going back there without me?"

"Neither of us is going back until I talk to Nicole." I lowered my voice to a whisper, as if speaking the words softly would make them less real. "Michael, I think Nicole might have done it."

"Stolen the puppies? Probably. But at this point, who cares? I'm certainly not going to turn her in. Legally she may have committed a crime, but ethically? She seems like a hero to me."

"I agree, but I'm not talking about the dogs. I'm afraid that she might have killed her stepfather."

Michael looked confused. "How does anything you saw today indicate that?"

"It gives her more motive. You didn't see Dr. Dick the night Nicole stole his money. He threatened to send her away over fifty dollars. If he ever found out she'd stolen dogs worth five thousand dollars from his business partner, he'd have kicked her out for sure."

"I can't imagine dumping a kid over some rescued puppies."

"Me neither. But Nicole wasn't his daughter, and he didn't want her living with him in the first place. I got the feeling he was looking for an excuse to get rid of her." I slumped heavily into the couch cushion. "I'm not sure what to do. I hate to point Martinez toward Nicole without more information."

Michael sighed. "There's nothing we *can* do, at least not tonight." He stood. "It's late and I'm tired. Let's go to bed. Maybe we'll come up with a brilliant idea in the morning."

I remained sitting. "Honey, we need to talk about the puppies."

Michael sagged back down beside me. "Tiffany told me." He averted his eyes. "How could you tell *Tiffany* that we have to get rid of Mutt and Jeff before you told me?"

My heart deflated like a two-day-old balloon. *That's* why Michael was so upset. And he was right. He deserved to hear the bad news from me. More importantly, he deserved to hear it first.

"I'm so sorry, Michael. You're right. I should have talked it over with you before I told anyone else. I was upset, and Tiffany was there. I guess I needed some sympathy."

"You don't even *like* Tiffany."

I smiled. "That's where you're wrong. I *do* like her. I don't know when it happened, but your plan worked. Tiffany's not nearly as bad as I made her out to be." I circled the conversation back to the puppies. "The vet thinks Bella's digestive upset was triggered by stress—that she doesn't like living with other dogs."

Michael sighed. "Honestly, I'm not surprised. I started to wonder when she trapped the puppies outside."

"I know you wanted to keep them. I did too, but … " I couldn't finish the sentence.

"I get it, Kate. Bella's my dog now, too. She has to come first." He glanced at the ex-pen. "They're healthy enough to have their shots now. I'll call to make an appointment tomorrow." His lower lip trembled. "A couple of days after that, we'll take them to Betty's."

I glanced at the puppies, curled up together in a perfect yin-yang symbol. "There's something else." As I told Michael about Betty's littermate policy, his entire body seemed to grow small. He looked almost as stricken as he had the night of his father's car accident, before the doctors knew he'd pull through.

"I can't imagine separating them, Kate."

I leaned over and kissed his cheek. "I know. I can't either." I grabbed his hand and pulled him to standing. "Let's go to bed. We'll figure out something tomorrow. I promise."

The five of us retired to the bedroom in heartbreaking silence. When I fell asleep three hours later, Michael was still staring at the ceiling, both puppies curled up asleep on his chest.

———

Sleep provided no solutions. Michael dejectedly made an appointment for the pups' first round of vaccines. We agreed to give ourselves the weekend to come up with an alternative plan, then we'd turn Mutt and Jeff over to Betty. For today, they'd hang out with Aunt Rene and Uncle Sam.

The antibiotics had started to kick in, so Bella's digestive issues were blissfully waning. She was too stressed to stay home alone or hang out with the puppies, so Michael took her to work with him. He promised to park in my indoor parking spot and to take her for a walk every couple of hours. That left me free to focus my busy day on birth planning, mystery solving, and working with my clients at the Lake Washington Medical Center.

First up was wrangling Rene into finally creating her birth plan. I coached Mutt and Jeff as I carried them up the stairs to her front door. "Listen up, you two. No destructo-puppy antics today—at least not until after I leave. This is a business meeting. I have to focus."

I was surprisingly nervous about today's meeting. I had learned just enough in doula training to feel completely incompetent. The best I could do was talk Rene and Sam through a list of birthing options while not revealing my own preferences. Not that I had any yet.

Sam opened the door. The puppies wiggled out of my grasp and delightedly dive-bombed his shoes, growling and yanking at his laces.

"Come on you two, knock it off!" He swept them into his arms, carried them to the living room, and deposited them unceremoniously inside a child's playpen.

"Sam, they're not housetrained. If you plan to use that for the twins, I'd get them out of there. Pronto."

"It's not for the twins—it's for the fur balls. I bought it last night. It's super-portable but sturdy. I plan to trap the little destroyers inside, so they can be near us without causing trouble." He mistook my pained expression for disapproval. "Don't worry, Kate. They won't be stuck in it all day. I'll take them out every hour to play with them and give them a potty break."

"That's not it, Sam," I replied. "I'm grateful. It's just that the puppies won't be coming here much longer."

Sam's eyebrows narrowed. "Why not?"

A beach ball-sized lump formed in my throat. "Can we talk about it later? After the birth plan?"

Sam didn't look happy, but he acquiesced.

Rene peeked her head out from behind a fort-like pile of papers, fabric swatches, and catalogues stacked on the couch. "Sam was about to make my breakfast smoothie," she said. "Do you want one?"

Oh good lord, not another food fight.

I shook my finger at my friends like a grumpy old school marm. "Let's get one thing straight, you two. There will be no arguing over food this time." I gave them both a direct, Alpha Kate stare. "I mean it."

Rene flashed me her best impression of a submissive grin. "You don't need to worry about that, Kate. Sam and I had a long talk after that unfortunate incident at the hospital, and we realized that we were both acting silly."

"She's right," Sam replied. "I was so worried about the twins after Rene's premature labor scare that I went a little crazy. I wanted to keep everyone safe, you know? Dictating her diet made me feel in control."

"Well, I *am* a junk food addict, hon. Making sure the twins get adequate nutrition isn't all that silly." Rene swept the makings of Fort Baby into a pile and stacked them on the floor. "We came up with a compromise: I drink one of Sam's smoothies every day, and he allows me one junk food meal. My other six meals are up for negotiation."

Sam nodded his head like a mustached bobble head doll. "That way we're both equally unhappy."

Rene smiled at him sweetly, but I could have sworn that her right eyebrow twitched. "Honey, why don't you make that mondo-nutritious avocado-apple-dandelion smoothie you keep raving about? I'm sure Kate would like to try it, too."

I backed away from them both. "No thanks. I already had breakfast. I'm not hungry."

"Nonsense," Rene admonished. "It's liquid. It's not filling at all." She swished her hand through the air. "Hurry up, honey. I'm hungry." As Sam left for the kitchen, Rene wiggled her eyebrows at me and yelled, "Make Kate's a big one!"

A blender's ear-piercing screech sent sharp stabs of pain through my teeth. I leaned toward her and grumbled, "What are you up to?"

She picked up a magazine, licked her index finger, and flipped through it. "You'll see."

Sam returned three minutes later carrying two sixteen-ounce glasses of sludge the color of Aunt Rita's 1973 avocado-green refrigerator. It smelled like something left in her vegetable drawer the same year. He set one in front of Rene and handed the other to me.

"I've read that this recipe isn't as tasty as some, but it's packed with nutrients," Sam said.

I tipped my glass to the side. Foul-looking liquid adhered to the glass like a thick layer of pond scum.

"Go on," Rene said. "Give it a try. Smoothies taste best when they're cold."

Sam's eyes begged for validation. Rene's demanded revenge.

I closed my eyes, held my breath, and took a tentative sip. It was all I could do not to gag.

Rene took a sip of hers and offered pretend sympathy. "It has a little bit of a vomit aftertaste, but I'll bet you get used to it. It's probably better if you chug it straight down."

A little? Aftertaste?

The gelatinous goo tasted like something Bella would upchuck after raiding the garbage can. As for aftertaste, my tongue would still be polluted six days from now.

Rene has to drink these every day?

I mentally vowed to sneak in enough gummy bears to last until the twins started kindergarten.

She kept teasing. "And it provides so much energy, doesn't it Sam?"

Sam didn't answer. He looked so disappointed, I thought he might cry.

I considered taking a second drink in an offer of solidarity, but I couldn't. My jaw spasmed shut at the thought.

"Sam, maybe you should put some extra apple juice in Kate's drink. She's a smoothie virgin, after all." Rene's eyes followed her husband until he disappeared inside the kitchen. As soon as the blender started whirring again, she swung her legs to the floor, leaned over to the ficus tree, and poured a third of her drink into the soil. Then she glanced over her shoulder to make sure Sam wasn't watching, pulled a metal flask from her bra, and added two ounces of clear liquid to the goo.

I opened my mouth in horror. "Rene, you can't drink alcohol. You're pregnant!"

She placed her index finger against her lips. "Shhh, he'll hear you! It's not alcohol, silly. It's simple syrup. Put enough sweetener in this crap and it's almost drinkable." She pointed to the flask before nestling it between her breasts again. "I have to hide the syrup in this. The bottle it comes in won't fit in my bra."

I had to admit, this level of guilt-free deception was impressive, even for Rene.

"How are you getting simple syrup into the house? I thought Sam did all of the grocery shopping now that you're on modified bed rest."

"I called a grocery delivery service while he was at work the other day. You should see the junk food I have stashed in the twins' diaper pail."

I gave her a stern look.

"Come on, Kate. This arrangement serves all of us. It makes Sam happy. My lab tests are great, so it's not hurting the babies. And I feel guilty enough that I eat vegetables two meals a day now. I actually had oatmeal for my first breakfast this morning."

Who was I to argue?

Sam returned and handed me a now-more-diluted glass of pond scum. I picked it up and barely touched the fluid to my tongue. This time I couldn't suppress the gag.

"Oh for goodness sake, Kate!" Sam snapped. "You act like I'm poisoning you. It can't taste *that* bad." He grabbed the glass from my hands, took a deep swig—and retched. "Oh my god! It *does* taste like vomit!" He swiped a glass of water off the end table, chugged it, and wiped all traces of smoothie from his lips. "Rene, honey, how do you drink this stuff?"

She sipped her sugar smoothie and smiled. "No sacrifice is too small to keep you happy, honey."

"Well, I'm proud of you." He tilted my glass up to the light. "As for this disgusting ... whatever it is ... it's going down the sink."

He returned from the kitchen a minute later and handed me a Diet Coke. I popped the top and guzzled several deep, long drinks. I could still taste sewage sludge at the back of my throat, but at least it had a sweet aspartame aftertaste.

"Thanks." I pulled out my birth plan template and gave a copy to Sam, who sat on the couch next to Rene. "Are you guys ready to get started?"

Rene nodded yes.

"We have quite a few things to discuss."

Rene thumbed through the multi-page document, frowning. "You know, you're making this way more complicated than it needs to be. Considering how hard it's been to keep these kiddos inside me, they'll probably slide out halfway across the parking lot." She winked. "Sam will have to wear a catcher's mitt."

I smiled. "Let's make a contingency plan, just in case." I pointed at the *General Information* section of the form. "I pre-filled the document with your names, contact information, and doctor's address, but I left the twins' information blank. Have you two agreed on names yet?"

They both stared at me, clearly avoiding eye contact with each other.

"For goodness sake," I chided. "You have two babies. Why don't you each name one?"

They gaped at me like I was Solomon suggesting they cut their infants in two.

"The names have to go together!" Rene exclaimed.

"Which is why we should name them after your grandmothers," Sam countered.

"Gertrude and Matilda?" Rene pretended to stick her index finger down her throat. "They're babies, not little old ladies."

Sam turned to me, eyes begging for me to take his side.

"Sorry, Sam. I'm with Rene on this one."

If we kept this up, we'd be here all day. I decided to move on. "Let's switch topics." I pointed back to the form. "What about the birth itself? Have you thought about pain control?"

Rene nodded decisively. "Yes. I want an epidural, ideally before the first contraction. Do they have some sort of drive-through option? I want to be good and numb before I hit the hospital bed."

I thunked my pen against the notebook and frowned at my friend. "Did you read *any* of the childbirth books I gave you?"

She rolled her eyes. "Yes, Kate, I read them. I'm kidding. Sheesh! You're taking all of the fun out of this." She leaned forward. "In all seriousness, though, I *do* want an epidural."

I picked up the pen again and made a note. "Got it. You should know, an epidural may increase your chances of needing a C-section. And once you have the epidural, you won't be able to walk around. They likely won't let you eat, either."

That got her attention. "What do you mean, not eat? I never go more than two hours without a snack. You don't want to be around me when I have low blood sugar."

Sam's face grew serious. "Rene's right, Kate. She's a monster when she's hungry." He pointed to the center of her chest. "Maybe we should sneak in her sugar-water flask."

Rene's face flashed bright red. For the first time in the twenty years I'd known her, she'd been punk'd.

Sam had been vindicated.

"Sweetheart," he said, "I'm not nearly as clueless as you think."

I interrupted before Rene picked up her glass and made me a smoothie fight victim. "I don't know what—if any—food they'll let you have, but your options diminish as you have more interventions. There are other pain control methods you can try if you want."

I went down the list of options I'd learned in doula training, starting with Demerol, passing through morphine, and ending with Stadol. "Stadol's popular because it starts working in five minutes, and it's also a sedative."

"I'll take that one," Rene said.

I made a note in my binder. "The doctor will decide the specifics, but I'll write down that you're open to trying narcotics. Would you like to start with those first or go right to an epidural?"

"Can I decide that day?"

"Absolutely."

We continued discussing options, including when Rene would want labor induced, if she hoped to have skin-to-skin contact with the babies, and whether Sam planned to cut the cords.

He shuddered. "I'm the one who's going to need drugs during all of this."

I had a feeling I would, too. We wrapped up the futile-but-important work of planning for the unplannable, then moved on to talking about murder.

"Is Rachel still under arrest?" Rene asked.

"Yes, and I'm getting worried. It's been a week since the murder, and I'm not anywhere close to solving it. I have lots of suspects, but so far nothing that points to one over another." I paused, then spoke to Rene. "Don't let it go to your head, but I miss having you as my sleuthing partner."

"I'm barely allowed to lift my butt off the couch," she replied, "but I'll bet Sam and I can still help. Why don't you tell us what you've learned so far? We might have some ideas."

I outlined all of my suspects while Rene took notes on the back of her birth plan. Sam listened intently. When I got to Liam, the stillborn baby's father, he sat up straight. "Wait a minute. You said he was at the open house, right? And that he has a goatee? Is his hair dark?"

I nodded my head.

"Do you know him, Sam?" Rene asked.

"No, but I think I saw him. While you two were planning the great cake caper, I was in the hallway returning Peggy's nonexistent phone call, remember?"

Rene blushed.

"Anyway, a man with a dark goatee was prowling the hallway, obviously looking for someone. He looked like he was about to explode, so I watched him. He skulked around for a while until he saw another man. They argued. I didn't hear their entire conversation, but the bearded man called the other guy a quack."

"What did the second man look like?" I asked.

"I don't know, six feet tall, maybe? Handsome, I guess. Rene would have ogled him." Rene playfully kicked Sam with her bare foot. "He had one of those purposefully messy hairstyles."

"Like George Clooney?" I asked.

"Now that you mention it, yes."

"That sounds like Dr. Dick."

"The murder victim?" Sam shuddered. "That gives me the creeps. He was dead a few minutes after I saw him."

"What else happened?" I asked.

"The guy you think was Dr. Dick eventually got fed up and left. The last time I saw him, he was walking toward the sky bridge."

"What about the bearded guy?"

"I don't know. I lost interest when the fight ended. That's when I finished my call with Peggy and came back to the party. I'm not sure if the bearded guy followed Dr. Dick to the sky bridge or not."

"If it was Liam, he probably did. He had to cross the sky bridge to get to his wife's room."

"Honey, why didn't you say anything about this sooner?" Rene asked.

Sam shrugged. "Honestly, I didn't think much about it. People get into arguments all the time. I had no idea a minor yelling match might have something to do with the murder." He turned to me. "Does any of this help you, Kate?"

"Maybe. At the very least, Liam lied to me—and to the police, for that matter. He claimed he never saw Dr. Dick except at the party.

He certainly never admitted that they had an argument shortly before the murder."

"Do you think I should call your detective friend and tell her?" Sam asked.

"It couldn't hurt. But I doubt a minor scuffle between them will convince Martinez that Rachel's innocent." I tapped my pen against my lower lip. "I'd like to get more information out of Liam. Maybe I can come up with an excuse to talk to him when I see his wife this afternoon."

"Careful, Kate," Sam said. "He seemed a little unbalanced. If he *is* the killer, confronting him could be dangerous."

"I know. I'll make sure we're not alone."

We spoke for fifteen more minutes, but we didn't come up with any other useful insights. Mutt and Jeff woke up from their nap and began serenading us with their *release us from prison* song. Sam picked them up, set Mutt on Rene's nonexistent lap, and cradled Jeff in his elbow. "Why did you say these guys can't come here for much longer? Did you find them a home?"

"I wish." I shared what I'd learned yesterday at Bella's vet visit. "So as sad as it makes me, we'll have to surrender them to Betty's rescue in a few days."

Sam gazed down at Jeff for several long seconds, then looked up at Rene. When he spoke, his voice was determined. "No one is taking Lucy and Ricky to a shelter."

Rene and I both frowned at him, confused.

"What on earth are you talking about, Sam?" Rene asked.

"Mutt and Jeff are dumb names. I've been calling them Lucy and Ricky. And I'm not letting them end up in a shelter. We're taking them."

He set Jeff—aka Ricky—on the floor and scooted closer to Rene. "Think about it, honey. We talked about getting a dog for the twins in a year or two, anyway. I know it won't be easy raising puppies so soon after the babies come, but I'm taking a couple of months off from work and we're hiring a nanny. If anyone can make it work, we can."

I desperately wanted to say yes to Sam's offer, but I couldn't set my friends up for failure. "That's sweet of you, Sam, but adopting two puppies from the same litter is a terrible idea. There's even a term for it."

"I know," he replied. "Littermate syndrome."

"How do you know about that?"

"I formed a software company, Kate. Google isn't exactly a challenge. Rene and I will have to enroll Lucy and Ricky in separate training classes, but we'll make it work."

"They're puppy-mill puppies," I countered. "Betty also told me that they'll likely have expensive health issues as they get older."

"Another reason Rene and I should adopt them. We can afford vet bills." He turned to Rene. "Honey, you know the best thing? They're hypoallergenic. They haven't bothered your allergies at all."

Rene set the golden pup on the ground. "You're serious about this, aren't you?"

"I am. I was planning to talk to you about adopting them, but I wanted to wait until after the babies came." He winked at me. "I didn't know Crazy Kate here was planning to adopt them out from under us." He pointed at Ricky, who was growling and tugging at his shoe laces again. "I don't know how, but these two little monsters have wiggled their way into my heart. I think we were meant to have them."

I gaped at them both in delighted shock. If anyone would stick through the tough times with littermates, it would be my two amazing, crazy, wonderful friends. Best yet, they wouldn't have to do it alone. Michael and I would help.

Sam continued. "Raising twins isn't going to be easy, Rene, and the timing sucks. But these puppies need us, and I know we can help them." He shrugged. "Who knows? I might even score some points with Bella."

A slow smile lit up Rene's face. "And here I thought I was going to have to strong-arm you. Of course we'll take them." She heaved herself up to standing and glared at me with mock stubbornness. "Kate, are you going to leave these puppies with us willingly, or does Sam have to wheelbarrow me over to your house so I can steal them while you're asleep?"

I stared back and forth between my two friends, never having loved either of them more. "I need to call Michael and make sure he's okay with it, but I'm pretty sure you guys just bought yourself two new puppies."

I wrapped Sam in a long hug, so overjoyed that I barely noticed his mustache touching my cheek. Perhaps I was making progress overcoming my beard phobia after all.

"Thank you, Sam." I squeezed Rene's hands. "Thank you, too."

"No problem." She flashed her trademarked I-got-my-way-again grin. "You know the best part?"

Sam closed his eyes and groaned, as if he knew what was coming. In retrospect, I should have, too.

"What's that?" I asked.

"Sam named the puppies. That means the twins' names are all mine."

TWENTY-FOUR

MICHAEL WAS, IF ANYTHING, happier than me. We agreed that Mutt and Jeff—I mean Lucy and Ricky—would stay with us until Rene and Sam settled in with the twins. In the meantime, Sam would provide daycare and continue potty training.

I was so excited that I practically floated from Rene's house to the hospital for my afternoon yoga sessions. I was almost to the old perinatal unit when I saw Justine scurrying down the hallway. She seemed to be in a hurry, so I skipped the small talk.

"Hey, Justine. I was hoping to see you today. Do you have a minute to look at something?"

"If it's quick."

I rummaged around in my purse until I found the crumpled note from my windshield. "Is this Nicole's handwriting?"

Justine took the page and examined it, wearing a puzzled expression. "It looks like it, but she's never mentioned knowing anyone on Bainbridge. What are the 'answers' she's talking about?"

"That's what I want to ask her. I'm beginning to think she knows more about her stepfather's death than she's letting on."

Justine's lips tightened. "I can't imagine what. If she knew something, she'd use it to get her mother out of jail." She glanced at her watch. "Sorry, Kate, but I have to go. I'm working a double today. If I don't hurry, I'll be late. I'll text Nicole and ask her to call you." She rushed down the hallway and disappeared onto the sky bridge, heading toward the new building.

As I checked in at the perinatal unit, the normally friendly blonde nurse at the desk shuffled through charts, oddly refusing to meet my gaze. She handed me the day's client list without speaking. I was so distracted by her uncharacteristic aloofness that at first I didn't notice an important name was missing.

"Only two clients again today? I don't see Kendra. Did she have the baby?"

The nurse made a note on a chart without looking up. "No, but she's not on this floor anymore. She was one of the first patients transferred to the new wing."

"She didn't schedule a yoga session?"

The nurse set the chart to the side and started entering data into a spreadsheet. "No."

Not having a scheduled visit would make questioning Kendra and Liam more difficult, but not impossible. "What's her new room number? I'd like to stop by and say hi. Maybe take her some flowers."

The nurse stopped typing and frowned. She lifted her eyes and steeled her shoulders. "I'm sorry, Kate, but I can't tell you which room she's in. Something about your last session upset her. Kendra specifically asked that you not be allowed to visit her anymore."

I cycled through multiple emotions. First I felt wounded. Then frustrated. Then suspicious. No yoga teacher worth her mat wanted to find herself on a client's do-not-visit list. That's why I felt wounded. Kendra's no-contact request quashed my plans to quiz Liam, unless I was willing to risk my hospital teaching privileges, which I wasn't. That was the frustrated.

Suspicion, however, trumped all. If what Sam told me was true, Kendra and Liam had lied, both to the police and to me. Liam *hadn't* gone straight back to Kendra's room after seeing Dr. Dick at the open house. He'd followed Dr. Dick and Rachel out of the party, then waited around long enough for the two men to have an altercation. The fight—and Liam's lie about it—made him seem awfully guilty. Was Kendra afraid I might jump to the wrong conclusion about Liam—or the right one?

A familiar female voice interrupted my thoughts.

"You're Kate Davidson, right?"

"Tamara? Hi! I didn't know you worked here."

"I don't, at least not officially. I work for Sound Nursing. I mostly pick up shifts at ABBA, but I catch some here occasionally."

Of course. Summer had mentioned Tamara's temp agency. Still, it had never occurred to me that I might see her at Lake Washington. Was running into her today a blessing or a curse? I'd planned to question her, but not until I'd come up with a reasonable cover story. My mind spun through options, trying to create a story that was both spontaneous and convincing.

Nothing.

Maybe that was a sign. Thus far, my ruses hadn't worked nearly as well as the truth. Why not stick with that?

"I've actually been hoping to talk to you. About your ex-lover's murder."

She raised her eyebrows. "Don't beat around the bush, do you?"

I shrugged.

"I like that. No bullshit. Justine told me you were looking into Richard's death. I figured you'd show up on my doorstep eventually—me being the bitter ex-lover and all. Especially since I was on shift here last Saturday."

"You were here at the hospital the day of the murder?" That was new—and interesting—information.

"Me and about two thousand other people. I don't think I have anything relevant to tell you, but I'm willing to give it a shot."

I glanced at my watch. My first private session was scheduled to start in fifteen minutes. Hopefully my client wouldn't mind if I was a little late. "Do you have a minute now?"

"I have forty-five of them. I'm on lunch break. If you're willing to talk in the cafeteria while I eat, I'm all yours."

We rode the elevator down to the cafeteria in relative silence. Tamara headed for the food line while I grabbed a quiet table in the large, mostly empty eating area. The bland, rubbery-looking meatloaf she brought to the table smelled about as appetizing as one of Sam's smoothies.

"Before we start," she said, "I need to apologize."

"Apologize? For what?"

"For my behavior last week at ABBA."

"When you confronted Dr. Jones and his mistress?"

She frowned. "That too, I suppose. But I meant for my behavior with Summer. I normally work more effectively with doulas than I did that night. Summer pushes my buttons in all the wrong ways. We have a history."

"The baby that died."

Tamara's eyes widened. "She told you about that?"

"Yes. Were you at that birth, too?" I knew she wasn't, of course, but I wanted to compare her story with Summer's. The less she thought I knew, the better.

"No, I was still on staff at Reproductive Associates back then, but that baby's death impacted me all the same. Richard was never the same afterward. The night that baby died, our relationship died, too. I just didn't know it yet."

Part of me wanted to tell her I was sorry, but I couldn't. Dr. Dick should never have been in a relationship with Tamara to begin with. That privilege rested solely with his wife. I stayed silent and waited for her to continue.

"The baby's parents blamed Richard, but Summer was at least partially at fault. And she learned nothing from the experience. She's good at her job, but doulas aren't medically trained—not to the extent that a doctor or midwife is. Not to the extent that nurses like me are, for that matter. That doesn't stop Summer from spouting off her opinions, though. Her clients trust her, sometimes more than they trust their doctors. She claims that she fights for the rights of the mother, but she's kidding herself. She's pushing her own agenda."

Tamara stabbed a desiccated Brussels sprout with her fork. "She calls herself a natural childbirth advocate, like that makes her better than the rest of us. We're *all* childbirth advocates. Some of us simply have a different definition of the word 'natural.' Tell me, Kate, what's so 'natural' about needless suffering?"

I didn't reply. This was one of the few controversies about which I *didn't* have a strong opinion. I refocused the conversation instead. "I understand what you're saying, but I still don't see how you can blame Summer for the baby's death. I know she doesn't approve of most medical interventions, but how did refusing Pitocin lead to the stillbirth?"

Tamara paused for a moment and stared over my shoulder, as if formulating her thoughts on the blank wall behind me. "Remember, I wasn't there that night, and I only heard the story from Richard's perspective. But I believed him. The labor was way too slow, and Summer fought Richard every time he suggested trying something to speed it up. I mean, seriously. Forty hours? That poor woman went through agony, and there was no reason for it."

"I spoke to the parents. They told me there was no evidence of malpractice."

"There wasn't. There couldn't have been, not with Richard." Tamara laid down her fork and pushed her plate away. "Richard had plenty of faults. He certainly wasn't husband of the year." She grunted. "He wasn't lover of the year, for that matter. But he was a brilliantly talented physician. He knew something was going wrong that night. He couldn't pinpoint what, but he knew it. He wanted to speed up the labor, maybe transfer the mother to a hospital. Summer wouldn't hear of it."

"Isn't that the patient's decision?"

"Summer got inside that woman's head so deep, she wouldn't listen to anyone but her. She'd convinced her that drugs and other interventions might hurt the baby. And she was adamant that unless the baby was in distress, there was no need for a hospital transfer. Summer gave lip service to the fact that it was the mother's decision, but she made sure everyone in that room—especially the laboring mom—knew her opinion."

Tamara picked up a cafeteria-beige coffee mug and cradled it in both hands. "Look, I'm not saying Richard was right. No one knows for sure what happened to that baby. But Richard still blamed himself. He was convinced that if the baby had come sooner, it would have survived. I think the guilt drove him to Mariella."

"You seem pretty gracious for a woman who was trying to sue the pants off of him."

Tamara stopped talking. Her lips thinned; her jaw clenched. She stared at the liquid inside her cup for so long, I thought she was going to douse me with it. Instead, she lifted her eyes to meet mine.

"I was angry. Richard was more than my boyfriend, you know. He was my boss."

I involuntarily winced at the word "boyfriend."

"You can't stop judging me, can you? You think I'm some marriage wrecking whore, but you're wrong. Richard's and my relationship was more complicated than that. We were friends for years—long before he married Rachel. They never had a perfect marriage, but it fell apart when her daughter moved in. Our affair started shortly after that. By then, everyone but Rachel could tell the marriage was over."

"Why didn't he leave her?"

"I like to think he would have, if the baby hadn't died. He needed time to find the courage."

I couldn't hide my skepticism.

"There's that sanctimonious smirk again. Richard's and my relationship wasn't a casual fling. I loved him."

"Then why the lawsuit? To punish him?"

"Yes, but not for throwing away our relationship. For destroying my career."

That surprised me. "What do you mean?"

"When Richard dumped me for Mariella, I quit Reproductive Associates without notice. I expected him to be mad, but I had no idea he'd blackball me."

"Blackball you?"

"He put the word out that I was a bad hire."

"Why would he do that?"

"I suspect it was Mariella's idea. What better way to make sure Richard and I never got back together?" She set the mug on her tray and stacked her plate and utensils beside it. "Let me assure you, it's not easy to land a decent job when you don't have references. None of the local clinics will hire me as an IVF nurse. I've been forced to go back to my original specialty—labor and delivery. Only this time, I'm stuck at a temp agency, grabbing whatever shifts I can get, hoping I scramble together enough hours to pay rent. That lawsuit was my best chance to get my life back on track again." She sighed. "And now it's over."

"Couldn't you still go after the clinic?"

"I could, but I won't. I always liked Dr. Steinman. He didn't have my back, but I don't blame him. He was trapped in the middle of an unwinnable battle. There's no reason he should be punished for something that Richard did."

"Perhaps not." Though seeing him punished wouldn't have bothered me. Not after seeing what he'd done to that dog. I kept the thought to myself. Instead, I asked, "Where were you at the time Dr. Jones was killed?"

She smirked. "I figured you'd get around to accusing me at some point. I was riding the bus to the hospital. By the time I arrived, Richard was already dead."

"Can you prove that?"

Her face remained expressionless. "Probably not."

I stared into her eyes, trying to decipher whether or not she was telling the truth. After several moments of uncomfortable silence, she spoke again.

"I can see that you don't fully believe me. Ask yourself this: Richard's and my relationship ended a year ago. I was suing him, and I was going to win. I was better off with him alive. Why would I kill him?"

The question sounded familiar. "Mariella said the same thing. But in her case, she said Dr. Jones was planning to marry her."

Tamara's cheeks turned bright red, but she didn't reply. She curled her fingers into fists, then slowly released them.

"At first I believed her," I continued. "Believed that she had no reason to kill Dr. Jones. The more I think about it though, the less sure I am. Something's off with Mariella. She seems cold."

"Damned right she's cold," Tamara snapped. "Mariella's a heartless gold digger, and everyone knew it. Especially Richard. That's what made me so angry."

"Why did he choose her over you?"

"I've asked myself that question a thousand times. Part of me thinks he was trying to punish himself. Like taking up with a user was some sort of masochistic penance. The other part thinks he was simply being a man. You have to admit, that little slut has plenty of sex appeal."

I kept my expression carefully neutral. "Could she have killed him?"

Tamara laughed, but with contempt more than humor. "Mariella does whatever it takes to get what Mariella wants. But why would she kill him? You saw them at ABBA. They seemed pretty darned chummy to me. I don't see a motive."

She pushed back from the table and picked up her tray. "Personally, I think the police are right. If anybody had a reason to kill Richard, it was his wife."

With those final words, she moved to the bussing area, placed her tray on the conveyor belt, and headed back to the elevator.

I stood, but I didn't follow her. Our meeting hadn't gone as I'd expected, but it had been illuminating all the same. Tamara would never make my most-laudable-humans list, and Mariella seemed

267

downright despicable. But why would either of them have killed Richard? Unless they were lying, they didn't have a motive, as Tamara had pointed out. I reluctantly moved them both to my "low" category of suspects and headed back to the perinatal unit.

My cell phone rang halfway to the elevator. I didn't recognize the number, so I let the call go to voicemail.

The message was from Tiffany.

"Hey, Kate. My cell phone's out of juice, so I'm using Chad's."

Tiffany was still with Adonis? I smiled. Last night's smoothie date had evidently turned into a sleepover.

Voicemail Tiffany continued. "Nicole stopped by my apartment this morning. Chad and I were, well, you know. Totally embarrassing. Anyway, she says you keep calling her, but she's afraid to answer. She left the note about that dog on your car. I promised her we wouldn't tell anyone that she stole Mutt and Jeff. Let's not get her into trouble, okay?"

Damn.

The mystery note *was* about the dog, after all.

I couldn't talk to Liam and Kendra. I'd pretty much eliminated Tamara and Mariella. And my one remaining lead (or at least potential lead) had turned out to be a big, fat zero.

What was I supposed to do now?

TWENTY-FIVE

THE PHONE'S METALLIC RING jarred me awake at midnight.

Michael mumbled something unintelligible, rolled his back to the sound, and covered his head with his pillow. Bella lay sprawled out beside him, snoring. I reached across them both and pulled the phone to my side, so sleepily churlish that I forgot to say hello.

"This had better be good."

A low moan seeped through the phone line.

I sat up straight, all crankiness forgotten. "Rene, is that you?"

Sam's voice replied. "Sorry, Kate, it's Sam. Rene's gone into labor." He whispered, "She started having contractions a couple of hours ago, but she wouldn't let me call. She wants to wait until morning to go to the hospital, but I don't think we should. The contractions are already three minutes apart."

"Get her to the hospital. Now. I'll meet you in triage."

Rene yelled in the background, "I told you the twins would come as soon as we talked about the birth plan!" She stopped talking and moaned again, louder this time.

"Don't take too long, Kate." Sam's voice disappeared, replaced by a dial tone.

I almost cried. I'd had four hours of sleep in the past twenty-four hours. Why couldn't babies arrive at a more civilized hour, like noon?

I jumped into sweats and a T-shirt, threw a couple of protein bars and my doula binder into a gym bag, and prepared Bella's food so Michael could simply add water and incubate. My car pulled out of the driveway fifteen minutes after I hung up the phone. A new record for me.

I drove strictly on autopilot, not thinking at all. Certainly not remembering that I could park in the visitors' parking lot close to the emergency entrance. I parked in the staff parking area on the tenth floor of the garage and sprinted from there to the new birthing center. Rene had recently graduated from triage to a delivery room, where she was arguing with the admitting nurse.

"What do you mean I can't order room service? I'm starving! All I had was a freakin' smoothie for dinner!" She hugged her three-person belly, leaned over, and groaned. A minute later, she stood upright and pointed at me. "Kate, tell Nurse Ratched here that you promised me full meals in my birth plan."

I winced at Rene's wildly inaccurate recollection. "I didn't promise you meals. I told you we'd ask about food."

The nurse's lips pressed into a stern line. "As I already told your friend, twin births are at high risk for C-section. She won't be allowed to eat until the babies are delivered."

This was going to be a very long night.

As I helped Rene crawl into the bed, Sam offered her a paper cup. "Here, honey. They said you could have ice chips." Rene curled into a fetal position and wept.

The door opened and Justine strode through it. The admitting nurse gestured to her and said, "Rene, this is Nurse Maxwell. She'll be your labor nurse tonight." She sidled next to Justine and whispered, "Good luck. You'll need it."

Justine smiled and kneeled next to Rene's curled-up body. "Hey, Rene. Call me Justine. I'm a friend of Kate's. I promise, I'm going to take good care of you." She squeezed Rene's arm. "Your labor's progressing quickly. Good for you, Mama. We'll have those twins out of there in no time."

She moved to the foot of the bed and barked out confident-sounding instructions. "Kate, I'm going to check on Rene's progress. Coach her through some of those breathing exercises you taught me in yoga class." She glanced at Sam, whose face had blanched to the color of bleached egg shells. "Dad, you look like you could use some breathing, too."

Great idea—one I should have thought of myself. I whispered to Justine, "I'm so glad it's you tonight. I'd be a wreck with a stranger."

She smiled. "I asked for your friend's case when I saw you come in. You're going to do great." She gestured with her chin toward Rene. "Start by helping her calm down. While you're at it, try to keep her husband from passing out."

Sam's birth coach training had obviously drained out of his brain, along with the blood that normally oxygenated it. His body swayed back and forth, about to topple. "She's in pain, Kate. Do something."

I pulled a chair next to the bed, pointed at Sam, and barked Bella's favorite command: "Sit." To Rene, I said, "Inhale as I count to four ... "

Justine gave us a thumbs-up sign when the contraction was over. "Six centimeters. You're doing great!"

I continued my coaching, pulling from my yoga toolbox. "Tell you what, Rene. Let's try some of the chanting we did together in

Prenatal Yoga. The next time you have a contraction, we'll chant the word 'oh.'" I hoped chanting would slow down Rene's breath, which would calm her. The "O" sound would vibrate low in her belly. "Think of the word 'open' when you chant." Sending a subliminal message to her cervix couldn't hurt, either.

Ten infinitely long minutes passed. Minutes filled with pained groans, rejected ice chips, and a mercifully short visit from the on-call obstetrician. Each of Rene's contractions lasted longer and seemed to get more painful.

"The pain doesn't go away after the contractions anymore," Rene moaned. "My back is killing me."

I whispered to Justine, "Is that normal?"

Justine hesitated. "It's not abnormal. I suspect she's having back labor."

Great, just our luck.

Back labor—in which significant pain was referred to the mother's back—was widely considered the most painful kind of labor.

Justine pointed to Rene's chart. "She told the triage nurse that she didn't want an epidural."

"Really? When we created her birth plan, she asked for the drive-through option."

Justine chuckled. "Women often change their minds once labor begins. I don't like to push drugs on my patients, but some pain control might help her a lot."

"I'll ask."

I joined Sam next to Rene. His face had turned from bleached-shell white to a sickly greenish yellow. "I can't stand to see her hurting like this," he whispered.

"Then let's do something about it," I replied.

I took Rene's hand and asked, "Do you want that epidural we talked about?"

She gaped at me like I'd suggested crushing her spine, not injecting it with painkillers. "You told me that epidurals increase the risk of a C-section."

"Sometimes, but—"

"Nobody's cutting into my belly. Nobody. I plan to walk out of this hospital wearing my skinny jeans."

"Rene, that's not realist—"

She sat up and squeezed my hand so tightly, I expected to hear at least three metacarpals shatter.

"I said no!"

Justine shook her head at me from across the room, clearly warning me off.

So much for that idea.

I'd never felt more impotent. I wanted to help my friend. I *needed* to help my friend. But how? I nervously suggested every birthing option I could think of in rapid-fire staccato.

"Do you want to walk around? Do you want to get in the jetted tub? Do you want to squat? Do you want to get on the ball? Do you want me to rub your back? Do you—"

"I want you to shut the hell up and let me concentrate!"

Sam grabbed Rene's hands, probably to keep her from punching me.

Justine took me aside. "Give her a minute to get through this contraction. Don't take anything she says personally. Women say all kinds of things in labor."

I knew that, of course, but Rene's words still stung.

Justine continued. "When she's ready to talk again, ask her if she wants some Demerol. It will take the edge off and help her relax."

I cautiously tiptoed next to my friend. When the contraction was over, I spoke.

"Rene, what would you think about Demerol?"

Rene released Sam's hand. He shook it, as if making sure his fingers were still connected.

"Yes, or that Stadol stuff you told me about," Rene replied. "Something that'll help me relax. I swear these little buggers are chiseling their way through my spine." She groaned again.

"I'll talk to the doctor," Justine said. She picked up the phone, mumbled some words into the receiver, and hung up again. "Hang tight. I'll be right back."

Evidently "right back" meant shortly after the twins graduated from college. Or at least that's what it felt like. Fifteen infinitely long minutes later, Justine injected the merciful brew directly into Rene's IV line.

Which would have made me feel a whole heck of a lot better if her hands hadn't been shaking so hard that she almost dropped the syringe.

I eased next to Justine and whispered, "Are you okay?"

She smiled. "I'm fine. My blood sugar's a little low. I took some glucose a couple of minutes ago. It should kick in soon."

Deep down inside, I had to have known she was lying, but I couldn't admit it to myself. Not then. I needed to focus all of my energy on Rene.

The next hour passed in a million-year heartbeat. Rene rested off and on, but the contractions became longer and closer together. A mere three hours after she'd been admitted, she was almost ready to push—and to give up.

"I can't do this anymore," she wept. "I'm going to be a terrible mother."

Sam stroked her hair. "Rene, honey, you're going to be a fabulous mother."

"He's right," I said. "You're in transition. Remember, we talked about this. Transition is the stage in which laboring women want to give up. That's good news. You'll be ready to push soon!"

As the next contraction began, Rene sobbed. "The drugs aren't working. Please, I changed my mind. I need an epidural. Now."

"I'll talk to Justine."

Justine made another phone call, then took me aside. "Anesthesiology is really backed up. The anesthesiologist will get here as soon as he can, but that could be thirty minutes or longer. I'm pretty sure the first baby will already be here by then."

"Can we give her more Demerol?"

"Sorry, the doctor already ordered the maximum dose. Try to keep her calm."

Rene cried out, over and over again, begging for an epidural.

She certainly wasn't acting like a woman on the maximum dose of pain medication. True, Rene could be melodramatic—over-the-top, sometimes— but when it counted, she was surprisingly stoic. This was no act. Rene was in agony.

I smiled and whispered sweet assurances to my friend, but my mind spun in circles, refusing to remain in denial even a minute longer. Rene said the drugs weren't working, and I believed her. Was that because she'd never received a full dose to begin with?

I looked into Justine's glassy, unfocused eyes, and my dream's metaphor became suddenly clear. The dream hadn't been about Bella after all. In spite of her challenges, I'd never considered Bella a burden. Not once. Bella was the greatest joy of my life. The staggering burden that my subconscious mind had shown me was Justine's.

Clues I'd refused to acknowledge flashed through my mind in a dizzying, fast-forward slide show. Justine talking in yoga class about the unbearable pain of caring for a parent with advanced Alzheimer's while mourning the loss of her husband and child. The red eyes. The stumbling gait as she crashed into the studio's book shelf. The syringe she'd dropped in the bathroom. The extra-large piece of cake she'd swiped from the party—a cake loaded with more sugar than any conscientious diabetic would ever ingest.

Justine hadn't injected herself with insulin that day in the bathroom. It had been Demerol, or morphine, or Stadol, or one of the many other narcotics she had access to during all of those double shifts. At best, Justine was a drug addict. At worst, she was a thief, stealing drugs from the hospital or—worse yet—from her patients.

Justine needed this job. She needed to take care of her mother. If Dr. Dick ducked into the break room to hide from Liam and saw her shooting up ...

She might very well panic and kill him.

The hollow ache in my belly assured me that I was right. But despite my certainty, the theory was still conjecture, and career-ruining conjecture at that. I'd call Martinez and tell her my suspicions tomorrow. For now, I needed to keep Justine calm, focused, and hopefully sober for the remainder of Rene's birth.

I was about to volunteer to get her some coffee when Rene had another contraction. She pushed Sam away, sat straight up in bed, and snarled in a voice straight from *The Exorcist*, "Either get me an epidural now or rip these demon spawn out of me!"

Justine took some measurements under Rene's gown, picked up the phone again, and mumbled words I couldn't understand.

When she hung up, she spoke to Rene. "Hang on there, sweetie, the doctor's coming now."

Rene pinned her to the wall with wide, hopeful eyes. "To give me the epidural?"

"No, hon, to deliver your babies. You're fully dilated. It's time to push."

TWENTY-SIX

RENE PUSHED OUT BOTH babies in an action-packed forty-five minutes. Moments after the second baby was nestled against her chest, Justine disappeared. Not long after, a new nurse appeared.

"Nurse Justine became suddenly ill. I'll be with you for the next couple of hours."

The doctor gave the new nurse a questioning look. She shrugged in return. If Justine had a drug problem, I had a feeling it wouldn't stay secret much longer.

Rene, Sam, and what seemed like a thousand hospital employees oohed and aahed over the tiny humans. None of us could seem to stop smiling.

"Alice and Amelia," Rene announced.

"What?" I asked.

"Their names." She pointed to the blonde. "Alice, after Alice in Wonderland." She nuzzled the brunette. "Amelia, after Amelia Earhart. They're going to be adventurers."

"Honey, that's perfect," Sam said.

"It's more than perfect. It's inspired." I cooed at the bitsy beings. "They were cute in the ultrasounds, but that was nothing. They're gorgeous." I smiled at my friends. "They look exactly like the two of you."

Rene's lips fluttered, as if they couldn't decide whether to form a smile or a frown. "I know," she hiccupped. "One blonde, one brunette. They're not identical." Her hiccups turned into sobs.

I wrapped my arm around her shoulders, careful not to touch the breakable creatures. "Oh, honey. I'm sorry. I didn't realize how much you wanted them to be identical."

"Don't be silly, Kate," Rene admonished. "Who cares about that?" She covered her mouth and smiled through her tears. "Don't you get it? One blonde, one brunette. Just like the puppies. The four of them are going to look awesome on my next catalog cover."

Sam laughed. "That's my girl. Always plotting. Maybe you should add puppy accessories to your baby line."

I playfully punched him in the arm. "Don't give her any ideas."

Sam lifted Amelia off of Rene's chest and reached her toward me. "Here, hold her."

I longed to cuddle the doll-like creature more than I cared to admit, but she seemed too fragile—like porcelain. If I breathed, I might shatter her. I held up my hands and backed away. "No, I can't, I—"

"You'll be fine," he insisted. "Hold your arms this way." I pantomimed his position, and he laid her body so that it was fully supported by my forearm. "Don't let her head drop."

I cuddled that brunette sweetheart next to my chest and fell madly in love. In that moment, I made up my mind: Michael and I were going to talk about kids.

Soon.

I stayed with them for forty-five more minutes, then called Michael to let him know I was on my way home. I promised to visit the next afternoon and left Rene to bond with her new family.

I staggered up to my ancient Honda around five in the morning, so exhausted I felt like weeping. Even my fingers felt tired. So tired, I could barely lift my keys. A noise startled me from behind and I jumped. The keys clattered to the cement.

"I was beginning to think you wouldn't get here in time." Justine's voice echoed through the empty parking garage. Her complexion was waxy. Her eyes were dulled in a narcotics-induced haze.

All feelings of exhaustion vanished, replaced by adrenaline-laced trepidation. Why was Justine waiting for me in an empty parking garage? More importantly, how long would it remain empty? Shift changes happened at seven, which meant that no one else was likely to be on this level for another hour at the soonest.

"I thought you went home sick?"

She didn't reply.

I looked pointedly at my watch. "I'm exhausted. You must be, too. Whatever you want to talk about, let's do it later, after we've both had some sleep." I reached down to grab my keys, but Justine jerked my arm away and kicked them under the car.

"I'm afraid I won't be available later." She released my arm, pulled a knife from her jacket pocket, and pointed it at my chest. "I won't hesitate to use this, but I think you already know that." She pointed at my gym bag. "Hand me your bag and your jacket. We wouldn't want you pulling out any weapons, now would we?"

I complied.

I should have been frightened, and honestly I was. But I wasn't terrified. Justine's energy—in spite of the weapon she pointed at my sternum—was defeated. Done.

She spoke in a monotone. "You know, I think I wanted you to figure it out."

"Figure what out? Your low blood sugar?"

"Please, Kate. We're done with all the pretending now. I saw the expression on your face when I put the Demerol in your friend's IV. You know I'm not diabetic."

She was right, of course. Just wrong about the timing. My subconscious mind had figured out Justine's addiction when I saw her hands shake. My conscious mind had refused to admit it until an hour later. Not that the timing mattered now.

I tried to back away, but I bumped up against my car.

Justine stepped closer. "I don't want to hurt you," she said. "If you behave long enough to hear me out, you'll come out of this fine." She lowered the knife, but only by an inch. "I didn't think I wanted to get caught, but I must have. There's no other reason I'd have made so many mistakes." Her eyes grew wistful. "Your friend's babies are beautiful, by the way. I'm so glad I got to be part of their birth."

"Are you high now?" I kept my voice low, hoping to soothe her, but it still echoed across the quiet garage.

Justine smiled. "Oh yes, but don't worry; I only took half of your friend's dose. I needed to be functional for her—for both of you. I took the rest of my stash after the babies were born. I've been saving up for today."

"What's happening today?"

She ignored my question and kept talking.

"Please don't judge me too harshly, Kate. I'm a good nurse. Ask any of my patients. I simply couldn't stand the pain anymore." A weak smile lifted her lips, but the expression looked broken. "The yoga you taught me was great, but it's no morphine."

"What pain? The pain of losing your family?"

"Yes, and knowing that I'll never have another child of my own." Her words slurred. "The first time was so simple. Mom had been up all night, and I was exhausted. My patient needed Stadol, but not the entire vial. We're supposed to have another nurse present when we discard the remainder, but we were busy, so she entered her number and left. I put the vial in my pocket and took it home. I finally got a full night's sleep."

"But one night wasn't enough."

"Not even close. You don't understand how powerful these drugs are. I went from being in agony to being...numb." She slowly shook her head. "Blissfully numb. Soon I was stealing anything I could get my hands on. Stadol, Dilaudid, morphine...Once I even licked a fentanyl patch before I put it on a patient."

I flashed back to Rene's desperate pleas during her last hour of labor. "You claim you're a good nurse. How could you steal from patients in pain?"

"I didn't. At least not always. Sometimes the other nurses signed off on drug disposals without witnessing them, like that first time." She stared down at the floor. "Occasionally, like tonight, I gave patients a partial dose of their medicine. But never, ever if they lost a child. That pain is too unbearable."

Her fist slackened around the knife's handle. I reached out my hand. "Justine, give me the knife. You're not violent, you're sick. We can get you help."

She tightened her grip again. "It's too late for that, Kate." Her words grew slower, more halting. "My mother...I picked out a facility. She doesn't want to go, but it's time." She forcefully squeezed her eyes shut, then opened them again.

I hesitated, conflicted. Justine was dangerous, that much was certain. But she was also heavily sedated. If I rushed her, could I get to the knife before she cut me with it?

It was worth a try.

I leaned forward, slowly bent my knee, and placed my sole against the tire, preparing to push off with my foot.

Justine quickly pressed the tip of the knife against my throat. "Don't even think about it, Kate. I don't want to kill you, but I'll cut you if I have to. Don't make me hurt anyone else."

I held up my palms and lowered my foot to the floor.

She moved the knife back a few inches and tossed two envelopes on the hood of my car. "The top letter outlines the health care provisions for my mom. Make sure the lawyer on the envelope gets it. Give the other one to the police. It's my confession. I killed Richard, but you already knew that."

"Why?"

"I didn't plan it. I was feeling blue last Saturday, so I gave myself an extra bump. I got the dosage too high, and I passed out for a second. Richard must have heard me collapse. He came in the bathroom and caught me picking up the syringe." She shook her head. "What was he doing in the break room? He didn't have any births at the hospital on Saturday."

I didn't tell her, but given what I'd learned, Dr. Dick had most likely ducked inside the employees-only area to hide from Liam.

"I panicked. He would have turned me in. I'd have lost my job, probably gone to prison. All I could think about was my mother. What would happen to her without me?" She laughed, but with no humor. "The same thing that's going to happen to her now."

She forcefully blinked her eyes again, clearly fighting to stay awake. "I need you to know, Kate, that Richard's death was an accident."

"An accident?" Shoving a knife into someone's heart seemed pretty deliberate to me.

"It all happened so fast. I ran past him, but he came after me and cornered me at the sink. I grabbed the knife and told him to back off, but he didn't stop. He lunged toward me, and … " She didn't finish the sentence.

"Your story doesn't make sense. If it was truly an accident, why didn't you call for help? They might have been able to save him. Instead, you dragged him into the bathroom and left him to die."

Justine shook her head. "I have no idea how he ended up in the bathroom, but I didn't put him there. When I left, he was on the floor, right where I stabbed him." Her words slurred. "You're right, though. I should have called for help. I just needed to get away. To have time to think."

"Rachel's your friend. How could you let her go to prison for a crime you committed?"

"I couldn't. I won't. That's why I wrote the confession." Justine's body swayed, but she kept talking. "Rachel's no innocent, though. You saw her that night at the yoga studio. Richard threatened to send Nicole away, and Rachel just stood there. She never protected Nicole. It's a mother's job to protect her child … "

Justine's knees buckled. She grabbed my arm, trying to stay upright. That was my chance, and I took it.

I shoved her and she fell, hitting her head solidly against the floor. The knife slipped from her fingers and clanked against the cement. I kicked it away and dove for it, praying Justine wouldn't reach it first. My wrist slammed into the ground. The blade sliced my palm when I scooped up the knife, but I had it! I whirled around, ignoring the searing pain in my hand and the blood oozing between my fingers. I was prepared to defend myself if I needed to. I hoped against hope that I wouldn't.

Justine was still where I left her, lying in a crumpled ball on the cement.

No, no, no, no, no. Not again. Not another death.

I should have run away, but I couldn't. I had to make sure Justine was alive. I ran back and kneeled next to her, knife at the ready if needed.

It wasn't.

Justine was barely conscious. I shook her—hard. "Wake up! You have to wake up!"

Her eyes fluttered open. She smiled. "It won't be long now. Please don't leave me. I don't want to die alone."

Any impulse to save myself vanished. The only person Justine planned to kill today was herself. I wrestled my gym bag out from under her and desperately rummaged through it, searching for my cell phone.

Please let it work in the garage.

Zero bars.

I tossed it to the side.

"Justine, hang on. I'm getting help."

I tore across the parking garage to the elevators and pounded my fist against the call button, barely noticing the bloody marks I left behind. What was taking so long? I glanced back to check on Justine.

She was gone.

I found her fifteen feet from where I'd left her, crawling toward the edge of the ten-story parking garage.

"You can't save me, Kate. No one can. Please, let me go."

If I left her to get help, she'd try to climb over the guardrails and jump. She might very well succeed. I pinned her to the floor and screamed.

"Help! Somebody help!"

I screamed for help over and over and over again, watching helplessly as Justine's breaths became shallower and further apart.

My pleas echoed through the empty space for what felt like eternity. They haunted my nightmares significantly longer. As Justine slipped into unconsciousness, I prayed that she would finally find peace.

TWENTY-SEVEN

As it turns out, a hospital is a terrible place to attempt suicide. But I think deep down inside, Justine already knew that. The emergency room staff arrived seconds after the first Good Samaritan heard my calls for help. They were able to save Justine, though the ending to her story was far from happy.

I did what I could to help her, which didn't feel like nearly enough. I delivered the first letter to the police—who released Rachel a few hours later—and the second to Justine's attorney. I visited her mother at the new nursing home and explained what had happened, but if the elderly woman's empty, unaware eyes were any indication, she didn't understand me. In this case, Alzheimer's might be a blessing.

Two days later, I did one final good deed: I reunited a family. Michael watched Bella while I drove Rachel, Nicole, the pups, and myself to Fido's Last Chance for a visit.

Nicole sat in the back with the puppies curled up asleep in her lap. Her mother rode up front with me.

"Nicole, I still don't understand why you were so secretive about the dogs," I said.

"I didn't know what else to do. If I'd taken them home, Richard would have made me return them. I didn't want them stuck in those awful cages. I figured that if I left them at the pet store, someone would help them. I hid until I saw your boyfriend open the box, so I knew they'd be safe. That's why I was so late to class."

"I get that part, but why did you leave me the cryptic note about their mother? Why not just tell me about her?"

"The puppies are valuable. I was afraid that if you knew I'd stolen them, you'd tell Justine. She might have turned me in to the police. When we were at your house the day Mom got arrested, you told me you wanted to find the person who'd dumped the puppies so you could kill him."

Those weren't my exact words, but I didn't correct her.

She continued. "As soon as you said that, I knew you'd never take the puppies back to that shed. I thought you might save their mother. I figured the note would point you to the dog without implicating me."

"Justine would never have reported you to the police," I said.

Rachel's voice sounded bitter. "She had her own crimes to conceal."

"That's not what I meant," I replied. "What Justine did to Richard—what she did to you, Rachel—was inexcusable. But she would have protected Nicole. She told me someone needed to."

Rachel's cheeks reddened, but she remained silent. I glanced in my rearview mirror at Nicole, who was happily cradling a puppy in each arm.

"How did you know about the dog in the shed?" I asked.

Nicole hesitated.

Rachel prodded her. "Go ahead, Nicole."

"Richard and Mom made me go to a dinner party with them at Dr. Steinman's house. I was so bored I thought I would die, so Dr. Steinman told me I could go swimming. I shouldn't have snooped in the shed, but I heard the puppies whining." Her voice caught. "He had them trapped in that awful cage like prisoners. They looked sick and sad. What kind of man does that to innocent dogs?"

One who should be locked in a cage himself.

"I couldn't let them rot in there like that," Nicole continued. "I had to help them. So I stole fifty dollars from Richard's wallet the next day and took Mom's car back to get them."

Rachel turned to face the back seat. "Honey, why didn't you tell me any of this?"

"I didn't think you would do anything. You always took Richard's side."

Rachel reached back and grasped the teen's hand. "I was wrong. I'm so sorry, honey. Never again."

"I was stupid, though," Nicole continued. "I didn't think to bring leashes. I grabbed the puppies first. I was planning to go back for the mother, but Dr. Steinman came home. I hid and waited, hoping that I could go back and grab her, but he must have heard me. He went into the shed and noticed the puppies were gone. He stomped back into the house, came out with a padlock, and locked the cage. I couldn't get to her then."

We turned onto the long gravel driveway that led to Betty's rundown house, which was also the main shelter for Fido's Last Chance.

Betty greeted us in the yard. The petite yellow lab stood on leash next to her. She was still thin, but otherwise cleaner, healthier, and happier-looking than I would have imagined possible.

I'd barely come to a stop when Nicole jumped out of the car. The lab broke her stay next to Betty and pulled toward the teen, wearing a huge doggy smile.

I carried Ricky and Lucy into the yard, closed the gate behind us, and set the two wiggling monsters onto the grass. They scampered to their mother, who sniffed them cautiously, at first, then lay down and began patiently grooming them while they chewed at her legs. Nicole and Betty hovered nearby.

Rachel and I watched from a distance. "Thanks for bringing Nicole here," she said. "The closure is important for her. I know she caused you some trouble. I don't condone what she did, but I can't bring myself to punish her."

"Punish her? I think she should get a medal." I hesitated before speaking again. I wasn't sure I wanted to know the answer, but *I* needed closure, too. "If I ask you something, will you answer me honestly?"

Rachel held her breath. When she replied, her voice sounded cautious. "Yes."

"Was Richard dead when you moved his body?"

Rachel's mouth opened, then closed again. For a moment I thought she would walk away without answering. Finally, she spoke. "Yes. There was no pulse. How did you know I moved him?"

"Justine said his body was in the break room when she left, and she had no reason to lie to me. She'd already confessed to the murder. Besides, it explains the blood the police found on your shoes. Are you going to face charges for tampering with evidence?"

"My lawyer doesn't think so. Not if I fully cooperate with the investigation."

I lowered my voice to make sure we wouldn't be overheard. "You thought Nicole killed your husband, didn't you?"

Rachel bit her lower lip, then nodded. "It was the only thing that made sense. Nicole and Richard had a huge fight that morning, after he told her he'd arranged to send her to a boarding school on Monday. I never would have let it happen, but Nicole didn't know that." Rachel's eyes watered. "She's right. I always took Richard's side. I couldn't let her throw her future away because I didn't protect her. I had to help her … I needed to buy some time before anyone found him, so I could figure out a plan."

"And your red purse?"

"Wow, you don't miss much, do you?"

I smiled. "I have a source in the police department."

"Most of Richard's bleeding was internal, but not all of it. I used paper towels to clean up what I could and shoved them inside my purse. I tossed it into a dumpster about thirty miles outside of Seattle."

"But you didn't dispose of the knife?"

"Stupid, right? I couldn't bring myself to pull it out. I wanted to go back and get it later, but you'd already found him." Rachel glanced over her shoulder at Nicole. "Please, Kate. Nicole can never know I suspected her. It would crush her."

"She'll never hear it from me."

"Thank you."

We stood together for a few idyllic moments and watched the animals play. The lab ran in circles, barking and play-bowing. The pups bounded clumsily behind her. Nicole ran with them, clapping her hands and laughing.

"She's going to be all right, you know," I said.

"The lab?"

"No, Nicole. I know she's had troubles, but she's a good kid. I think she'll surprise you."

Rachel smiled. "She already has."

Rachel left to join her daughter. Betty meandered over to me and nodded at my bandage. "How's your hand?"

"It still hurts, but it should start feeling better once the stitches come out. Luckily there wasn't any nerve damage."

Betty's eyes sparkled mischievously. "So let me get this straight. You got into a standoff with a knife-wielding murderer, and the only injury you got was the one you gave yourself?"

I smirked. "Pretty much."

"Since you insist on hanging out with killers, I was going to recommend that you get a gun. But on second thought, maybe that's not such a great idea."

I nudged her with my elbow. "Maybe I should be like you and hire my own bodyguard."

"Don't get any ideas about Jamie. He's mine. You'll have to find your own veterinarian gangster." She nodded in the direction of the dogs. "That lab looks pretty good now, doesn't she?"

"Wonderful. Do you think bringing the puppies here was a mistake?"

Betty wrinkled her eyebrows. "Why would it be a mistake?"

"She's so happy. It might be hard on her when I take them home again."

"Nonsense. Those pups are weaning age now. Mom will be more than happy to say goodbye to them in an hour or so. Now that she's seen them, she'll be more content. I told her they were in good hands, but she needed to see it for herself."

"You talk to her? And you think she understands?"

"Of course. Don't kid yourself. Bella understands you, too. Dogs are a lot smarter than people think. We humans are the dumb ones."

I couldn't disagree.

Betty eyed the pups closely, but I had a feeling she was actually watching Nicole.

"So, what's next for the lab?" I asked. "Have you found someone to adopt her?"

"Nope."

I felt unaccountably sad. "She'll go to foster care, then."

"Nope. All of my fosters are full."

My chest tightened. That meant the lab was destined for an animal shelter. After rescuing her from a cage in a shed, I couldn't imagine her story ending in a cage at the pound. It was too cruel.

"Maybe Michael and I can take her for a few weeks. She can't stay at the house with Bella, but Michael might be able to keep her at Pete's Pets. Maybe one of his customers will adopt her."

"Not this one, Kate. She's had enough trauma and change in her life. Her next home needs to be her forever home."

"I thought you didn't have anyone to adopt her?"

Betty didn't reply. I had a feeling that meant we were standing in the yard of the dog's new home.

"Thirteen, Betty? Are you sure?" The last time I'd visited Betty, she'd had twelve dogs living on site.

Betty shook her head adamantly. "Nope. Not with me, either." She looked pointedly at Nicole and the lab, then back at me. "Those two are good together, don't you think?" She met my eyes, silently asking for my opinion.

At first I was surprised. Betty didn't know Nicole or her mother, and she didn't place dogs unless she knew they'd never come back.

Then I watched them for a few moments. Two mothers and a daughter bonding in a way that seemed important—for all of them. When Nicole collapsed on the grass and the yellow lab flopped down beside her, I realized Betty was right.

I looked back at Betty, smiled, and nodded my head yes.

"Let's go make it happen," she said.

Betty and I walked across the grass to join what we hoped would be a new family. She kneeled on the ground next to Nicole. "You saved this dog's life. I'm going to give her another few days to get stronger, and then I'll have my veterinarian friend Jamie spay her. After that, she'll be ready for a new home."

"I'm glad," Nicole replied.

Betty touched Nicole's shoulder. "I think that home should be with you."

Nicole stared down at the lab's fur, refusing to look at either Betty or her mother. When she spoke, her voice was so soft, it was barely audible. "I can't have pets."

Betty gave Rachel a stern look. "Is that true?"

Rachel shook her head. "Not anymore. That was Richard's rule. I like animals. But what makes you think we're the right home for her?"

"I have an instinct for these things. I won't lie to you, though. This dog has been through hell. She'll need a lot of love and even more training."

The teen looked up at her mother, eyes begging. "Mom, can we? I'll train her, I promise."

Rachel crouched on the ground and rubbed the lab's ears. "I don't see why not."

"Well, great. It's a deal then," Betty placed her hands on her thighs and stood. "You'll need to fill out some paperwork, and I'll want to come to your house for a site visit. But something tells me this is all going to work out just fine."

The teen scrunched her fingers into the dog's fur and buried her face in its neck. The lab leaned against her and slowly thumped her tail on the ground. I'd never seen either of them look happier.

I would never understand why my dharma was chasing down murderers, but in that instant, I stopped questioning it. If solving crime led to moments like this, it was worth it.

Nicole glanced up from the dog's fur. "Kate, do you remember what you told me during our last yoga class?"

To be honest, I didn't. I shook my head no.

"You said that if my future felt dark, I needed to lighten it. When I asked how, you said I had to find hope."

I smiled. "I remember now."

"You were right." She gently kissed the top of the lab's head. "That's what I'm naming her. Hope."

THE END

© Jason Meert

ABOUT THE AUTHOR

Tracy Weber is the author of the award-winning Downward Dog Mystery series. The first book, *Murder Strikes a Pose*, won the Maxwell Award for Fiction and was nominated for the Agatha Award for Best First Novel. *A Fatal Twist* is her fourth novel.

A certified yoga therapist, Tracy is the owner of Whole Life Yoga, a Seattle yoga studio, as well as the creator and director of Whole Life Yoga's teacher training program. She loves sharing her passion for yoga and animals in any way possible. Tracy and her husband, Marc, live in Seattle with their mischievous German shepherd puppy, Ana. When she's not writing, Tracy spends her time teaching yoga, trying to corral Ana, and sipping Blackthorn cider at her favorite ale house.

For more information on Tracy and the Downward Dog Mysteries, visit her author website at TracyWeberAuthor.com.

WWW.MIDNIGHTINKBOOKS.COM

From the gritty streets of New York City to sacred tombs in the Middle East, it's always midnight somewhere. Join us online at any hour for fresh new voices in mystery fiction.

At midnightinkbooks.com you'll also find our author blog, new and upcoming books, events, book club questions, excerpts, mystery resources, and more.

MIDNIGHT INK

MIDNIGHT INK ORDERING INFORMATION

Order Online:
• Visit our website www.midnightinkbooks.com, select your books, and order them on our secure server.

Order by Phone:
• Call toll-free within the U.S. and Canada at
  1-888-NITE-INK (1-888-648-3465)
• We accept VISA, MasterCard, American Express and Discover

Order by Mail:
Send the full price of your order (MN residents add 6.875% sales tax) in U.S. funds, plus postage & handling to:

> Midnight Ink
> 2143 Wooddale Drive
> Woodbury, MN 55125-2989

Postage & Handling:
Standard (U.S. & Canada). If your order is:
> $30.00 and under, add $4.00
> $30.01 and over, FREE STANDARD SHIPPING

International Orders:
> $16.00 for one book plus $3.00 for each additional book

Orders are processed within 12 business days. Please allow for normal shipping time.
Postage and handling rates subject to change.